# Lily Ariane

# Vincent, Miles & Mozart

America Star Books

Softcover 9781632496249
PUBLISHED BY AMERICA STAR BOOKS, LLLP
www.americastarbooks.com

Printed in the United States of America

'Whenever you don't understand why nobody does anything,
it is upon yourself to do something.'

*Vincent, Miles & Mozart* is my something.
—*Lily Ariane*—

*** 

If the boys had known beforehand, they wouldn't have remained in the park this late Saturday night. If they had just stayed at home, none of it would have happened, but they hadn't known and so they were there, unsafe and bored to death.

The three hung around a bench beside the local swamp, a place they had claimed to be theirs years ago. All were drinking from a bottle of whisky that the eldest boy had stolen earlier. They were pretty drunk by now and looking for trouble.

First, they had set fire to a public dustbin, with the use of a can of hairspray and a lighter, and now tried to burn the bench next to it. They couldn't, for it had been wet by the misty fog that covered the park all night so dense, it even blocked the light from the street lamps to touch the ground.

Continuously, burning cigarette ends were darted away in the beautiful swamp in front of the boys, which they referred to as 'Quagmire' among themselves. If anyone noticed the many cigarette filters that were thrown in by now, somebody might have had it cleaned. Unfortunately, nobody did. Nobody, except for the fish, the frogs, the turtles, the daphnia, the snakes, the salamanders and all other animals that lived in it, but they were all down-and-out. The swamp remained helpless. It couldn't do much more than to pray Mother Nature for urgent help. For the rest, it beheld its own suffocation with envious eyes.

Finally, the boys gave up their attempts to set the bench on fire and looked around for something else to burn. 'Hey, you know what?' the eldest after a few minutes said. 'That lady who gave me a push near the pet shop today, I know where she lives.' His friends looked at him surprised. It encouraged him to continue, agitated. 'I've been thinking about it all day, but I still can't figure out what had gotten into her. She even stuck her tongue out at me! Until today, nobody, I mean, nobody…' He held still and pointed his finger in the air while staring into nothing, as if his mind was miles away. His face turned angry. He went on, whispering this time, '…nobody in this town has ever had the guts to treat us like that, especially not a tiny woman like her. We have to straighten it out, for this whole thing can ruin our reputation.' He now looked straight into the eyes of his friends. His head nodded from one face to the other, punctuating his point. They knew he meant business. Slowly, their faces changed as well. Both gained the same determined look in their eyes.

'Let's go to her house!' the youngest suggested. 'I'm pretty sure we can find something to burn there!' The other two silently nodded and after a last empowering glance at each other, they left.

When they were younger, the boys used to fill their days with rather harmless devilment, but now they were thirteen, fourteen and fifteen years old and thus too old for childish play. Over the years, and out of boredom, they constantly had annoyed people, increasing the violence used, and had built a very bad reputation ever since. People feared them. Instead of being ashamed, the boys were deliberately living up the standard of their reputation. They were proud of themselves and glad to be somebodies in a town where they figured all good citizens to be nobodies. It had resulted in seclusion, which bored them even more.

They had just left their favourite hangout and walked alongside the field upon its path, when the youngest felt a cold shiver throughout his body, as if someone was watching him. He hesitated. For the first time in his life, doubts crossed his mind. Was it really a good idea to follow through with his friends? It frightened him and he stood still. His friends walked on, so he fell behind, plunged in thoughts, meanwhile trying to find out what it was he had felt earlier. The eldest turned around. 'Hey slug!' he yelled. 'Hurry up, man. We haven't got all night!' It encouraged him to continue. He shook his feelings off, took a short sprint and caught up with his friends in no time.

A few yards in front of them, a little hedgehog crossed their path. The moment it saw what it had come across, it curled up its head against its belly in protection. Even in the animal world their reputation had rushed them ahead. The boys instantly forgot their previous plan of burning a house down.

'Let's see how fast that beast can burn,' the eldest suggested. He pulled the can of hairspray out of his jacket. The others laughed as they had finally found something to play with. They never noticed how the murky fog moved away. It gathered into a dense cloud above the swamp.

'Look, it's disguised as a football,' the youngest pointed out. 'Bad choice, hedgehog, bad choice!' He was just about to give the prickly ball a kick, when something hit him in the back. It brought his tipsy body out of balance.

He fell against the eldest who was about to light the gas. They almost fell together. Annoyed with his gawky little friend, the eldest dropped the can. With a primal scream he then grabbed the bungler at the collar of his jacket, just in time to prevent a landing on top of the hedgehog. It crouched a little further.

'Hey!' the eldest yelled at his friend. 'Watch what you're doing, will you? I had nearly set myself on fire because of you!'

The youngest wanted to explain that he had miraculously been pushed, but his two friends had already gone back to focusing on their instrument of torture. He forgot about it the moment the can expectorated its huge ray of fire.

The hedgehog still lay curled up at their feet. It quaked a little. None of the boys saw its trembles, nor did they see the tiny strings of bluish, almost white light in between its spines. They orbited around like planets to a star and were of an indescribable beauty. The boys were too preoccupied to notice.

'Are you cold, little hedgehog?' the eldest asked with a cruel grimace. 'Let's keep you warm then!' whereupon he slowly pointed the beam of growling fire down.

In gloating anticipation, his friends uttered a squeal. They hardly could await the moment the prickly ball would catch fire.

'We are inventing a new game,' the youngest joked, 'which will be called 'Hot Soccer' in a few years time, let's build a goal!' For a moment his two friends gazed at him. They smiled next. 'That's a great idea!' The eldest let go of the spray nozzle. 'Let's build us a goal!' he repeated majestically and took off his coat. The youngest did the same. They laid their jackets next to each other in a six-foot distance at the field and returned to the hedgehog. The eldest picked up the hairspray from the wet grass. He lit it and with a resplendent 'Let the games begin!' then solemnly pointed the fire towards the ever-curled-up hedgehog.

To his surprise, the beam was deflected about a foot above the animal. Instead, it now burned his trousers. He stared at it. Still the spray was spitting fire. Then, finally, he felt the heat at his legs and let go of the nozzle for the second time. About the same time his friends laughed, he started screaming. 'Ouch...help... aaaai...aaai...aii...I'm...on fire...On fire...Help me!' Wildly, he started hitting the flames, jumping from one foot to another in an attempt to extinguish the raging fire that was eating his pants. To his friends, the jumping increased hilarity. 'Don't you stand there laughing!' he now screeched. 'Do something! Help me!' but his friends couldn't help doing anything else but shriek with laughter.

'Run...Ffff...Forest...rrr...Run...' the youngest finally joked, spluttering. It made his fourteen year old friend crack up again, but fortunately, this drunk mind also realized the seriousness of the situation. Hiccupping, the boy pointed a finger in the direction of the morass. 'Quagmire...' he screeched, whereupon he gave himself over to the laughing fit. The eldest did not persist in the moment, nor did he say anything. He just turned around and started running.

He had thought to reach Quagmire in a fraction of time, since the boys hadn't walked much until their encounter with the hedgehog, but to his surprise he saw that it was now situated in a far bigger distance than before. He didn't wonder why, just ran a little faster. It didn't matter. The boy could just as well be running on a treadmill, for the swamp moved itself miraculously away from him with every step he took. He never came closer, so he increased his speed. The swamp did too. He started running at maximum velocity, but Quagmire knew no mercy. No matter how fast he ran in his attempts to overtake it, the distance in between them stayed the same. He finally foresaw he wasn't going to reach it this way and ceased the chase. The fire had reached his shirt by now.

Both his legs and abdomen were covered in flames. Even though he didn't feel any pain, he was too scared of being burned alive to think straight. Exhausted, he started hitting the flames again until he noticed his polyester shirt had melted. Hot drips stuck on his hands, burning his skin instantly while big blisters upholstered his abdomen. He looked at it and became increasingly certain he was going to die, so he scanned around for a last solution. He even prayed for salvation. Although he hadn't been in church for years, it was the only thing that came to mind. 'Please God, help me…' he repeatedly mumbled, '… help me. Don't let me burn alive. I will change!'

'Drop yourself in the wet grass,' a voice suddenly whispered in his ears. 'Give up resistance and you will remain unharmed.' The boy never questioned what voice he heard, nor did he wonder where it came from. He just responded to its suggestion and dropped himself on the ground, where he expected to feel the wet grass upon his damaged body. He didn't. Instead, he felt the cold waters of Quagmire enclosing him. The flames quenched instantly.

During all the commotion, the hedgehog saw its chance and took off. Much quicker than anyone would expect, it ran towards the swamp, into the safety of tall grass and shrubs. There, two gentle hands picked it up.

The boys on the field had totally missed the severe life-threatening situation their friend had come across. They were just roaring in the grass, while holding their bellies. Laughter had started to hurt. Finally, one of them stopped and looked at something in front of him, amazed. Before his eyes hung a cigarette filter in the air. It was wet and covered in dirt. Aside its body, two tiny white wings were violently flapping alike the wings of a hummingbird. Just as he wanted to point it out to his friend, the filter hit him hard in between the eyes. 'Ouch!' he shrieked astonished. It hit him again. He kept silent this time, but his friend realized something was going on and got up on his knees too. He crawled aside, where he also got hit. 'Hey, leave it!'

he said. Again it hit him. 'Knock it off!' He swung his arms like he was scaring off a wasp. Both boys were now mowing the air.

Meanwhile, more filters rose up from the swamp, all like the first one. The boys froze when they saw what was rising. A huge cloud grew above the waters and started floating towards them. It grew from the filters all three of them had ever thrown in. In it, strings of bright bluish, almost white lights were orbiting around. The two stopped their waving and stood up. The single filter continued its ferocious task, but the boys were too stiff with fear to pay it any more attention. Petrified, they stared at what was coming their way.

They gasped for air when all the sudden two bright blue eyes appeared in its middle. Now a spooky face was rushing their direction. It gave them a very angry, even mad gaze.

They started running, but the cloud gained on speed and had quickly overtaken them. Immediately after, cigarette filters pounded their heads like a severe hailstorm. No matter where they ran, the cloud followed them and hailed its filters wherever it could strike. Soon, there was nothing else the boys could do than to let themselves drop on their knees in the wet grass. They curled up their chins to their chests, like the little hedgehog had done earlier, and protected their heads with their arms. When the youngest just lay down like that, he heard a voice, whispering. It sounded a lot like his own, but seemed several years younger and gave him the creeps.

'Hey, it looks like you are imitating a football now!' the voice said. 'Some funny coincidence, don't you think?' The boy shivered. 'Bad choice, little boy, bad choice!' He felt a kick at his right side that hit him straight in the liver. He sighed when he felt the stabbing. Afraid to be kicked again, the young boy crouched as far as he could, meanwhile ever protecting his head from the harsh pounding that never ceased. Next to him, his friend went through the same ordeal. After the kick, he cried. The youngest started praying. He hadn't prayed for years and hardly knew how to address Him. On top of that, he wasn't really sure God would listen after all the rotten pranks he had pulled, but he gave it a shot. His friend soon joined him. Both promised to better their lives and even prayed for remission.

The pounding stopped. The friends stayed on their knees and kept their heads low for a while. It was the youngest who dared to look up first. The cloud had changed. It still hung above them, but its eyes didn't look as angry as before anymore. Besides that, a large mouth had manifested itself in its bottom regions, smiling an evil grin.

'Boo!' it bellowed suddenly. Out of fear, the boys screamed back, whereupon it laughed a childish giggle that gave them the creeps all over again until its eyes regained seriousness and the titter stopped.

In the meantime, the eldest boy had now sank to the bottom of the swamp, being unaware of what his friends were experiencing at the same time. He was struggling because the mud dragged him down. Wildly, he tried to escape its grip until he realized his movements were dragging him down only more. When he finally succeeded in remaining calm, he could feel solid ground under his feet and stood up, all wet and covered in dirt. To his amazement, his body hadn't suffered a bit from the burning. The blisters and red marks simply had vanished, even though his cloths remained severely damaged. He looked up at the sky and smiled in gratitude. 'Thank you, Lord!' Then he heard the voice again.

It didn't whisper in his ear this time, but now came from a distance, somewhere from above the field. It was tittering.

He crawled upon the dry land and wanted to look around in order to find out where it came from, but his gaze got stock upon the path next to the bench. He had expected his friends to be on the spot where he had caught fire earlier, but they were now nowhere to be seen. It made him furious. First, they hadn't helped him in extinguishing the flames, and next they had let him drown in mud! Determined to address their lack of friendship, he was just setting foot at the path when he heard the voice aloud for the second time.

He turned his head towards it, to the other side of the park, and couldn't believe his eyes when he saw the cloud. It hung in the air above his friends. Both lay on their knees in the dirt underneath, both in absolute despair. Tears dripped down their faces as they looked up, their eyes fixed upon the cloud above. It looked down parentally for a while until it turned around and stared at him in a piercing gaze as well.

He fell on his knees and showed it his greatest respect by bowing his head too, when something stung his knee. He sighed a short hiss and moved aside to see what had hurt him, even though the eyes in the cloud were ever looking strictly into his direction. It was a stone; a white rock with a green blaze that moved in flames, as if it was on fire itself.

Under different circumstances, he probably would have gazed at it for a while, but now he was in no condition to behold anything other than the cloud. Without knowing why, he grabbed the stone and put it in his pocket. He heard the voice again. 'All three of you have made a promise,' it resonated in his ears. 'Hailstones and flames will return the moment you break it. Remember! For my eyes are always everywhere…' It sniggered again and then took off, leaving the air filled with its giggle, as if it echoed in the park.

His two friends stood up and dried their tears. They walked towards him. Neither of them spoke a single word. Not because they didn't want to, just because they couldn't yet. All three hugged. The youngest silently picked up both soaked coats from the field and gave one to the eldest in order to put it on. After a short nod at each other, they next went their separate ways, each plunged in their own thoughts. The boys went home.

None of them had seen the old man in the swamp. He held the little hedgehog in his arms and cuddled it. Thick white hair curled around a friendly face with bright blue eyes. It waved a little in the wind. The man smiled.

His boy had done well, even better than he could ever have imagined. The strength was more vigorous, his power gigantic. 'A little boy has changed these lives for good,' he said in whisper to the hedgehog. 'For good, these three now learned their lessons and for that, my little friend, we have to thank you too.' He kissed the hedgehog on its tiny head and stooped. Gently, he let it step off his hands. He remained his position and looked at the little creature in loving tenderness for a while. It looked back in gratitude. Next, the old man stood up straight and started to disappear. Slowly, his silhouette evaporated into the humid air above the morass, leaving the hedgehog behind to resume its little life as if nothing had happened.

\*\*\*

He was a unique young boy, yet people in town knew him to be retarded because his social life was mainly filled with the animals that lived on his parental farm. He poured his heart out to them daily, mostly without the use of any words, and so he was simultaneously raised by goats, chickens, cows, horses, rabbits, cats, sheep, bugs and Mother Nature, even though his own mother tried to interfere with his life wherever she could.

His family had understood that he was special and never knew him as complicated as the rest of town did. They loved him dearly, even though they were unable to level with him. Instead of squeezing him into their lifestyle, they had let him to explore life the way he preferred. He grew up outside; on their land, in the stables, in the barn and anywhere but inside the house. Only indoor meals and school kept him from growing up completely wild.

He lived in a warm, loving family full of secrets, for neither of his parents ever told him anything about his grandparents, who all had died before he was born. His father only told him a little, mostly about the Friesian horse he had owned as a little boy, his mother never a word. No matter how hard he had tried to get her to talk, she simply wouldn't give in. He really wanted to find out though, oh yes he did, because the little that he knew made him wonder, as if both his parents were keeping an enormous secret from him.

This is what he knew:

The parents of his father had left them their farm, the parents of his mother nothing more than an old book containing Greek mythology.

His father had been born out of a thirty-seven year old mother, his mother's mother had only been eighteen years old at given birth.

His father had been born the oldest of fraternal twins, his mother was an only child.

His father's parents had planned the birth of their children precisely while, rumour had it, his mother was born out of a short affair with an older man nobody knew anything about. Soon after his grandmother had let the old man go, she had met a local farmer to whom she would be happily married a year later, shortly after given birth to a beautiful baby girl. Her husband then raised this daughter as his own, since the couple would never have any more children.

His father's parents had died of old age, his mother had lost hers in a car accident at the age of twenty-one. Her father had been instantly killed, her mother had remained unfound until this day. She was supposed to have been thrown out of the car while it made its lethal roles off the steep cliff and was declared dead after being a missing person for ten years.

The boy had tried to ask his mother about her biological father on many occasions, but she had never responded to his questions other than by telling him that he would find out some day, but that he was too young for it now. He had stopped trying, although he hadn't really let the subject go. Always, somewhere in the back of his mind, slumbered the exciting feeling that there was a chance that he could still have a grandfather, a grandmother, or even both somewhere.

He was very font of his only aunt, Angela, because out of all family members he resembled her the most. In behaviour that is, not in appearance. The woman had thick black hair that curled around in a long pony tail and deep brown eyes with long eyelashes. She was astonishing beautiful, but had never been married, nor did she have had any boyfriends. She had lived alone in a huge apartment down town all her life, accompanied by four cats and five fish tanks. Whenever his family went down to visit her, the boy always played with the cats or watched the fish while nibbling the potato chips she usually bought for him especially. She had been a vegetarian all her life, a lead the boy had followed from babyhood on. She also hardly had any human contact and came over to visit his family on very few occasions. Her only friend he knew about was a woman, Simone. This lady lived in France, so he had never met her.

There was something special about this friendship because, without ever visiting each other, the two women regularly seemed to meet. His aunt never told him much about her friend, even though he asked, except that she worked as a psychic massage therapist in Carnac, an area in France that was likely to have very special energetic power. Since Angela had never owned a phone, he had become very curious about Simone and how they then would meet, but he had never gotten any logic explanation other than, again, that he would find out some day.

He had two outgoing younger brothers to whom he differed the utmost thinkable. They were monozygotic twins, three years younger and the opposite of him, in appearance and in behaviour. Both were very loud, not calm for a single moment and always together. They had thick, straight brown hair, chubby cheeks and deep brown eyes, just alike their father.

Their mother was a very beautiful woman to whom the boy resembled most in appearance, as she was also thin, had the blue eyes and the curly blond hair as well and alike showing cheekbones in her face. People called her a real stunner.

He never questioned why he differed so much from the rest of his family members, but rumours about his origin were spread all over town.

For having breakfast, lunch and dinner all together, his mother daily had to search her eldest for a while. She had found him reading his ancient book in the barn, resting in between goats, chicken, cows and horses or hanging upside down on the biggest branch of the old apple tree. Mostly, she had found him alone in the haystack, his favourite hideout.

It lay inside their biggest barn, where aside tractors and other farm machinery were parked. In the high roof, a big skylight was placed because her son liked to look at the stars at night. Each evening, after he was excused at the dinner table, she watched him rushing off to his haystack, back to the stars, back to his book and back to the fantasies. She knew he then would fall asleep there, not bothered by cold, nor by the many insects that usually crawled around him. In winter times, she gave him thick woolen bedding to stay warm, although the rick already isolated him from cold. Often, he kicked the blanket aside in his sleep.

On top of the haystack, their rooster stood guard. The moment the first sunbeams showed up in the morning, it would wake up her boy. First, it would softly crow to awaken him gently. Then, it would raise its voice to wake up the humans indoors.

Their three cats hunted mice in daytime, but kept him warm by curling up to his side at night. The animals secured him. If anything wrong, they would warn him in time, she had always known. Besides that, the sweet spinning sound of cats and the light snoring of the rooster made him fall asleep easily each night.

After his discovery of sleeping in the haystack at the age of two, her son had never slept in a bed anymore. Whenever she laid him in, he quickly crawled out and ran to the barn after she had left his room. The first couple of times, she had desperately searched the farm for her missing son, convinced that he must have been sleepwalking, but soon she had learned that he really chose to be outside at night. Since all of her attempts to get him to sleep in a proper bed failed, she finally gave in, knowing deep in her heart that she had given birth to a child that was different. Each night, before going to bed herself, she went to the barn to check on him. Each night, she found her boy deeply asleep with his head upon an open book and their three cats curled up at his side. Every night confirmed her that they were raising their child the right way. She saw her son growing up happily, just as any parent would want their child to grow up like. She knew that they had served him right by letting him.

He was born on the eleventh of November, just a few days after a horrible snow storm had afflicted their farm. Fortunately, it wasn't very thoroughly damaged, but still, the boy's father and mother had been working hard for days to repair all the necessary damage in time. His mother, highly pregnant, knew that her baby could come any minute now, but persisted in helping her husband. She was born a true farmer girl who had always been prioritizing the needs of the farm above her own, and so she had even climbed up the roof a few hours before the baby was born.

After they were done, she went down to prepare for lunch while her husband went into the barn to start butchering rabbits for the following Christmas. He was a little early this year, but because of a huge demand of rabbit meat around these times and the fact that his wife soon expected their first, he rather started early than late. On top of that, she cooked the best rabbit stew in the wide surroundings and he wanted her to have some extra time in preparing. Maybe, she would even be able to cook a few more than usually because at the market where he sold his meats, milks and eggs, her stew was a very popular dish.

He was about to give the first rabbit's neck a good twist, when he heard his wife calling from the house: 'Honey, come quickly, my waters just broke!' Startled by this sudden news, he accidently half twisted the neck of the poor animal. It produced an agonizing sound, so loud that the neighbour who lived three farms away crumbled his head between his shoulders. Next, the old man smiled and jumped on his bike to assist, even though the terrible noise had stopped by then. He came just in time to help delivering a baby. It was a boy with the bluest eyes he had ever seen, even brighter than his own.

They named the boy Vincent.

Vincent liked to read a lot. At a very young age, his father had read him the stories over and over again, but soon, he knew them by heart, recognized the words and read on his own. He could read by the time he was four years old.

The book that he fancied the most was the ancient book his grandparents had left him. It told the story of Heracles, a Greek man and son of chief god Zeus, who had concurred demons and gods on behalf of mankind, but was considered a bad boy by Greek humanity. He was a demigod, born out of a fling his father had with a mortal and stronger than many gods. Unfortunately, he was also drunk and outrageous very often, so people hated his attitude. Finally, they brought him to trial, where the misbehaving hero was condemned to perform twelve feats.

He showed tremendous courage, patience and endurance throughout his ordeals, so Vincent forgave him his impetuous character soon. Even though his idol had killed his three sons in rage and madness, he couldn't stop fantasizing about him. The thought of Heracles made him look forward to the day that he would find the courage to stand up against evil too. He knew he was too young for it now, but he had always felt that, somewhere deep inside, the same strength rested.

Often, he dreamed about his future actions. Every time, his dreams would end in kissing a beautiful girl with whom he had fallen in love by now. He could picture her precisely: She would have the darkest hair that curled around her face and neck in sophisticated twists. Thick, silky soft locks would crawl over her brown shoulders, where her skin would be smooth and shiny and her hands as soft as butter cream. Her eyes would be two of the lightest lights that he had ever seen; two deep green shiners with a little twist of white within.

Each morning, he had woken up with the image of this girl burned into his brain. The more mornings he woke up, the more determined he became in finding her. Somehow, he knew that he was going to meet her some day. By then, he would have possessed his powers, he also knew, even though he hadn't yet discovered them.

Pretty soon, it started to look like he was right.

***

They lived a simple life in a rural town, just outside a big city area in Southern England. Breeding rabbits was their main occupation, although they only sold their meats in the weeks running to Christmas. All other weeks, eggs and milk were brought to the market.

Vincent loved the rabbits and had played with them a lot until the day that he accidently had spotted his father on butchering his beloved cuddles, shortly after his fourth birthday.

'No!' he had screamed in shock, 'No, dad, don't hurt them!' but it had already been too late. His dad had just killed the last one and was about to skin furs before he would rest the meat. The screaming of his son had startled him and he had felt sorry for the poor kid straight away, even though he was about to show him this annual ritual some day soon anyway. However, he would never have shown him this way, unprepared and without any explanation. It simply hadn't occurred to him that the door stood wide open and that his eldest was able to see everything.

He had to calm Vincent down. It took him a while because his boy was very upset, but in the end, Vincent understood: His parents took really good care of the rabbits, but once they were big enough to provide their family with meats and furs, his father had to kill them, as quickly and painlessly as he could, in the most humane way possible. They wouldn't notice a thing and were always killed while nibbling a fresh piece of carrot. It was important that all rabbits died that way, for it made their meats more healthy and tasteful for the clients.

Even though he really believed that his father never hurt them, from that day on, he decided to stay away from the rabbits, for he wasn't allowed to get emotionally attached to animals that served for food purposes. His family never saw him in the shed ever again, at least, not until the day that he turned eleven years old.

The school the three boys eventually went to was nearby. To get to it, they only had to walk two miles on a straight road that lead them from their courtyard directly into school. It didn't know much traffic. Before his two younger brothers were old enough to go to school too, his mother had always accompanied Vincent on his walks, meanwhile leaving the twins at home with their father. Pretty soon after his first year, Vincent had asked her if he could go all by himself, just as he preferred. Because of her two sons at home and a husband too busy to watch them, she had reluctantly agreed to it. Vincent was only five years old then, but a special child and very independent for his age too. Besides that, she knew that they lived in a social community and that her son was well known in town. If needed, he could always ask for help everywhere.

So it happened that Vincent, already at the age of five, walked to school alone. He loved it. Even when his younger brothers were old enough to go as well, he kept on going alone. Way earlier than his brothers would leave, Vincent departed from home on school days. He didn't feel very comfortable around a lot of other children, so he always tried his best to dodge everybody in the schoolyard and therefore always came in the classroom first.

It was a bright room with large windows on one side and big shelves of books alongside the walls. Students were allowed to pick a book once they were done with their homework. At one of these shelves stood a huge globe with a light inside. Whenever they were taught Geography, the teacher would dim the lights, light the globe and show the various continents of the Earth. Vincent had always enjoyed these classes.

Often, in the mornings, when he was the first to enter class, he studied it thoroughly, turning it around and trying to find his own hometown. Sometimes, he imagined being a traveller who discovered new worlds. Playing with the globe became one of his many morning rituals. It comforted him.

Fortunately, he had a teacher who came in early each day as well. She considered him a bright student and far ahead of his classmates because of his huge love for reading.

Each morning, he picked a book from the shelves and dove into a world of fiction, after greeting her politely first of course. The old teacher had always known about Vincent's peculiarities, so she had let him.

After school, she even stayed in late on behalf of him only. Both enjoyed each other's company, even though they hardly spoke. The teacher then corrected assignments or prepared for new lessons, meanwhile always keeping her reading glasses on top of her greyish white hairdo, while Vincent read his books or did his homework. Once every now and then, his teacher looked at him with great compassion. Her brown eyes poured him love as if he was a son of her own. He never noticed, nor did he think that it was a strange phenomenon to have the same teacher each year, while the teachers of his brothers, who were in the same school, constantly varied.

Every day, he stayed in class as late as he could until it was time for his teacher to catch the bus. Then, he calmly walked home for dinner, glad that he succeeded in evading his classmates for another day.

It happened on his way to school, when he was only seven years old. He first saw it in the distance, the big black spot on the courtyard of the neighbour who lived three farms away. He wondered what it could be for a while until he saw it was a dog.

He loved all animals, except dogs. He never knew why, but he had always assumed that since he had spent so much time in the company of prey, he had developed an instinctual fear of big predators.

The beast was huge. It appeared to be very strong and had a thick, black and bristly fur. He was glad the dog lay on the neighbour's courtyard and assumed it to be tied down somewhere, although he didn't see a chain or rope attached to its neck. This frightened him a bit, but he knew that these types of farm dogs weren't allowed to come off the property, so his fears diminished a little.

He was just about to recommence his walk to school, when the dog looked at him. Vincent froze and stared at it fearfully, straight into its eyes. It went mad.

Unexpectedly quick, it jumped on its feet and started ferocious barking. Vincent couldn't move. It was like his gaze was captured by the big black creature that was staring back at him, meanwhile still barking violently. Then, it moved forwards, all the sudden silently. It crawled as if it was stalking prey.

With no one in sight, Vincent realized there was no one to turn to for help. He didn't dare to scream, too afraid it might trigger the dog to attack. He remained helpless. The only creature he could turn to was the big oak aside the entrance of the courtyard. He pressed himself tight into the security of its body, awaiting the moment the beast was going to eat him. By now, he had started to cry.

The dog, in the meantime, had never meant any harm. It just had become curious about the little boy that had crossed their land. Normally, it would have happily greeted such an unexpected young guest, but this one stood so still, it didn't know what to think of him.

The boy smelled a little bitter, it concluded after picking up his scent, carried a strange energy and a weird gaze in his eyes. It wasn't sure what to expect of this odd creature. Was it really a human being, or was it something else, something he should warn the boss for? It was a little bit afraid, but still decided to investigate further, meanwhile taking precautions by approaching very cautiously.

By the time it was only a couple of yards away, it saw water running out of the eyes.

'Aha!' a high voice whispered its ears. 'Now I know what's wrong. This child is broken!' The dog didn't wonder where the tiny voice came from, for it knew very well. It came from the flying creature on its head. It was just about to answer, when the kid collapsed.

'Ah well,' the flying thing sighed. 'In the end, sleep is always the best remedy.' The dog looked up and nodded. 'Now,' its voice continued, 'off you go, back to the farm. You scare him in a way. I'll repair the boy in the meantime.' And so it was done. The dog shortly sniffed the boy's face and turned around to the farm. 'Maybe there's some food around,' it muttered. 'After all this excitement, I could use a good bowl.' With these reflections on its mind, it left the passed out boy under the big oak, entered the courtyard and went into the farm of the neighbour who lived three farms away.

Vincent awoke by a fly that had landed on his nose. It tickled. He waved his hand at it and opened his eyes. He saw nothing because the bright sunlight blinded his view. The incident with the dog came back to mind, so he startled, convinced that it must have bitten him to death, but after his eyes had adjusted to the light, he saw that he was still at the spot where he had passed out earlier. He could now see the leaves and branches of the big oak he fainted under.

A black crow was watching him curiously. Its shiny feathers reflected the bright light in such a way, he had to squeeze his eyes again. In shock he then looked at the sun. 'Wow, is it that late already?' he asked no one in particular. 'I'll better get myself to school as soon as possible or I will be too late!' Quickly, he stood up.

He had just grasped his rucksack from the grass, when the crow drew his attention. It scratched a range of sounds that Vincent never had heard before. For a moment, he stayed under the big oak and looked above until he remembered his rush. He swung his backpack over his shoulder and started to run for school, but almost instantly stopped because the crowing started for the second time, this time louder, as if the animal had something to make clear to him. He walked back, looked up again and now discovered it's amazing eyes. Afresh, he was captured in an animal's gaze, only this time within full admiration. The eyes appeared to be blue, but when he took a closer look by squeezing a little, he saw strings of yellow, green, purple, orange, pink, red and blue lights circling around the irises. If the bird hadn't moved, he would have stood there for hours, in full disbelieve of what he was witnessing. He then definitely would be late for school. Fortunately, the bird saved him the disgrace. It jumped off the branch and elegantly landed in front of Vincent's feet. There, it dropped a white stone in the grass, whereupon it crowed three times before taking off.

Vincent watched it fly high up to the sky, straight up, as if it went straight back to heaven. His eyes followed the bird until they couldn't distinguish it anymore in the blue lights of the sky. He then bent over and picked up the stone from the grass.

In his hurry, he quickly inspected it, but saw nothing special. With a shrug, he put the stone in his pocket and crossed the road. He didn't understand the crow's intentions with it, but decided to hang on to it anyway.

One last time, he looked over his shoulder to see where the dog was, only to find out that it was nowhere to be seen. He heaved a sigh of relieve and climbed the fence of the field opposite to the farm of the neighbour who lived three farms away. He would never take the road to school anymore.

Vincent was so taken aback by the whole event, he continued his way to school sufficiently plunged in thoughts to never notice that a man had been monitoring him from a window. He had a pair of the brightest blue eyes ever seen in a man's countenance and a grey, curly hairdo that swarmed around a friendly face. He smiled.

'The boy I once helped coming into this world is truly on his way now,' he said to the big black dog next to him. 'Finally, he's in possession of the stone.' He turned his face away from the window, for he had a lot of things to do in only little time. He'd better start as soon as possible.

In one gulp, he hit his now cold coffee back, stroke the dog on its big furry head and told him to stay. He took his long black leather coat off the hanger and went into the shed. There, he took a small box off a shelf, wiped it clean and tied it to his bike's carrier. He jumped upon the saddle and cycled through the shed's open door.

'It is about time for it to be energized, after not being used for ages,' he said to himself, 'Fortunately, there is still a capable relative left.'

The old man quickly cycled through the village. After passing the school, at the crossing of Main and Second Street, he turned left, to the city. He was in the greatest rush ever. Breathing heavily, he pushed himself to go faster until he went at full speed. He knew that there was little time, for this crystal sphere needed a long time to energize. They only had four years left, as the legend had stated, only just enough.

*** 

The moment Vincent arrived, the schoolyard was crowded. Children were running around everywhere.

They made noise and touched each other constantly. Boys pushed, wriggled, swarmed and played soccer, while girls clapped hands, sang songs and screamed jokes at each other. None of them did anything silently. To Vincent it seemed the schoolyard was specially designed for making noise, loudly exchanging information and constantly touching each other. He didn't like it at all.

It seemed to be a good thing school hadn't started, yet a bad thing he now had to go across the yard, having never experienced so many children at the same time before in his life. To his own surprise, this all didn't frighten him, he just wondered, standing still at the school's gate, not knowing how to act or where to go, and for the second time this morning he saw nobody to turn to for help. Some of his classmates he recognized, but he had never said anything to them before, so he wasn't going to speak to them now. He just stayed there and stood still, hoping nobody would notice him. The opposite happened. All noticed him.

First, a blond girl with big glasses and pigtails gazed at him. Her mouth fell open when she laid eyes on him. She seemed amazed. 'What's wrong?' he heard one of her friends asking. The girl never answered, only pointed at him silently. Her friend walked up to her side and gazed at him as well, meanwhile more children joined them. Soon, in front of Vincent gathered a group of astonished little people. Quickly, it grew larger until all children were present. All had their mouths open, all were amazed. They stood at the schoolyard, Vincent on the threshold, opposite of each other. Nobody moved.

At the back of the crowd, Vincent recognized his two younger brothers. Glad to see familiar faces, he looked at them in full expectation of an enthusiastic, immediate response. It never came. Second, he tried to draw their attention by waving at them. Still no response. They only stood still at the back of the group and stared at him, straight through. Both appeared to be frozen. Everybody else too.

In the schoolyard, where earlier the sound of playing children had dominated its surroundings, now wasn't a single sound to be heard. Then, the school bell rang. Nobody moved. Vincent wanted to go to school, but didn't know how to. After a while, he tried. Carefully, he took a first step into the yard. The crowd moved back. Everybody stared, nobody spoke. Silently and simultaneously all children took two quick steps back, similar to the military keeping pace. Nobody said a word, everybody stared. He took another step. Again the crowd moved back. A little braver, he walked two steps to find out the crowd dived in halves, leaving him an alley through. Afraid to be an easy target for possible bullies, he carefully set another two steps to see if anybody would move now. Nobody did. Nobody spoke. Nobody touched. Everybody gave him passage.

Uneasy about their behaviour, but confident they wouldn't harm him, he more firmly walked through now. After he had passed, the alley closed and people followed him. It gave him the confidence to pass through the school doors without a doubt. The silent mass behind him passed them after.

Once inside, all finally went his or her way, without even looking at him anymore. Shortly after the children were seated, they all forgot the incident, even Vincent's two younger brothers. Nobody remembered. No one, but Vincent.

Before falling asleep in his haystack that night, he realized he had learned two things that day. First, he had learned never to walk past the neighbour's courtyard ever again and second, that crossing the schoolyard truly was a weird experience, but nothing frightening. Happy and reassured by these two conclusions, he curled up in the hay and prepared for sleep until he felt something. It glowed and vibrated in his pocket.

It took him a couple of seconds, but then he realized that through all events at the schoolyard, he had completely forgotten about his stone. In protesting its lack of attention, it now glowed and shook a little. Ashamed that he hadn't remembered his queerly meeting with that awesome bird more carefully, he reached in his pocket. He felt it immediately. It sparkled tickly, although warm and pleasantly soft in touch. The moment he pulled it out, it glowed a firing soft green blaze.

Now, finally, he had the opportunity to truly see it. He held it in between his thumb and forefinger and lifted the stone in front of his face, near his eyes, to investigate how it glowed and why. Then, he gasped for air. He saw things moving!

Little strings of light were orbiting each other alike he had seen in the eyes of the crow earlier. All had different colours, all moved. The white glassy material he earlier couldn't see through, had now slightly evaporated and showed a colour changing flare; first a clean golden blaze, then a bright green bloom. Either way, Vincent couldn't stop looking at it. It was so beautiful.

After a while, sleep overcame surprise. Vincent first tried to fight it, but soon had to give in. With the stone still firmly in his hand, he fell into a deep sleep. It would be the first time his vivid dreams occurred.

*** 

A woman stood in her backyard. She hung laundry in the wind. It was a sunny day, so she expected her white clothes to dry bright, which gave her the best mood ever possible. Her deep brown eyes showed a sparkling light.

The normally cranky spick and span housewife had finally found some time to do her regular household jobs. After the big move, she had finished unpacking the last boxes yesterday. It had set her mind at ease. She was all alone at home and deeply enjoyed the quietness of the house as well as its surroundings. Her twelve year old daughter was at school and her husband at work in the city. They daily travelled together and weren't supposed to come home any sooner than dinnertime, so she had the whole house by herself all day long. She was totally at ease and even happily whistled a tune. Climb Every Mountain from The Sound of Music sounded throughout the backyard. She loved that musical, had seen the movie many times and knew all the songs in it by heart. For a moment, she even felt like Maria because they had recently moved into this detached house in the hills, just alike she had dreamed when she was little. The fact that they finally had been able to fulfil this great wish of hers had made her tremendously happy.

Her husband ran an Internet business of his own. His office was situated in the big city they lived before. Being born on a farm in the country, the woman had never gotten used to city life. The constant noises of cars, trams and people had gotten on her nerves, even as the gasses that hung around everywhere. Their former apartment lay in a narrow street. It didn't matter from what window she looked outside, at each and every one of them, she looked straight into their neighbour's houses, as they did into their house likewise. She constantly felt being watched, longed for fresh air and was in desperate need of a wide, quiet view. The lack of it made her day by day increasingly depressed.

Her daughter had, already at a young age, tried everything she could think of in an attempt to make her smile. She never knew how to respond and could hardly perform a little grimace. She had seen the disappointment in her little girl's eyes, but truly couldn't help her inability to smile. It broke her heart over and over again.

Her husband also saw his wife languishing, but he couldn't do anything about it, for they simply couldn't afford moving. Until, one very special day, he had a surprise for her. His business had contracted several huge clients, so all the sudden there was plenty of money around. He came home with the folder from a broker who sold houses in the rural area nearby. She couldn't believe the news and threw her arms around his neck, kissing him passionate. 'Thank you,' she whispered in his ear. 'Thank you for saving my life!' The next morning they went house hunting, together with their daughter.

It had been quite an organization, the whole rehousing, but the prospect of living rurally had given her the strength to manage. During drives in between the old and the new house, she had hated to go back to the city. Soon, only her husband and some helpful friends drove up and down between houses. She stayed in the new house and organized things there, as she liked best. It had made her a different person right away. They had only lived in the hills for two months, but everyone already noticed a big difference in her personality. She finally was able to be her own self and loved it.

The house was the first one they had looked at. She had fallen for it immediately. It wasn't big, but bigger than their previous apartment, totally made of wood and painted in dark brown colours. It lay on a small hill, which made the view even more spectacular than one could ever dream of, and in front of the windows, on the outside of the house, little shutters were placed to keep the light from shining in too early in summer time. She absolutely adored them. They were painted in a lighter brown colour and had small clover figures carved in the middle. In the morning, these clovers would bring spectacular rays of light in the bedrooms, the living room and the kitchen. It was as if they helped her awaken slowly, as she liked best. Most of the mornings, she took her time to enjoy the game of lights before opening the shutters. Only then, she would make breakfast, pour coffee and wake up her husband and daughter. It became a little ritual of her own.

The only downside of life was the dog. When they finally were settled in their new house, her husband had brought it home. It was a huge German Shepherd.

'Living rurally comes with a certain risk,' her husband had declared. 'Here, we are more vulnerable to burglars and other scum, so we need protection. This dog will provide us that.' He then had grinned at her happily, the dog had barked affirmative and her daughter had clapped her hands in pure joy. She, however, had felt her heart palpations accelerating.

'No!' she had tried to make clear. She had even stamped her feet with it. 'No, no, no! That dog is not coming into our house! I will not clean after it. Do you have any idea how many hairs a dog shed daily? Do you have any idea how much sand and dust that dog will bring in? Do you have any idea what its nails will do to our brand new sofa, our carpets or our nicely painted walls?' The dog had looked questioningly at her, in full expectation of the boundaries she was about to set to its newly found freedom.

'But darling, we really need some sort of protection,' her man had tried again. 'If a dog like this barks, no burglars even consider breaking in the house, nor would they come on the terrain. And, look how much fun Britt is having with it already!' Indeed, she had seen her daughter teaching the dog tricks, rubbing its fur and kissing its big head. She then simply couldn't sent it away anymore. 'Okay,' she had sighed, 'the dog can stay, but on one condition: It stays outside, and I will not have it in my way in daytime!'

And so it had happened. Father and daughter had built a huge kennel in the front yard with a large doghouse inside. In daytime, when she was at home alone, the dog stayed inside its kennel. Every morning and every evening, her husband took it for a walk, after their daughter had fed it first. She never had to do anything with it, which was a huge relieve since she had always feared dogs deeply. No one knew, not even her family. Still, she saw no need for such a revelation. She just was glad the dog stayed locked in all day.

But, as the weeks went by, it started to seek her attention. All by itself in its cage, it became lonely in daytime. She began to feel sorry for it, and often sat near its kennel, but never had the nerves to touch it, let alone pet it, or unlock the door. Although her fears had decreased a little by the gentle way it treated her young girl, she still didn't dare to go one step further with it, at least not until this morning.

She was just hanging the last sock on the hanger, when she heard its querulous bark again. It was the good mood that gave her the idea to go up to its cage and open the door, as it well deserved.

For the first time, she truly wanted to give it some real attention. After all, this dog was responsible for fulfilling both her husband's and daughter's life with greater joy. She had to repay it somehow. Fear or no fear, by now she knew for sure their dog was not going to harm her.

As in a dream, as if she wasn't truly doing what she was about to do, she turned around and walked into the house. There, she automatically went to the kitchen. She took the tin of dog biscuits from the top of a cupboard, picked some big ones out and walked to the front of the house. On the doorstep she hesitated, as if she had an inner fight, but something in her was determined to carry on. She stepped outside. This time, she wouldn't let her fears stand in the way of happiness. The dog belonged to her family now as well and her fear was not enough reason to keep further excluding it like this. Again she made up her mind. She straightened her back and firmly walked to the kennel. She was going to bring her family back together, the whole family this time. It was about time she took this next step, she somehow knew. It was about time she connected to the dog, even though she felt as if she was a spectator of her own life right now.

The dog had made a big improvement by moving from the shelter to this household, even though it was lonely in daytime. At least here, the lady came to talk, whilst in the shelter people used to bypass it regularly. The only downside to its newly found life was that its boss woman wouldn't let it out during the day. The rest was all perfect.

It knew she was afraid, but was also confident that she would turn around one day. Patiently awaiting the moment she could shed her fears, it only drew her attention by barking. The first moment she finally came over, and later each time she approached its bars, it showed her the sweetest dog in the world, as it had learned the hard way: The more it had tried to get attention from the visiting humans in the shelter in its early days, the more it had scared them off.

First, it had tried jumping against the front grill of the kennel, which had shied them. Next, it had tried ferociously barking, which had spooked them off as well. In the end, after trying several possible ways to get someone to look at him, it had learned that wagging its tail, keeping its head low and tilting it to one side worked the best. It was a clever dog. Its name was Utopy.

It was the day of his jubilee in the kennel that Utopy's tremendous efforts finally paid off. Exactly one year ago, his boss had brought him here to put him up for adoption. Today, he could still feel the energy and still hear the voices of his former pack. He missed the pride where he belonged, knew his place and fulfilled his duties. He felt useless and wanted to contribute.

In the year that had passed, the dog had kept on trying to draw the attention of every visitor that bypassed his kennel to boost his reputation into 'well recommended' and enhance his adoption possibilities. He treated the people, especially those who volunteered to work in the shelter, with the greatest possible care, not only to get their good recommendations, but to receive a lot of fun time too. They sometimes came in to cuddle him, play with him or take him for a nice long walk. He loved being in touch with them. It often made him forget about his missing pack. He daily prayed the staff members to bring him home themselves, but they never heard him, even though they did understand that he was getting more and more miserable in his kennel. However, none of them had considered bringing him home themselves. He was simply too big, even though he sympathized everybody who worked with him a lot. It had made him tremendously depressed by now.

Except for one good morning, this morning, Utopy was in high spirits. Today, he felt, was going to be a good day. Wagging his tail, he had greeted the morning staff that came to hose down his kennel with ultimate joy. He had greeted the feeder with even greater enthusiasm next. Happily, he had finished his meal and had just taken place in the dog basket when it happened: Two humans held still before his kennel. One was middle aged, the other younger. They were male and female. Both carried the energy that immediately reminded him of his former pack. He recognized the energy of love, bonding and tender care, which made the dog want to go home with these humans in particular right away. He made a huge effort in looking his best and pulled out all the stops.

Acquiescently, he waited until all four human eyes were focused on him. He sat on his buttocks and tilted his head to the right. Both his ears pricked up to show interest, while his eyes affirmed goodness.

'Utopy,' the big male read out loud from the sign at his kennel door. 'What a nice name. That certainly suits us, don't you think?' The female nodded. Then, both looked at him. With a perfect timing, Utopy took one foot of the ground and lifted it, as if he gave paw. The young female uttered a scream of pleasure. She clapped her hands. 'What a nice dog,' the older male now said, 'and so big as well! This dog is perfect for us.'

The young one clapped her hands again. 'Daddy, can I pet the dog?' she asked. Utopy stood up. He wagged his tail and slowly approached her. Meanwhile, he kept his head low and his ears back in utmost respect. He then gently pressed his wet nose to the grill of the kennel door and smelled their scents with tremendous precision.

'I think that is a great idea in getting to know Utopy a little better,' the dad answered, 'but first we need to get someone from the shelter to open this kennel door. Don't stick your fingers through the gate yet!' He took the girl by her arm and pulled her towards the office at the end of the hall, leaving Utopy behind.

He wondered where the humans were going and pressed his nose through the gate a little further to follow their scent. Fortunately, it didn't last long for them to return. They had brought the feeder with them.

'It is a very nice dog,' he heard him tell the older male, 'its previous owners brought it here in deep sadness, but they were too preoccupied by a severe divorce to fulfil its needs. After their separation, neither of the former weds would be able to take care of it on their own, so it ended up here.' The older male now looked at him with great compassion. 'It is about time for it to be adopted,' the feeder continued. 'Utopy needs more attention than the shelter can provide, it is such a lovable animal.'

He opened the gate to let both humans walk in first and came in after them next, leaving the kennel door open. The female ran into the kennel. Within a split second, she dropped at her knees in front of Utopy and threw her arms around his neck. 'I want you to come home with us,' she whispered. Utopy licked her face. The father looked at them approvingly. He patted Utopy on his head and then came down on his knees too. He took his daughter's head in his hands and looked her deeply into the eyes. She looked back. None of them spoke. None of them needed to. Utopy lay next to them a silent witness. He understood what was going on and knew his faith was sealed. It was a done deal, he was sold.

After a while, the father stood up and nodded to the feeder. Both grown up males walked down the hallway to fill out all necessary forms in the office. They left the kennel door open and the girl, with Utopy flat on the ground next to her, behind. He had finally found home.

He loved his new place. He loved being outside, loved his pack, the young female in particular, and truly adored hiking with New Boss.

Boss was a true dog lover. Each morning and each evening of each day, Boss had let him explore the wide surroundings of the house, being unleashed. He could hardly believe what was happening to him, but didn't give it too much thought. He enjoyed life to the fullest.

He had been given food of the highest quality and had played the funniest new games with Young Boss. Every night, before his bedtime, she brought him a delightful bone to brush his teeth. At night, the gates of his kennel remained wide open for him to guard the terrain. He didn't go out a lot though. Most of the times, he stayed inside his doghouse and slept on his soft dogbed. He always had one ear straight up in the air, in case of emergencies. He knew how to guard the yard while sleeping, even though he dreamed a lot. He knew all very well because he was bred to know.

Most nights Utopy dreamed about Female Boss. He didn't trust her, for he didn't know what to make out of her energy yet. At their first encounter he had picked up some scents from her he couldn't place. Every day, he tried to connect to her in an attempt to make her feel at ease, but she hadn't let him. Instinctively, he knew her energy was unhealthy. He felt that she wasn't on the same level as the rest of the pack and that the pack needed to be united. Therefore, his instincts had saddled him with the task of balancing her mind.

He daily barked for her attention, but until now, his attempts had remained unanswered, although he did manage to get her to approach his kennel a couple of times.

Today, finally, he saw the woman standing in the front door opening. She had such a determined look upon her face, it took him by surprise. Next, he felt glad, instinctively knowing that change was going to come.

He had sat down and tilted his head as he had learned so well. She looked at him for a while and then stepped outside. She walked up to him. In front of his kennel door she held still. He wagged his tail in supreme joy, not only because he had finally succeeded in getting her to approach him this close, but mostly because her energy had made a huge change. He looked up to her eyes and uttered a surprised barking when he saw the colour. They were now the most bright bluish lights he had ever seen. It didn't frighten him, but gave him a pleasant feeling instead.

He rolled over to his back in showing more respect, when the woman opened the cage and fell on her knees, just like her daughter had done in the shelter. She petted him for a while. He proceeded the lying on his back, while his eyes watched hers as if he drowned in them, until their colour changed back to brown. Instantly, her energy changed as well. It brought him out of balance, but soon he regained his trust. He kept on looking straight at her, in the most loyal gaze a dog could ever give.

The feeling of being a spectator disappeared. She woke up and found herself, sitting on the knees, next to the seventy-pound-weighing dog that had recently moved into her household. She was petting it.

The dog lay still on its back, but its eyes were focused on hers. In its beak she saw the huge sharp teeth, an image that had brought her to fear dogs in the first place. She pulled her hand back and fossilized for a moment, but then her attention went to its eyes. They sent her a message of pure love and loyalty, she now could see.

No longer was she spooked off by his appearances, so her hand went back to its side and stroke the thick fur again. It was a very pleasant feeling that went throughout her body. 'I'm sorry I acted so weird,' she whispered, 'and sorry for not trusting you. I know you are a good dog, now I know. I'm just sorry for not seeing it earlier. Will you forgive me?' She leaned forward and kissed him on his big head. He got up and sat down next to her. She threw her arms around his neck and cuddled him for a while. Tears were dripping down her cheeks in big black currents that her mascara had caused. She let them. Polluting her face was now the last thing on her mind. She got in touch with their dog.

She gave him the biscuits. He took them from her hand with great care. She felt his teeth, but because the dog was so careful, it never frightened her. Instead, she felt a click in her chest. It was the click of love and tenderness, of unbounding loyalty. From that moment, she decided to give this dog the best life she could ever provide.

She got up from her knees and turned around, leaving the gate of the kennel unclosed. The dog followed her. She went into the house. He followed her there as well. She let him be inside, went to the sink to wipe her face clean, dried it and took her purse of the living room table. Then she turned around, towards Utopy. 'I'm going to be away for a short period of time, but when I return, I promise, your life will be the best life a dog could ever have.' She petted him on his head, went outside and got into her car, happily whistling Climb Every Mountain again.

Nothing could ruin her day today, not even the three pesky lads who were well known in town for causing trouble. They were the local brats nobody could handle; their parents couldn't, nor could the police. She encountered them nearby the local pet shop. The three boys were walking the side walk next to each other and had deliberately left no room for her to pass. She kept on walking her side in a straight line, opposite to the eldest. He also walked the straight line and was definitely not planning to go aside for her. It didn't bother her, for she felt strong today.

He was about to walk in on her, when she suddenly stretched her arm. It touched his shoulder hard and made him step back, meanwhile giving room for her to pass. The boy turned his head and looked her into the eyes the moment she walked by. She watched back. He had an amazed look upon his face. His friends also stood still and watched. Nobody moved, none of them spoke. They weren't used to people showing guts like this because, until now, nobody had ever dared to go against them. She had been the very first ever. It took the three totally by surprise.

After she had passed them, she looked over her shoulder. All three were motionlessly watching her, eyes wide open. None of them spoke, as if they had lost their tongues. For a brief moment, she felt sorry for causing these three dazzled faces. Then, to break their tension a bit, she laughed at them and stuck out her tongue. It only caused a bigger amazement.

Normally, she would never do anything like that, but today was different. Today, she felt a changed woman who had just overcome her fears. She was in the right energy to teach these three a lesson. Now was the right time because, somewhere deep inside, she felt like she had her back covered.

Then she walked on, still smiling. She felt good, strong, in touch with herself and back in the real world. She knew that she had to thank the dog for that. It had been the reason she had gone into town.

She went into the pet shop and took the biggest dog basket she could find from a shelf, whereafter she went to the counter, dragging the basket along.

An old man stood before her in line. When he finished paying for his goods, he turned around and looked straight at her. She said to him a friendly hello, meanwhile admiring his beautiful blue eyes and his long curly grey hairdo. He friendly nodded back and showed her one of the greatest smiles she had ever seen in a man's face. Although she was sure she had never seen him before, she had an odd feeling she knew him. It only didn't occur to her wherefrom. For a moment she kept trying to remember, but then she quickly let it go. It was her turn at the counter. Meanwhile, the man left the pet shop, still smiling.

Utopy wagged his tail for her when she came back in the house. He loved his basket right away. She placed it in the living room, next to her side of the couch, so she could pet him as much as possible during evening family time. He straight went in and never came out, not even when Boss and Young Boss came home later that day. They couldn't believe their eyes when they saw Utopy happily greeting them from out of his basket in the living room.

Her family members flew around her neck, after admiring the beautiful dog basket first. They kissed her wherever they could simultaneously, both tremendously glad the dog was allowed indoors from now on. She started to cry. For the second time that day, she cried her happy tears, for she had finally managed to get her family close together.

The kennel in the front yard was demolished after several days. A nice pond with fish and frogs came in its place a week later.

\*\*\*

All the sudden, Vincent stood in the kitchen. At least, it looked a lot like the kitchen. The normally red colour of their kitchen cupboards had changed. They were brown now. He recognized the same kitchen chairs, but not the table. It was round instead of the rectangular one he knew from home. Besides, it had a thick Persian rug on, the kind his mother absolutely loathed, he knew.

He wondered for a while until he noticed the window. Behind, the familiar leaves of their old apple tree were waving in the wind. He felt relieved, knowing for sure now this was his home. A little dazzled, he walked over to the window side to greet his favourite tree, as he always did in the morning. Instantly, he looked for its biggest branch, the one he liked to hang on upside down so much. He startled. It was gone.

Vincent rubbed his eyes in making sure he saw it right, but nothing changed. His favourite branch was only a small twig. In fact, the whole tree was little. No one would ever consider climbing this tree since its trunk would immediately break. He examined it further. Was it even an apple tree? Fortunately, he saw a tiny card waving in the wind. It was attached to the top branch and showed a big red apple. It certainly was an apple tree, but how come it was so small? This tree clearly had been planted recently. He looked past the tree and discovered their courtyard. It looked familiar. Opposite to the farm laid the meadow, the road was still at his left hand side and at his right, in the distance, he discovered both sheds; one for the rabbits and one with his haystack.

He stretched his neck a little further and was even able to see the stables. He sighed in relieve and was just about to explore these strange yet familiar surroundings, when a horse walked out of its stable. It was a beautiful black Friesian horse, unknown to Vincent, but exactly alike the one his father used to have as a young boy. Its fur was shiny, as if it was rubbed with oil and it showed a massive strength. It was huge, but calm, almost royal. For a while, Vincent forgot his previous astonishment and gazed at the horse that calmly walked into the meadow and started to graze. Suddenly, he felt a huge urge to go outside and connect to it. He was just about to turn around, when he heard footsteps on the stairs. They were coming down. Immediately, Vincent felt like a stranger in his home again. Afraid of who might walk into the kitchen, he wanted to grab the window's curtain in order to hide behind. He couldn't. Every time his hand was about to touch it, the curtain slipped through. The footsteps, in the meantime, had now reached the end of the stairs and walked in the hallway. Vincent heard they were of more than one person. He became increasingly afraid. Since he wasn't able to hide behind the curtain, he sat on his haunches and dove away behind the kitchen chairs, meanwhile praying not to be seen.

A woman walked in. He didn't recognize her. She held the hand of a young boy and dragged him into the kitchen by his arm. The boy was screaming and crying. 'No, I don't want to go to school today,' he yelled. 'I don't feel good.' 'Stop it!' his mother screamed back. 'You have to go, or you will grow up a vagrant. Take an example of your twin sister, for she is already gone to school. Now, stop whining or I have to tell your father.' Still holding him by the arm, she dragged him to a kitchen chair, shoved it back with her free hand and pulled the boy upon it.

Only then, she let go. 'Sit and eat, for I've had quite enough of your behaviour.'

Vincent panicked because both mother and son were so close, they only had to look his way to discover him. He crouched a little further, but it was already too late. The boy at the table looked straight at him with a very angry gaze upon his tearful face. Vincent looked back, dazzled. He didn't know what to say to the boy, nor how to explain what he was doing in their kitchen, so he said nothing. Slowly, he came up straight. The boy said nothing. Meanwhile, his mother turned around from the kitchen dresser, holding a plate in her hands. As she walked over to her son, she placed it upon the table. Her eyes briefly crossed Vincent's. No reaction. Vincent waved his hand at both humans. Again, they didn't react. It was like they never saw him. He started to explain. 'I'm sorry for being here, but I don't know how...' Still, both humans continued their morning ritual at the table. The boy shoved his plate away. 'Don't want to go to school!' he cried out, whereupon his mother smacked him at his cheek hard. It was done with such a force that the boy's head bounced to the side at impact. Instantly, his cheek showed a deep red mark. His mother clearly had hurt her hand with the wack too, for she hissed and shook it immediately after.

The boy shoved his chair back and jumped up. Tears were running down his cheeks in massive currents. He was hurt and very angry now. 'Why do you always have to hurt me? I hate you!' he yelled as he turned around to run out. Vincent didn't know what to think of the situation. Instantly, he forgot his fear of being discovered. He stared at the scene in front of him, in absolute despair. Never in his life, his own parents had slapped him, not even softly. Witnessing this young boy being smacked, made his stomach twist. He felt deeply sorry for him right away.

The boy had almost reached the kitchen threshold, when a man showed up. He was huge, had big hands and a sun tan all over his skin. Obviously, he worked outside a lot. Immediately, the boy ceased his run and took a step back. His eyes were big as he was clearly frightened. The man said nothing, just stood still in the doorstep until he started to unbuckle his belt. He pulled it off his trousers next and wrapped its empty side around his hand, leaving its buckle to dangle.

The young boy froze as the man's angry gaze fell upon him. 'Johannes,' he spoke to him in a strict voice, 'how many times does your mother need to tell you this? You clearly don't want to listen. Do you know what we do with boys who don't listen? Do you?' Johannes shook his head. Fearfully, he looked at his father. When the big man took a step forward, he turned around and hid behind the table, right next to Vincent. Still, he didn't notice him. 'You don't know? Are you sure? You've forgotten? That's strange! I clearly can remember teaching you yesterday that we make them feel, boys who don't want to listen. Can't you?' 'Mom, help!' Johannes now turned to his mother for help. 'Johan,' his mother tried to stop her husband, 'don't, please, for I have already smacked him one. He's had enough.' 'Nothing to do with that,' his father answered her. 'If we want to turn this boy into a man, he's got to be punished like a man.' He turned around to his son next. 'Now, don't run. Every extra second that I have to chase you, I will smack you one extra, understood?' His son nodded. 'Come over here and drop your pants.' 'No,' his mother now firmly protested, 'not on his buttocks. You've already slapped him there yesterday. It's still damaged too much. Take his back instead!' 'Fine, I'll take his back. Okay then, Johannes, roll up your shirt and bend over,' he said as his arm swayed over his head, holding the belt in his hand with a firm grip. His son complied reluctantly. Sobbing, he slowly approached his father, meanwhile rolling up his shirt. In front of him, he turned around and bent over, his eyes firmly shut in preparation of the expected blows. They never came.

Since no one had noticed Vincent, he had lost his fears of being discovered. Clearly, no one was able to see him, so his fears gave way to anger. He was furious. Never in his life he had witnessed parents treating their child this bad, this violent and this harsh. His rage focused upon the man. It grew by every word he said, by every action he took. When he just had raised his arm, a green mist appeared out of nowhere. It covered the boy's back. Tiny strings of bluish, almost white lights were meandering in it. Nobody noticed, not even Vincent. He was totally focused upon the man, in mad rage.

The man swung his arm back. He even tipped on his toes in order to use a bigger force, slapping his improvised whip upon his son's back. It came down in a cruel whoosh and bounced back the moment it touched the green mist. It hit the father in his face, increasing his anger. Again, he swung his arm back. This time, he let the buckle come down in a bigger speed than the strike before, putting all his weight behind it. Afresh, it bounced back and hit him in the face, leaving Johannes unharmed. His father went crazy. He dropped the belt and stormed at his son, determined to continue the corporal punishment, but when he was about to grab him, the green mist grew drastically. However Johan never saw the mist, he bounced back from it and fell, hitting the back of his head against the tiled floor hard. It knocked him out.

Since his father lay on the floor unconsciously, Johannes dared to look up. He smiled first, but then became angry. 'Now see what happens if you guys try to hurt me all the time!' he yelled at his mother. 'You have to love me instead of hurting me. I hate you, both of you!' He started crying again. Fighting his tears, he turned around. He ran for the stairs, went up and into his room. The door slammed when he shut it. Next, Vincent heard its lock twisted. Johannes probably was not going to school today, he somehow knew.

He looked at the adults in front of him. Johan still lay passed out on the cold kitchen floor. His wife briefly checked on him. She sat down at his side on her haunches, quickly lifted an eyelid, shrugged and came up straight. She kept looking for a while until she turned around to the countertop and resumed preparing for breakfast, as if nothing had happened.

Her husband woke up a couple of minutes later with a severe headache. He said nothing, just rubbed the back of his head. Quietly, he stood up, picked up his belt from the cold kitchen floor and strapped it around his trousers. From that day on, he would never use it to punish his son, ever again.

\*\*\*

The next morning Vincent couldn't wake up. Normally, he never had problems getting out of his haystack, but this morning he had a very hard time. When the rooster first cried its soft alarm, he didn't even hear it. It took it by surprise.

Gently, as it ever took care of him, it tried again. Still Vincent didn't move. A little worried because the boy normally always reacted, it came down from the top of the haystack to check on the young one. Quicker than any human being would have found out, it noticed that he was still asleep. The bird pulled a little tuft of hair in an attempt to wake him. The boy didn't move. It took a bigger tuft and pulled a little harder. Now he swung his hands at it, as if he was chasing away mosquitoes.

He hit the rooster, but fortunately not very hard. It was caught by surprise and shouted a short cry. This finally made the boy come round. The three cats on his lap opened half an eye to see what the fuss was all about, but then went back to sleep, as they usually did in the mornings.

First, he didn't understand where he was. He looked around astonished until he realized that he had been dreaming, still in his haystack, and that he had just hit the rooster. He felt sorry for the bird immediately, before he even knew why he had hit it. He grabbed it and gave it the best hug he could ever give. The animal already forgave him. It nested in Vincent's arms and let itself be caressed by his tender loving care.

Then, Vincent realized the time, about the same time the rooster realized it hadn't woken the rest of the family. It cried aloud to let everybody on the farm know that it was way over time to rise and shine. In shock and still in pyjamas, Vincent's parents soon after arrived in the shed to ask him what had happened. Vincent first assured them that he was okay, went into the farm to look for some breakfast next, cleaned himself and then quickly dressed for school in his room.

While dressing, little pieces of his dreams occurred to him, but none were actually making sense. He tried to remember once more, but then let it go, for he was already late for school.

Soon after, in the days, weeks, months and years that passed, he never woke up easily anymore. Every time he woke up, he felt tired, as if he had worked all night. The cats stopped sleeping at his side because he moved too much for them to find a quiet spot. Even the rooster stopped being gentle with him in the mornings as the boy never heard its soft crows anyway.

He had come late in school each day and was now the last to come into class in the mornings. It had become his new way of dodging other children in the schoolyard.

He paid less attention in class, developed some puffiness under his eyes and yawned almost the whole day. After he had fallen asleep at the family dinner table during supper, his mom finally took him to see the doctor. It was the tenth of November, a day before his eleventh birthday.

Both were surprised to see the note on the doctor's front door:

*Dr. Rosenberg is on a holiday for three weeks.*
*A substitute doctor is working in the pavilion of the backyard until he returns.*

*We are very sorry for the inconvenience, but sure that the deputy takes care of you in the best possible way.*
*Please go around the corner and have a seat in the waiting room. He will be with you as soon as possible.*

*Kind regards,*
*Dr. Rosenberg and staff.*

'That is weird,' his mother said when she finished reading the note. 'We have been patients of Rosenberg for almost thirty years and, until now, he has always been present for us. I can't remember him ever taking the time off. Besides, his assistant didn't even mention it over the phone.' She first seemed to get a little angry about it, but then clearly gave the assistant the benefit of the doubt. 'Ah well, whatever, I phoned her very early this morning anyway. Maybe she was still a little sleepy and forgot to mention.' Then she asked Vincent: 'Do you have a problem with seeing another doctor today?' 'No, mom, I'm fine with it. It's alright, really.' 'Okay then,' she said while grabbing his hand, 'let's meet this substitute and see what he can tell us about your tiredness.' Still holding hands, they walked around the corner and into the backyard, meanwhile never noticing that the note upon the front door disappeared the moment they had turned their backs. It slowly dissolved into nothing.

When they arrived in the large backyard, they saw a big pond, surrounded by a nicely mowed lawn, but no pavilion and no waiting room. At both sides wild bushes and shrubs marked the garden's boundaries. They looked around for the pavilion, but couldn't discover anything that looked alike, not even in the bushes. They found it truly strange. Vincent saw the crow. Although he hadn't seen it again in four years, he was absolutely sure it was the same crow as the one that had given him his stone. Its feathers were as shiny as he remembered them to be and in its eyes he saw the strings of light orbiting around its irises. He looked at it with joyful recognition. The bird looked at him for a while likewise until it crowed three times and took off, directly into the shrubs.

'Mom, look!' Vincent pointed it out to his mother. 'I have met that bird before and I am pretty sure it is giving us directions!' His mother, not really surprised by this revelation of her son, first couldn't see it, for it had taken place somewhere in the thick bushes. Finally, she managed to see it too. 'Wow!' she said. 'That really is a beautiful crow. I can imagine you would want to get in touch with it!'

Vincent smiled at her. In the past years, she had come to know him better and better until she was his biggest human support. He had always found it a heart-warming idea that she had pulled all the stops in order to fully understand his world. Now, her efforts paid off.

'Let's see what that bird is pointing out to us,' she said and made her way through the bushes by pushing the front branches aside. She held them back and then signed him to go through first. She stepped after him next and pushed aside a second row of branches. She laughed. 'You would probably never have expected to be with me in the bushes like this, would you?' He shook his head and smiled. She laughed again. 'I figured,' she said as she pushed back yet another branch. 'Now, let's go on adventure!' Together they went in, deeper and deeper, until they couldn't see the doctor's backyard anymore.

He had never deemed the bushes to be this thick, this high and this wide. From outside, standing in the backyard, it had appeared to be just a small ridge of trees, shrubs and other wild plants, but once they were in, it seemed like a jungle. Both were working very hard in making way through, but because of the high density they could only make progress slowly. On top of that, they couldn't see the crow anymore. Fortunately, it regularly crowed its voice to show them its location.

'Wow, this really is a tough job!' his mother finally said. 'I have no idea how long we are trying to cross these bushes already, but it doesn't really matter. We're still having fun, aren't we?' Vincent confirmed and looked at his mother in full excitement, for she was a mess by now. Her hair normally had always been decently tight down in a knot, but now locks of it were sticking out as if they were living a life of their own. Little leaves and branches hung it almost everywhere and her face showed stripes and marks from the branches she had swept with her cheeks. Her skirt was torn by the many thorns that they had come across and her normally always shiny shoes were covered in dirt. She definitely had become dirty, but her eyes ever sparkled and twinkled.

'I know, I know,' she said when she saw him looking at her appearance, 'I am dirty now, but I haven't had this much fun in a long time, son. Welcome into your world, I would say!' She laughed again and kissed him on the cheek, whereupon she made further way through the seemingly never ending foliage.

They heard the crow again. It came from very nearby. 'Mom, do you hear that?' Vincent asked. 'Can you see it already?' Both stood still and looked around. They couldn't distinguish it, yet noticed something else instead. Not far ahead, the bushes seemed to thin. Vegetation grew lower to the ground progressively until only grass was paving their way. They looked at each other joyfully, for they understood that they had finally reached the end of their jungle hike. The last few yards were easily done, so they made their way to the field rather quickly. Once they set foot on the grass, they stood still and beheld its surroundings with baded breath. What they saw there, was truly unbelievable.

They stood upon a field, similar to the doctor's backyard, only without a pond this time. It was totally enclosed by the bushes they had just made way through and, no matter how hard they looked, they couldn't find any sign of an entrance.

At their right side, they finally saw the crow again. It sat on top of a small haystack. The moment they looked its direction, a shiny yellow brick road paved itself from where they stood. Golden blocks appeared out of nothing and laid themselves, tile by tile, forming a path from the noses of their shoes towards the haystack. When it reached its destination, it formed a tiny golden sill and likewise tiny door in the front side of the haystack. Meanwhile, big mushrooms with red roofs and white dots upon, popped out of the grass simultaneously aside. They were almost as big as trees and towered above their heads. Next, a dreamcatcher with bars underneath started to jingle its enchanting sound. It hung aside the tiny door, they now found out. However, it certainly hadn't been there earlier. Both wondered for a while and beheld how its small bars were producing the sound, for there hadn't been any wind at all.

They kept standing still to admire the wonderful spectacle that had taken place until the bird started crowing aloud nonstop, encouraging them to tread the path. Without any hesitation, mother took the first step. Vincent demurred a little. 'Come on, boy!' his mother heartened him. 'We do have an appointment, remember? And, besides, I'll stay with you all the time, so you're safe with me. Now, off you go!'

Awaiting her son's first step upon the path, she was just about to lick her appearance into shape, when she discovered there was nothing to fashion anymore. The moment she had set foot on the golden lane, all dirt had vanished. Even the rips in her skirt were gone. 'Look, I'm suddenly all clean!' she cried out to Vincent. 'Quickly, step on the path and you will become as well.' Although it was clear that the golden path hadn't harmed his mother, Vincent still hesitated. He searched his pockets for his miracle stone and firmly enclosed it. It gave him the power to go on.

When he first set foot upon the path, his tears and spots vanished immediately. Even his hair looked combed more neatly than it had ever been combed before. 'Wow, you look awesome!' his mother reacted while she grabbed his hand again. Together they walked the path towards the tiny door. Mother knocked on it. Silently, it went open. Behind, nothing was to be seen. She didn't await the moment, but dropped on her knees and crawled through. Vincent did the same after her.

The crow now had fulfilled its task and took off. It flew straight up, to the sky, as if it went straight back to heaven. Vincent wasn't able to set eyes on its flight this time. He was already inside, crawling behind his mother through a small corridor, where, at its end, awaited another tiny door. His mother had already opened the second one as well and was trying to get in. Vincent had to wait a while for her to get through it completely. It took her some effort because she hardly fitted. Once she managed to pull her behind after her, it was his turn.

When he came inside, he couldn't believe the small haystack to enclose such a huge space, but it did. After they had entered, they were easily able to stand up straight. They found themselves in the largest waiting room Vincent had ever seen. It was more than twenty yards wide and all around were its walls made of glass. Miraculously, they hadn't been able to see through the haystack earlier, but now they overlooked the whole outside surroundings. They could even see the sky above. High up, Vincent discovered a little black dot. It was the crow, ever rising.

'Do you want anything to drink?' his mother asked him. 'I'm pretty sure they will have something here.' As she asked, a huge machine appeared out of nowhere. It looked a lot like the coffee machines he had seen in gas stations, only this one offered soft drinks, hot chocolate milk and any fruit juice one could think of as well. Even though he was really thirsty, Vincent looked at his mom amazed. None of these wonderful things had surprised her, not even a tiny bit, like she had known what was about to happen all the time. He wanted to ask her about it, but it was not given to him. Suddenly, another door, they hadn't seen any sign of it earlier, opened in the middle of the glass wall.

Vincent could see the projection of the outside world stuck upon, as if it was printed. Once fully turned, its exterior side took over the same image as its wall behind. The door vanished, disappeared in its background, leaving a dark rectangle above its threshold. Slowly, a huge black dog walked through.

Vincent recognized it immediately, for it was the same dog that had made him pass out four years ago. He froze again. His heart pounded in his chest heavily as he wanted to run to his mother for security, but because the dog was heading her direction, he remained his place, frozen, even though the dog was happily wagging its tail, as if it was about to greet an old friend.

'Hello Hector!' his mother greeted the dog. 'How are you, my friend? It's been such a long time, I've really missed you. How nice to see you back.' She patted the dog on its head while it rubbed her thighs with its cheeks.

Vincent hadn't moved since the dog came in and couldn't believe what he was witnessing. He looked at his mom in disbelieve again. She laughed and said: 'It seems about time to fill you in, son. Just have a seat, we'll wait for the doctor first.' The moment she finished her sentence, humongous black leather armchairs appeared. Too astonished to say anything, Vincent dropped himself in one of them. Next to him, his mother did the same, while the dog took place at her feet. It never looked at Vincent, only attended to his mom.

'Here son,' a warm voice suddenly sounded. He looked up and saw an old man standing next to him. The man had appeared out of nothing, just as the chairs and the coffee machine had done earlier. He was a little taller than his mom, had a wild, grey hairdo and very blue eyes. The eyes looked at him in a kind and understanding way and even though Vincent had been taken quite aback by his sudden appearance, he liked the man straight away.

The dog stood up and went to the man's right side. It sat down on its buttocks there. Still, it showed no interest in Vincent whatsoever. The man laid his right hand on its big head. In his left, he held a small glass with a drink. It was bluish in colour and disseminated a sweet sent, like the blackberry juice he used to drink at home a lot. 'Have a drink, my friend,' the old man spoke. 'I know you must be pretty thirsty after your bushwalk over here.' He nodded questioningly and then handed him the glass. Vincent took it, but wasn't sure about drinking its content, so he looked at his mom. She still smiled, looked happy and, again, wasn't amazed at all. She stood up.

'Hi paps,' she said as she hugged the old man, 'nice to see you again, I've missed you.'

'It certainly has been a while,' the old man responded while hugging her back, 'but it has been better for the boy's development.' 'I understood something like that, but tomorrow that will change, I presume?' She looked at him interrogatively. 'Tomorrow that will change indeed,' he confirmed. 'On the day this young boy turns eleven…' he placed his left hand on Vincent's shoulder, '… we will turn him into the man he is meant to be!' His mother smiled again upon that statement, while Vincent looked at her in utter surprise.

He still sat in the armchair holding the tiny glass of bluish drink in his hand. He had listened to what his mom and the old man were saying, but he hadn't had a single clue what their conversation was about. Finally, he asked his mom, agitated.

'Why are you acting as if you've known this man all your life?' he said, being annoyed with all the secrets around his persona. He stood up from the armchair and started to shout: 'Why does nothing that has happened today seem to surprise you and why, for God's sake, did you just call that man "paps"?!' 'Easy, son,' his mother answered. 'I know you're getting upset right now, and I understand, but you must not get angry with me, for I have had a good reason to keep all this a secret. I was supposed to.' 'By whom?! Him?!' Vincent yelled as he pointed at the old man. 'No, not him. He is part of the same secret.'

'Vincent,' the old man interrupted his mother. 'You've read the book of Heracles, haven't you?' Vincent nodded, still angry, while the old man proceeded. 'Well, then you must be quite capable of understanding how it must be, for a spirit like me, to accidently not only fall in love with a mortal, but to impregnate her too.' Vincent didn't, for the words hit him like a bomb. He looked at the man next to him first and gazed at his mother next, amazed. She further explained. 'The man next to you is my biological father, Vincent. However he has never lived in the flesh, he is sometimes capable of appearing in it, just like Heracles' father was.' 'Yeah, I couldn't really help but falling in love with your grandmother,' the man continued. 'She simply was too beautiful for me to resist. When we found out she was pregnant, I had to withdraw myself and watched her, with envious eyes, living her life with another man in order for your mother to grow up normally. Once your mother was old enough, it was destined for her husband to die and for your grandmother to further live on my side. Technically, she has never died, for she went into spirit the moment that car made its deadly roles. However, we are still able to keep in touch with our relatives. Not all of them though, for you must grow up a normal boy first. The legend clearly has stated that…'

'Okay, dad, that's enough!' his mother interrupted him. 'The boy turns eleven tomorrow. Don't tell him any sooner, you're not allowed to.'

Vincent was in shock. He had backslidden his armchair and looked at both faces in front of him. His head nodded from one to the other, astonished. Neither of the adults gave him the time to process.

'Drink the drink, my son,' his mother urged him, 'not only will you like it, it will also make you feel better.'

Vincent drank. He hit it in one gulp back and fell asleep immediately. He never noticed how he rose up from his chair and gently floated through the seemingly glass roof. His mother watched him for a while as he went straight up in the sky. She hugged her father next, petted the dog on its head and took off through the ever-black rectangle. She never worried as she went back home, to her husband and the twins, for she knew she wasn't going to see her eldest any sooner than the next morning, the morning of his eleventh birthday.

***

When he looked around, he saw nothing. Pure darkness surrounded him. At his feet, he didn't feel a thing, not even the familiar touch of solid ground. It felt as if he lay flat in his haystack, except for the fact that his head told him his body was most certainly in an up straight position. Immediately after the realization, Vincent felt light, as if he weighed nothing. Then, a soft breeze of air stroke his hair gently and the smell of moist grass and fresh fallen leaves reached his nose. He looked up to the sky, but there was nothing to be seen. Thick clouds were guiding the night as if they were deliberately blocking him from getting to know his current position.

Suddenly, he felt a presence, an energy, somewhere nearby. He felt another one, yet another. The more he drew his attention to the sensations, the more presences he started to feel. It felt like he was surrounded by many other human beings, although he couldn't hear them making any sounds, not even a single respiration.

At home, on their farm, it was now dark as well. The same kinds of clouds had wrapped up the sky. They had blocked the stars from twinkling Planet Earth and had even prevented the moon from shining its cold silver lights. Not only did this happen at home, everywhere else on Earth the same phenomenon occurred. The whole planet was coated with a thick down duvet. Not a single ray of light was able to penetrate, at least, not from above.

A huge light beam rose from Vincent's shed. It cut through darkness as a warm knife cuts through butter, bright bluish in colour, so bright, it almost turned to white. If seen with the naked eye, one should have to squint to prevent it from blinding ones sight. It had a glare of unprecedented beauty.

There was another light to be seen in its direct area. Just at one farm, three farms away, the light of a candle distinguished itself from black darkness. In that light, one could see the contours of an old men. Locks of white hair were dancing around his head, his face turned to the window. Then, all the sudden, two eyes lit up. They started to shine. Two tiny purple beams cut through the window next. They rose high in the night sky and united with the big blue ray above the shed. Together, they illuminated the undersides of the clouds.

A young girl who worked as an au pair for a musician couple in France, in Carnac, Brittany, was the first to notice.

When her beautiful green eyes looked out of the window upon the second floor, her mouth fell open in amazement. Rays of bluish, almost white lights crossed the undersides of the dark clouds. They moved as if they were the Northern Lights, only now to be seen in Carnac.

In bated breath she stared at the meandering rays in the sky above. There was nobody around to notice the change in her eyes since her boy was already deeply asleep and his grandparents had gone to bed in their own house long ago. For a moment, her eyes dwelled off to a small house next door. Then she looked back at the sky, meanwhile catching her own reflection in the window. She smiled, for she knew it had begun.

Her eyes showed a deep green colour and included little twists of white within. As she stood there, a bright green blaze had entered her aura. Still smiling, she finally turned away from the window and took something out of her pocket. It was a leather string bracelet with a white rock within.

She took a piece of paper out of a cupboard, picked up a pencil next and wrote a small note for the boy she had come to love so much. Then she went into his room. She pressed him a kiss upon his forehead and placed both items upon his bed side table. It was time for her to leave. Looking at the boy again, she smiled as she started to disappear, slowly evaporating into the humid air of the bedroom, leaving him peacefully asleep and unaware of her departure. He would find out she had left the following morning.

In the meantime, all around the world, now literally everyone looked up at the sky and noticed the meandering rays of light that were displaying such an unusual scenery. Cars stopped in the middle of the highway, mothers and children stood still at the side walk, television stations stopped broadcasting, waiters stopped serving drinks and soldiers on both sides of a fierce firefight ceased fire in order to set eyes on this extraordinary spectacle. The only thing that came the world to mind was the beautiful game of light that took place in the sky. All people looked up, even those who were in deep sleep. However, they did it in their dreams. It allied mankind for a couple of hours.

Because Vincent couldn't see a single thing in the darkness, he closed his eyes. All his senses were now focused on determining what he had felt. He sharpened his concentration, his brains working overtime. Never in his life had the boy experienced such a strange form of awareness, even though he had always been very sensitive. He felt a brief twinge in his frontal lobe. It didn't hurt him much, only startled him a little. Without opening his eyes, he reached for his forehead to rub it, but on its way, his hand stopped just in front of his head. He gasped for air when he noticed that he could see it. With his mind's eye he kept staring at it, meanwhile moving his fingers. This surely was a strange perception. He looked around and could see more.

When he looked down, he found out that he was floating high up in the sky. Little houses were visible underneath. They were covered by a forest. He now could see that he was moving. While neatly remaining the same height, he was going in a forward direction. Still, he had no idea of where he was, although he did see the contours of a city in the distance. Big towers almost hit his feet as he flew over. Palm trees wove aside the streets beneath, in the little breeze he had felt earlier. He had no idea which city it could be.

Then he started to notice the people. Apparently, they had noticed him too, although they were not staring at him directly. All of them were gazing above. The more areas he oversaw, the more people he noticed. They all had stopped whatever they were doing. All looked above. Some of them held hands, others were hugging. He didn't know why, but all the sudden, automatically, he was sending his love to them.

People were feeling small and insignificant in comparison with such an event of unimaginable greatness. It made them seek support from one another. While still looking above, complete strangers were holding hands. Others were hugging or wrapped up in embraces. Everyone felt a deep love.

The sight only lasted for ten minutes at each and every location, but it shortly had made a deep impact on the whole of mankind. Its effect remained in people's minds for several hours. In that period of time, no one in the entire world had fired a single bullet, not a single kid had received a corrective slap, no animal was butchered and nobody had been angry. Instead, now people showed love and were sweet to each other. Even the soldiers on both sides of a long lasting war were sending each other food and refreshing water supplies, regardless it was theirs or those from their enemies. Enemies simply didn't exist in those hours because the power of love had spread the world. It had made the Earth the most beautiful place to live, safe and secure for all its inhabitants.

Little rays of bluish white lights came out of Vincent's hands when he stretched them out to the people below. It affected them. They lit up as his beams first made contact. He didn't know why he was doing what he did, but he knew, somewhere deep inside, that what he was doing was good, so he continued.

He went over snowy mountains, flat highlands and rocky terrains, as it seemed to him, for hours. Wherever he flew, the people looked up to him. He touched each and every single one of them and was just wondering how long he could go on like this, when he encountered a huge beam of light that rose up from a small shed. It cut straight through the clouds above him and was made of the same light that had come out of his hands all night. When he gave it a closer inspection, he recognized the shed. It was his favorite; the one with his haystack. He could now even see the farm where he assumed his parents to be deeply asleep since it must have been way over midnight.

He floated into the light and immediately sank down. The light pulled him, down to the shed and down to his haystack. Gradually, Earth came closer. When he hung only about thirty feet high, he noticed the light split. Two smaller beams separated the big one. First, they turned purple and then, as if projected by laser, they rayed towards the farm of the neighbour who lived three farms away. Vincent could only see them for a brief period of time, for soon the shed's roof rose in front of his ever-closed eyes. The separated beams disappeared next, leaving two holes in the neighbour's window.

After he had softly fallen through, the gap above his head closed. He felt the comforting stimuli of hay, which made him magically fall asleep immediately. He didn't noticed anymore how the big beam of light opened the clouds in the sky, nor did he see it taking off to heaven.

Soon after it left, the clouds dissolved all over the world. For several hours, the sky stayed clear. Then the Earth regained itself. Clouds came back, while life recommenced as it had ever done, leaving no further trace of the miracle.

Individuality took over. Soldiers shot at other soldiers, bombs were dropped randomly, animals were bullied and butchered, dictators and directors resumed raking money and parents went back to correctively slapping their children.

Only a few hypersensitive people remembered the loving sensation they had experienced. Those who did, tried to remind the world, but were declared insane. Strangely enough, not even a single newspaper wrote about the lights, nobody had recorded them, nor had any television station reported the occurrence. It was like it had never taken place at all.

Although nothing of the energy seemed to have remained in the world, in fact it only seemed. Around the nucleus of any random atom, little traces of the bluish, almost white, lights were meandering alike the big rays had done in the skies earlier. They had always been there, but because of the boost of energy that had occurred during Vincent's quest, they were now recharged with a new load; the batch of love, waiting to be empowered.

On the top of a small hill near the coast in Sri Lanka, an old Buddhist monk was meditating. His eyes were closed while his focus lay in another dimension. He went in, meanwhile repeating the humming mantra that had brought him in this state of mind. Before his closed eyes, a beautiful spectacle of bluish-white rays of light started playing its ever game. Their show warmed him. He smiled and stayed attuned to it for a while. Then he bent over and pressed his forehead to the solid ground in gratitude. He opened his eyes and smiled again. He knew change was going to come.

\*\*\*

For the first time in years, Vincent woke up easily. Whether it was caused by his eleventh birthday today or by the good sleep, he didn't know. He only knew that he had woken up without feeling tired for the first time in years.

When he looked up, he noticed the rooster was still deeply asleep. Its light snoring accompanied the sound of the first birds waking up in the area. Vincent stayed in the haystack for a while and dozed off again until it occurred to him he couldn't remember how and at what time he went to sleep the day before. In fact, the whole of yesterday seemed to be erased out of his mind. He vaguely remembered something about a potion, a doctor and his mom, but he couldn't figure out more, as if the whole day had happened in one of his dreams. It was a strange sensation. He wondered about it a little further until he decided to ask his mother later. For now, all he had to do was to be the birthday boy. Any minute spilled on vague thoughts meant a minute less of joy.

He quickly rolled himself out of the haystack and instantly awoke the poor animal on top that started its cock-a-doodle-do in shock right away. By this mistake, it woke up the whole farm an hour early. Vincent didn't really mind. He was already wide awake and longed for his birthday present. He was curious. Other years, always one of his brothers had slipped tongue days in advance, but this year the two had firmly kept their mouths shut. He had to wait until the moment his parents would reveal their surprise.

Fortunately, he didn't have to wait long. When he was just heading towards the farm for breakfast, his father came out. 'Hey son! Nice to see you ready for the day. How are you feeling this morning?' 'I feel great, dad, thank you. Finally, I woke up really easily and totally not tired at all.' 'Wow, that's great news! I am glad your little visit to the doctor yesterday paid off. I don't know what that man exactly did to you, but I wish he had done it years ago. Unbelievable!'

Vincent wanted to ask his dad about the visit, but his father went on: 'Do you know what else is truly unbelievable?' He shook his head. 'That you are already eleven years! Man, you're growing up fast, I can still picture you a little baby, how time flies…' He stood still for a while and looked at his son, clearly becoming emotional. He knelt down next and threw his arms around the boy, hugging him in a strong grip while pressing him against his chest. Vincent could hardly breathe, but enjoyed the heart-to-heart moment with his father tremendously, so he let him. He laid his head against the big shoulder and held still because he could hear his father snivel. His hair became wet from the tears dripping from father's cheeks into his neck.

'Congratulations, my boy,' his father whispered in a hoarse voice, 'I truly hope you may grow up to have such a nice family as well one day. You guys are the lights of my life!' He then invigorated his statement by firmer embracing his son. Finally, he let go. He took his peasant handkerchief out of his pocket and dried his eyes and cheeks. His neck still remained a little wet when he put it back.

'So!' he now happily declared. 'That's enough emotions for one day, let's bring you to your present. Hold on for a while. The rest of the family is about to join us, they're almost ready. I'll go and get them.'

With that promise he left Vincent on the courtyard and went into the farm to gather the family. Vincent still hadn't had the chance to ask him about the doctor, but that was all right. He could always ask his mother later.

The front door opened. His father stepped through first. Immediately after, his two brothers flew out. They ran up to him in a straight line and bumped into him simultaneously. All three boys fell on the ground. Vincent first was a little agitated by this harsh encounter, but soon regained himself and went for a revenge. He got up on his knees and tickled the twins wherever he could. Both were laughing and rolled on the ground while trying to keep his hands away from their bodies. They even shrieked for mercy.

Meanwhile, their mother had entered the courtyard as well. She saw her three boys having fun on the ground and couldn't believe her eyes. Amazed, she looked at her husband aside them. He laughed as well. She walked up to him, gave him a kiss on the cheek and laid her arm around his waist. He laid his around her shoulders. 'Is this really Vincent?' she asked her husband, laughing. 'Yep, it really is.'

Together they kept watching their boys until their boys watched back. They suddenly stopped their romp and rushed over, for they had never seen them in such a dovelike embrace before, even though they knew very well their parents loved each other a lot. All three now wanted to participate. The twins had started the running, but Vincent had quickly overtaken them. He was the first to arrive and immediately crashed into their waists. Next he threw his arms around both. Soon, his brothers did the same after him. 'Family hug!' one of them screamed. It caused everybody to laugh. Immediately after, the twins recommenced the tickle party, so the whole family ended up in the playful fight.

Finally, their mom had enough. 'Okay boys, that's it,' she said wheezy. The boys stopped immediately. All three were exhausted, but still laughed. Their mom and dad had a huge twinkle in their eyes. It made them look several years younger. His mom walked up to Vincent. She took his head in her hands and kissed him on his forehead. 'Happy Birthday, son,' she congratulated him. Next, she tenderly rubbed the top of his head and made way for her two younger sons who were already lining up behind her. One by one they hugged their older brother and kissed him to congratulate.

At that point, Vincent was the happiest boy on Earth. He felt so loved, he would have liked to stay in the moment forever, surrounded by his loving family members, but it was not given to him. Soon, one of his brothers snapped him out of it. 'To your present!' he commanded with huge exaggeration. His mom and dad nodded silently but smiling and together all five family members started walking into the back of the courtyard. The twins walked in front, their mom and dad behind while holding hands, as Vincent closed the procession. After all, he was the only one who didn't know where they were going.

To his surprise, everybody went to the rabbit barn. He hadn't been in for almost seven years and was taken aback by this unexpected location. One of his brothers opened the door and went in. Soon, the other followed. Their dad held still in front of the door opening and turned around. 'Don't worry, son,' he said. 'Nothing in here will ever spook you off anymore, I promise. Now step inside and behold your present.' He stepped aside himself and made way for Vincent to go through. Vincent hesitated shortly, but his mom felt his nervousness and guided him gently through the doorway until he was inside. There, she let go.

Once inside, it was too dark to see anything, but Vincent immediately sensed the absence of rabbits. He became frightened. Something in him wanted to run away because, over the years, an absence of rabbits had meant that they all had been butchered. Their skinned bodies would hang at the ceiling, which was something that Vincent never wanted to see ever again, until he realized he couldn't smell the scent of blood. He decided to stay. Curiosity overcame his fears. 'Surprise!' the twins yelled simultaneously and at the same time they turned on the lights.

At a farm three farms away from theirs, their neighbour had recently woken up as well. He had taken a shower, had fed his animals and just finished breakfast. He stood up from his chair, put his dishes at the sink and took a coat off the hanger. He put it on. Next, he went into his barn to come out a few minutes later with a big box in his hands. It had a blue ribbon tied around and several holes in the top. Something scratched its walls inside. The neighbour then walked out of the courtyard, told his big black dog to stay on the terrain and went on his way.

The lights went on and Vincent looked around. He saw no rabbits. Instead, he noticed that the cages were locked off with glass windows against the bars. Something else now lived there. He couldn't really find out what it was, so he walked over for a closer inspection. At the bottom of each cage lay a huge variety of vegetables. Vincent saw lettuce, leaved branches, carrots, apples and other fruits, whereupon and around enormous numbers of bugs were crawling, each kind in their own cage. He saw grasshoppers, caterpillars, larvae, worms, cockroaches, snails, wasps, ants and even scorpions and tarantulas. At the end of the line, he discovered a huge aquarium where hundreds of water beetles were swimming around while dragonflies danced above the water. In the left corner of the barn, a large fridge and some other machinery were placed.

Vincent looked at his family. All stood still near the door and looked back at him. They smiled. 'Do you understand, Vincent?' his father finally asked. Vincent didn't know what to say and kept staring at his family in disbelieve. His father walked up to him and took him by the hand. 'Come on, son. Let me show you around. I'll clarify things for you.' Meanwhile, he gently guided him towards the first terraria.

'Look, inhere we grow different species of ants. Each kind in their own cage. We have got lemon ants, red ants, honeypot ants and carpenter ants. In Australia, for example, the Aboriginals eat the honeypot ants as a sweet snack, people in Colombia eat ants toasted as popcorn and in Thailand the red ants, as well as their eggs, are considered a delicacy in salads and chutneys. All over the world, it is normal for people to eat insects, except for parts of the world that are considered civilized, as in Europe and some parts of the United States. In fact, insects are a very healthy food source, containing a lot of nutrition. We are going to promote the insect eating throughout the whole world, starting with our own surroundings. Your mother has even collected a large variety of tasteful recipes. She wrote them down in a cookbook that is about to be sold in the bookstores as we speak.'

He nodded to his wife. She immediately came over, as if she had awaited the signal, holding a present in her hand. Vincent wondered where she had hidden it earlier, but assumed she must have kept it in the barn somewhere. It was wrapped in a beautiful shiny green gift wrapper and had a big blue ribbon tied around. 'Here son,' she said as she handed him the gift, 'this only is a little part of your surprise.' He opened it and held the cookbook in his hands. It had a nice purple cover and several photos of insect dishes printed upon its front. They seemed rather tasteful and Vincent could feel how his stomach protested its lack of breakfast. If presented one of these dishes now, he certainly would have eaten it right away.

'That is the first copy of her book ever printed,' his father proudly declared. 'We hope that, by selling these books, we would not only make some extra money, but also make a difference in the world. We hope that less animals as rabbits, cows, chicken, pigs, sheep, goats and horses are suffering on behalf of human consumption by telling people about insect eating as a healthy substitute for meats. As for our own family, we will no longer eat any meats anymore. That is another part of your birthday present, but the best is yet to come.' He then looked at his son to see what he had to say upon all this.

Vincent couldn't believe what he was hearing, nor seeing. His eyes welled up. In gratitude he looked at each and every one of his family members. 'Thank you,' he whispered, 'thank you all. I don't know what else to say but thank you. You have made me so happy!' Instead of adding anything to that, he then silently hugged everybody intense. One by one he embraced his family members in huge relieve. All these years on the farm until now, he had not only felt the misery of their rabbits, he had also felt the mistreatment of other mammals that were globally used for food purposes. He had felt how they all had lived their unnatural lives in between bars and in great social pain, how all had lived without any possibilities to collect their foods as they were born to do and how all were living throughout huge anxieties, knowing instinctively that they would be killed by the same humans that had provided them with food first. It had been the reason he had stayed away from the rabbits, but he had still felt their pains. He hadn't been able to change their destinies, even though he had truly wanted to. Now his family had made this huge step on their own!

He looked at the insects again and started to feel sorry for them as well. In the end, they were animals too. Sure, they were in fact living their natural lives and sure, they didn't have as much consciousness as other cattle, but for a fact, they were serving for food purposes now.

His mother felt his change right away. 'Don't worry, son,' she set his mind as ease. 'These animals are not butchered the same way as mammals are. Come, let me show you.' She walked over to the grasshopper cage and picked one out. While holding it carefully between her fingers, she went over to the back of the barn, to the fridge and the machinery. Once there, she picked up a transparent cup with a lid. The grasshopper in the meantime looked at her surprised, as if she was about to take it on a trip. Vincent couldn't sense any fear or anxiety from the animal. It only was a little worried about being held.

His mother placed it into the cup, put the lid on quickly and enplaned it in the fridge. Next, she closed the door. 'Now it falls asleep, as insects do in winter times,' she said. 'They will become stiff and will be easy to handle after.' She waited for a while, opened the fridge and took the grasshopper out. In the cup, Vincent could now see it sat still. It was alive and looking at them, but quite sleepy. His mother took the bug out and put it back in its cage.

'This one is not ready yet,' she said. 'We'll now wait until it is fully grown, but normally, when ready, we put them in the freezer after they have been in the fridge for a brief moment. They then die without any recollection of what is happening to them. We make sure they won't totally deep freeze them though, or else their nutrition gets lost. We'll put them in this machine next.' She pointed at the machinery next to the fridge. 'It'll dry freeze them without loss of any body structure or nutrition. This way, we'll take all their body fluids out and conserve them. You can keep them well up to a year. However it is quite an expensive process, we are able to earn all those costs back in the price we sell them for. We already have a large amount of customers who want to buy our bugs for this price, mostly restaurants with a large foreign clientele, for we only grow insects for human consumption.'

Vincent clapped his hands. This really was a friendly way of killing animals for human food purposes. The animals underwent no pains and were even able to live their natural lives while staying in their cages. No harm was done to them. In time, his parents had promised him, they would even build a windmill next to the barn, so electricity for the dry freezer would be gained in an environmental friendly way as well. They couldn't yet afford it, but in time they would have made enough money to buy it, they had assured him. It felt like he was dreaming.

He walked around the barn for a while, meanwhile beholding his present with joyful eyes until his mother reminded her family it was time for breakfast. He was just standing in front of the cage with the bees when he saw a little hole was made in the barn's wall for the bees to fly in and out. He sighed. It was a big relieve for him to know that they were living their natural habitat too, even though he was a little worried about eating the protectors of plant propagation.

'Dad?' he asked his father. 'Aren't bees the most necessary animals for pollinating flowers and other plants? Isn't it harmful for Mother Nature when we start eating bees?' His dad laughed. 'Son,' he said, 'you are truly an amazing child for you really think of everything. Don't you think your parents haven't thought about that too? No, boy, we don't eat the bees that pollinate flowers, we only eat the drones!' Not knowing what drones were, Vincent looked questioningly at his dad. He continued his explanation. 'Drones are the ones who don't participate in any of the working processes in a bee hive. They only fly from beehive to beehive to see if there is any bee queen to mate. These are their good purposes, were it not that there are way too many of these drowns per hive. Often, they form a threat to the food supplies of bee colonies. For this reason, beekeepers take them out and destroy them or feed their larvae to the chickens. See, here inside, we have placed this special comb to collect only them. They are the only ones we take out for food purposes. The other bees we keep alive in order to keep up their useful task for Mother Nature.' Again Vincent looked at his dad in gratitude. He couldn't believe how well his family had thought the process through. It was surely the best birthday present he could have ever had, suiting him like a handmade suit. He could never have figured this solution out all by himself. He loved it.

His mother really started protesting. 'Come on now, family,' she said, 'let's have breakfast, for it is almost time for lunch by now!' She pushed the twins towards the door. 'Wait a minute,' father held her back, 'we are forgetting the biggest part of Vincent's surprise!' His mother sighed shortly, but then agreed. 'Okay, let's wrap it up quickly then, for I am curious about his reaction upon this one too!' His father took him by the hand and together they walked up to the end of the shed where Vincent discovered another door.

'Aren't you curious about where the rabbits went?' his father asked him. It hadn't come to Vincent's mind. He felt a little ashamed to have forgotten about the rabbits, but he had simply been too overwhelmed by his first surprise to be further worrying them. 'Happy birthday,' his father said, while opening the back door. 'Now step outside!' Both twins clapped their hands in joyful expectations.

Vincent stepped through the door and found himself in another cage he had never known before. It was huge! About ninety square yards were surrounded by netting. Inside, all the rabbits they had bred on their farm were freely walking around. He saw several hills in the middle, which had holes through underneath, old sewer pipes to crawl in, more than ten big rabbit houses high up from the ground and several gangways to their entrances. On top of that, two and a half yards above their heads, his family had even placed the netting too in order to protect the rabbits from birds of prey.

He had just stepped into rabbit's paradise. Everywhere stood food bowls, drinking bottles were placed around and in small nets just above the ground hung little bales of fresh hay. All rabbits were freely jumping the grass, humping each other or just lay happily side by side. It was unbelievable how much joy Vincent felt from these animals. They had all been given the greatest gift one could ever give a rabbit; freedom and a natural life. He loved it right away. 'All males have been humanly castrated to prevent them from further breeding,' his father explained. 'This last group of rabbits is able to grow old inhere. They are allowed to live their lives just as they like and we will never butcher any of them no matter what. They will stay on the farm as our household pets and you can visit them as often as you like. They are yours to keep now.' Vincent burst into tears for the second time. Finally, he had nothing to worry about anymore in his own home, finally, he felt understood by his family and finally, he could love the rabbits, even though he still felt deeply sorry for the ones that hadn't experienced the blessings of such an amazing residence. He thanked his family again. 'We will help you with the rabbits,' one of the twins said to him. 'Is it okay if we play with them occasionally too?' the other one asked. Vincent hugged them both. He dried his tears and said: 'The rabbits are a part of the family now. No matter how often you guys would like to come here too, you are as much welcome as I am.' He kissed both brothers and for the first time in his life he shared a feeling with them. The family finally started to connect as a whole.

Meanwhile, the neighbour who lived three farms away had entered their courtyard with the big box in his hands. Every now and then, squeaking noises came out of it.

The old man looked around for people, but couldn't find anyone until he noticed the door to the rabbits' shed was open. He smiled and put the box down. He sank his rear end on one of the small benches beside the front door of his neighbour's farm next. 'And thus we wait,' he said to the box.

'Now, let's eat!' mother commanded her family. 'There will be plenty of time later today for you boys to play with the rabbits, so chop, chop, off everybody goes!' She even clapped her hands in showing she meant business as she turned around to re-enter the shed. Her boys followed her meekly, as well as their dad did after them.

When Vincent walked through, he gazed around again to inculcate the sight into his mind. Everywhere he looked, he saw bugs happily crawling around, as if they were outside, only without the threat of any predators stalking them. He felt they were truly happy in their cages because there was plenty of good food around and plenty of fun things to do for them. They loved it here and that made Vincent as happy as he could be. He grabbed his mom's hand and frisked next to her in a joyful walk towards the door. She smiled at him and hopped the last yards along his side. Together, they skipped into the courtyard.

The old man stood up when he saw his neighbour and her son stepping out of the shed's doorway. They were happily skipping steps together. He smiled. Quickly after, also the twins and their dad came out. He picked up the box with the big ribbon, stood up and waited until the family arrived at the door. The boy and his mother were there first. 'Hello neighbour!' she joyfully greeted him as she let go of the hand of her son. 'Good morning, Maria,' he responded, 'and hello Johannes!' Father walked up to the neighbour with a big smile on his face and his right hand extended. 'Hello neighbour!' The old man grabbed the outstretched hand and shook it firmly. 'Congratulations on your son's birthday, Johannes,' he said. 'I truly hope he may grow up to become a man just like his father one day. It's amazing what you have done to please your eldest. Thank you for making the world a better place for all of us. I would really like to see what you have accomplished in the shed later. Just let me congratulate your family first.' He turned around next and gave mother a big hug. She hugged him back. 'Congratulations, my dear,' he now also said to her.

Vincent still stood aside his parents. Next to him, also the twins held silent. He wondered where this man all the sudden came from and why their parents were greeting him as an old friend. However he seemed really familiar, he couldn't figure out why. Meanwhile, the man turned towards him and handed him the big box that he was holding.

'Hello Vincent,' he said. 'Congratulations on your eleventh birthday, my boy. I hope you will enjoy the present I brought you, but let me introduce myself properly first. My name is Agnus and I am your neighbour from three farms away. I've known you since the day you were born, but we will explain all about that later. Open up your present now, but be very careful not to drop or turn the box!'

Vincent held the box in his hands and didn't know what to do with it. Inside, he could feel something moving around. Scratchy noises sounded and once every now and then, it shrieked. He wondered what it could be until he decided it was safe to open it since he was surrounded by family members. They were also curious about its content, urging him to open it.

He put the box on the floor and sank down on his knees next to it. He took the ribbon off. Immediately, the top went open and revealed a baby black dog. Its tiny blue eyes looked at him joyfully, its tiny ears flat on its head. It had thick black fur that grew in all directions. The moment it saw Vincent's face appearing above, it made noises and crawled to the side in making clear it wanted to be picked up. Vincent had just received a puppy. It was a baby boy.

The twins clapped their hands in pure joy and dropped themselves on their knees next to the box as well. They were just about to grab the puppy out when their mother pulled them away. 'Hold on a minute, boys. Don't touch it yet, for it is Vincent's present. He must be the first one to connect.' Both boys nodded that they had understood and came up straight. Silently they waited next to their mother, awaiting what Vincent was about to do with his present since he hadn't moved a bit after opening it. Nobody said a word, not even when Vincent gazed around at each and every one of them. Only the puppy kept shrieking for attention. All looked down to the boxes content. No one looked at Vincent. He was on his own.

He kept staring at his puppy for what seemed like ages. The little dog stopped shrieking the minute Vincent focused his eyes on it. It sat on its behind and looked back at him with a slightly tilted head, calmly awaiting his actions, just as everybody else did, until all heard a voice. It sounded familiar. Vincent looked up at everybody on the courtyard, but surprisingly none of them had spoken. He turned around.

In the door opening of the farm stood his teacher. She walked up to him when he layed eyes on her. 'The things that we fear the most in life, will always teach us our biggest lessons,' she said. 'Only those who are capable of overcoming their deepest fears are the true brave ones this world needs.' She stepped in between his father and the neighbour who lived three farms away. By doing that, she closed the circle of people around him, meanwhile making him clear that he wasn't alone, but that he had to do this on his own. She held silent after that, just as everybody else. Only the puppy had made a little noise when Vincent had looked away. It immediately went back to his previous position the moment he looked back.

He shivered at the thought of touching a dog, even if it was this young, but since it was so calmly awaiting what he was about to do, he dared to go a little further.

Carefully, he placed his right hand into a corner of the box, as far away from the puppy as possible. Slowly, he sank his hand to the bottom and left it there, in order to let it approach his hand first.

It was a little startled by the appearance of his hand, but soon it carefully approached. Vincent tried to hold his hand without moving it, but he couldn't help his knees had started to hurt from sitting upon them, so he moved in order to set himself in a more comfortable position. His hand moved too.

It frightened the puppy tremendously. With a loud bark, it jumped backwards, back to the corner and there it crouched, meanwhile keeping its little eyes on the hand that had acted so unusually strange.

The twins started laughing about its sudden movement, but a corrective push from their mother was enough to hold them silent again. Everybody in the circle around Vincent and his puppy now understood the importance of him overcoming his fears for this little creature, even though they couldn't understand the fear itself.

Vincent, in the meantime, had noticed that his uncertain action had frightened his puppy. It made his fears diminish. After all, this dog was very young and needed comforting. Since nobody else did anything, he was the only one to set it at ease. He melted down bit by bit and started to feel sorry for the baby when he realized it mistrusted him. His energies changed, fully aware that he was about to connect to his dog. His fears diminished more.

He pulled his right hand out of the corner and slowly moved it into the puppy's direction. When he was about an inch away, he held still. It crouched a little further, but then it became curious. It's head moved into the hand's direction as if it was pulled forward by its nose. It sniffed his scent carefully, obviously liking what its nose had experienced because, after that, it moved. Step-by-step, while keeping its body low and its tail stuck to its belly, it dared to crawl up to his hand. When it was nearby, it pressed its wet nose against. Vincent could feel its cold mark when the puppy pulled back. Next, it started to lick his fingers and at the same time, his animal communication skills returned. Never in his life had he been able to communicate with dogs the way he did with the animals on the farm, for never in his life he had tried to understand dogs the way he understood all other animals. He had always been blocked by fear, a door that had been shut for years. Now that door was opened.

He felt a click in his heart that went throughout his entire body. It tingled a little and gave him a very pleasant feeling. He looked at the puppy's eyes again, but now with a different gaze. It looked back.

He didn't await another second, but stretched both hands towards the little creature and picked it up. It crouched again, but then he could feel how the animal's energies changed too. It was done in seconds. He cuddled it for a while, petted its soft black fur while holding it carefully against his chest with his other hand. Silent tears dripped down both his cheeks. The puppy immediately laid its tiny head in his neck and closed its eyes, as he laid his wet cheeks carefully against its back. Finally, a bond was made.

'Well done, my boy!' their neighbour broke the silence first. He laid his hand on Vincent's head and stroke it gently. 'Only those who overcome their deepest fears are the heroes we need in this world,' he then repeated his teacher's words. 'You are a true hero now, my boy, a true hero now.'

Vincent, still sitting on the ground, stood up. He looked up to the old man's eyes, meanwhile holding his puppy to his chest. 'Thank you,' he said, 'for this wonderful present, I will take great care of it.' 'I know you are because I am going to train you. We'll do it together, for I can provide you with the best teacher there is.' He then put his fingers in his mouth and blew on them hard, producing the highest noise Vincent had ever heard. 'Now, don't be scared anymore,' he said next. 'Remember the lesson you've just learned. Feel and read your energy constantly when you are around dogs. It will be quite handy in other circumstances too.'

On the courtyard of the farm three farms away, the big black dog had awaited the signal since its boss had left. Slowly, it got up on all fours and left the courtyard. It went up on the road and turned left, left to where the signal had come from.

Vincent's brothers had now understood that it was done. They walked up to Vincent and congratulated him with this big winning. 'Can I hold it too?' one of them asked. 'And can I next?' the other asked after. Vincent nodded and handed the puppy to his brother, even though it fell him hard to let go. 'Bring the puppy into the kitchen, boys,' his mother said to the twins. 'I've placed some food and water on the floor next to a nice little basket. Put it in there. You can pet it for a little while, but in five minutes you must leave it. It needs to rest after everything it has been through. Puppies do need to sleep a lot. We'll stay here a little longer and then we will all come in for breakfast too. Now, off you go!' The boys nodded and went into the farm.

His mother turned around to Vincent. 'Well done! I am very proud of you and very happy we will have a dog around from now on. Do you have any idea how you would like to name it?' Vincent looked around to the faces of the adults that were ever surrounding him. All were awaiting his answer, curious about the name that he was about to pick. They gave him time. His teacher looked at him over her glasses, his father had crossed his arms in front of his chest and smiled, while his mother stood at his side with her arm around his shoulder. The only one who said something was the neighbour who lived three farms away. 'The first name that will come to mind is very often the best. Don't think too hard, for we all know you have a name prepared already, even though you had never expected to own a dog one day.' Vincent looked at him and nodded. 'I don't know why,' he responded, 'and I don't even know where or how I have picked it up, but I have always liked 'Utopy' for a dog's name.' 'Then Utopy it is', the old man stated solemnly. 'What a wonderful name you've picked for it!' his mother fell in. 'I really like it!' 'Utopy,' his father meanwhile repeated as if he wanted to taste the word. 'Utopy...I can get used to that.' 'Congratulations, Vincent,' his teacher now came up to him, 'on your birthday, your dog and the very extraordinary name you've just picked for it. I love it! Of course I have brought you a present too, but from your mother I have understood that you haven't had any breakfast yet. You must be very hungry after all this excitement, so I'll safe my present for later.' 'That seems very wise, thank you,' his mother now stated. 'Come on everybody, let's go inside!' She turned around and went into the farm. The teacher went in next.

Vincent was just about to follow them when he froze. The big black dog that lived three farms away, just sat food on their courtyard. It was coming their direction.

His fears of dogs returned instantly. He couldn't help it, but his body shook, while his legs felt like cooked spaghetti. All the sudden he had forgotten what he had just experienced with the little version of this big black monster. Fortunately, his dad and the neighbour stood still at his side. He grabbed his dad's waist and buried his face into his belly, away from the sight of the dog that had made him faint a couple of years earlier.

'Hello Hector,' his father said, as he bent over with quite some trouble since Vincent still clenched upon his side. His arms stretched to pet the dog on its big head while Vincent pressed his face into the soft belly deeper. He could feel how the dog sniffed his pants, his shirt and the back of his head. He wondered why no one bothered to get that dog away from him since he clearly was deeply scared of it.

'Well done, Vincent!' the old man said to his surprise. He clapped his hands in an attempt to give him an applause. Vincent looked up, amazed. How could he have done so well without even having the courage to face this dog? He turned his head up and looked at his father who smiled. 'Step one,' he said, 'never look at a dog when your energy is not right.' 'Correctemundo, neighbour!' the old man adjusted. 'Dogs only follow humans if their energy is balanced. If not balanced, they will do everything to correct it, for they see it as an unhealthy state of mind. They are highly sensitive and pick up on human energy in an instant. That's exactly why dogs are considered man's best friend. Living with an unbalanced human can cause a dog serious stress, so we owe it to the dogs among us to take good care of the energy levels within ourselves. Therefore, dogs are very healthy to have around. They never mean any harm; they only mirror themselves to our energies. If we are calm, they will remain too, so you have done very well by not showing your fears to Hector.'

Vincent released his arms around his father's waist little by little. He had understood, but still didn't feel very comfortable. The dog, in the meantime, had stopped sniffing him and sat next to the neighbour. It was looking at him curiously and held its head slightly tilted to one side, just as Utopy had done earlier. Vincent hardly dared to look at it, but when he did, carefully, he noticed a big green fly circling above its head. It flew around until it landed upon the neighbour's shoulder.

It was the biggest fly he had ever seen. To his surprise, the neighbour didn't seem to notice or mind. He let it stay there.

His father pulled his arms away from his waist. 'Take your time, Vincent,' he said. 'It doesn't matter that you are still scared, as long as you ignore the dog when you are in that state of mind. You will get used to it being around us sooner than you think. Just relax and let things happen. Hector will never bite you, that is for sure. I know because I've known this dog for a very long time by now and I trust it with all my heart. Will you believe me?' Vincent looked up at his dad again and now dared to smile too. He grabbed his hand. 'I promise, dad, I won't panic anymore, but I will take my time in getting used to it.' The old man smiled, his father nodded and the dog stood up. It wagged its tail. All five went into the house, meaning the fly still hadn't left the neighbour's shoulder. It went in as well.

Vincent went in last. He made sure he kept his distance from Hector, even though he was determined not to let it scare him off like before any more. In fact, he realized he now owned a dog that was probably going to grow the same size and the preview of becoming friends with the animal that had deeply scared him earlier, had made his heart pound in pure joy.

He was also looking forward to the breakfast table because his stomach roared by now. It was time to take care of it. He was going to eat, meanwhile facing Hector and therefore exterminating the fear for once and for all, just as his hero Heracles would have done.

Inside the kitchen, his brothers, the teacher and his mother had already taken place at the breakfast table. Both females sat on the side of the kitchen dresser opposite to Vincent's place, his brothers sat across from them, at their usual spots. In between, they had left him his place. Both his father and the neighbour who lived three farms away took place at each head of the table. The fly was nowhere to be seen.

At his right side, Vincent saw a small basket in which his puppy lay deeply asleep upon a soft velvet bedding. It was happily curled up, even snoring softly. On one side he discovered a bowl of water and a food bowl in a holder, on the other side Hector was just about to lie down. He calmly looked at Vincent for a brief moment, as if he wanted to reassure him again, whereafter he gently sniffed Utopy, laid his head upon the ridge of the basket and dozed off as well.

Quickly Vincent looked away from Hector. He hadn't experienced any fear for him this time, but he didn't feel comfortable enough to look him into the eyes yet, so his gaze went back to the food and water bowls.

The whole construction was placed in its lowest position for the puppy to reach it easily. The bowls were held by iron rings that connected in between. In the middle he saw a screw knob that held the rings in their current positions at a vertical bar, just above the ground. Later it could go way higher up since the bar towered half a yard above. 'Mom, what a lovely basket you bought for Utopy, thank you. I love the soft blue bedding as well. It must be very comfortable for him to lay upon since he is already happily asleep. I also truly like the food and water bowls. May I ask why Utopy needs a construction like this instead of just two bowls on the ground?' His mother smiled upon his question and looked at the neighbour. He then replied.

'Great question, my boy! Let me first compliment you on your observation skills, well done! It gives me the opportunity to start with your dog training lessons right away, if I may?' He looked around to all people at the breakfast table. After all adults had nodded approvingly he went on.

'Probably you two want to hear this too, for Utopy will become your family member as well. No matter whose present he is, he considers each and every one of you as a part of his pack, do you understand?' He now looked directly at the twins. His eyes went from one to the other until both boys nodded they had understood. Only then, he further explained.

'There are two reasons for using a construction for food and water like this. First, dogs, especially large dogs like Hector and Utopy, have very sensitive stomachs. If they eat in a straight up position, their stomachs will contain less air after the meal than if they eat it from the ground. These gasses namely can cause the stomach to widen or twist, which stops the blood stream. The dog will then die, so it is a very dangerous phenomenon we can prevent by feeding it in such a way.' He looked around again to see if everybody understood.

'Second,' he went on, 'dogs are known for protecting their food as wolves do in a pack. Naturally, it is normal for both dogs and wolves that the leader of the pack eats first, then the second in command takes his turn, then the next in line, and so on. If it is a dog's turn for food, the whole pack will let it eat in peace, no matter what position it has. For that reason, it is considered its right to defend its turn if any other dog approaches. It will claim its meal by standing over and will fight the dog that tries to steal its food. That is an instinctual table manner which you don't want to have in your human household. Therefore, you have got to make clear to Utopy that you don't mean to steal his food away if you approach him while he is eating.

Now, there are many tricks to teach him that, but best you can give him an extra tasteful treat when he is eating. Every time he looks up at you while having his meal, you give him something extra special, so he will understand that you don't mean to steal. On top of that, we make it harder for him to defend his food by standing over it since it hangs in this construction.'

Everybody held silent for a while since everybody now seemed to understand that raising a puppy required a lot of knowledge about dogs in order to prevent it from misbehaving. The old man smiled again.

'I never said it was going to be easy,' he spoke, 'but don't let yourselves be spooked off by all these rules, it will be as much fun as well. It is just that the more effort you put in, the more bonding and joy you will experience later. Nothing will ever come easily, for it is a saying that you will never get the dog you want, you will always get the dog you need instead. It means as much as that they truly teach you about yourself.' He now turned to Vincent. 'That's why we all agreed you needed a dog in order to show you what you are truly capable of. It will show you who you truly are, for...'

'Not yet, Agnus!' the teacher interrupted him. 'The boy hasn't had breakfast yet, so he is going to eat first. He has heard enough information by now. Only after his breakfast, we will proceed.' The neighbour looked at her and smiled. 'You're right. I'm sorry for letting myself get carried away like that. After breakfast it will be your turn to fill him in, so we men can finally have a look in that shed I am so curious about, all right boys?' 'Yeah!' the twins responded simultaneously. 'What about you, Johannes?'

He looked at Vincent's father who had just taken a big bite out of his lettuce and cheese sandwich. He grumbled a hardly understandable 'yes' with his mouth full. Wet blobs of ground bread, lettuce and cheese landed on his plate and the breakfast table.

'Johannes!' mother shrieked. 'Don't you ever speak with a full mouth again, please! How many times haven't you heard me say that to the boys, now look what you're doing!' The twins laughed, the teacher and their neighbour too. Meanwhile, mother stood up to pick a cloth from the kitchen sink. She wet it, wiped the blobs off the breakfast table and gave him a clean plate next, putting his dirty plate at the dishes aside the sink. 'Now sit,' she commanded Vincent as she took her place at the breakfast table as well, 'and eat because I have made you a fresh cheese sandwich too.'

Vincent obeyed his mother immediately and took place in between his brothers. Behind him, Hector briefly snored in letting everybody know he was utmost comfortable. Aside, Utopy lay still asleep. It was a delightful sight and Vincent loved the big dog for it. He somehow couldn't understand anymore why he had feared it as tremendously as he had done before. He looked back at both dogs for a while, smiled and felt really proud of himself in overcoming his fears this fast. Finally, he took a big bite out of the sandwich, for he was really hungry by now.

***

Mozart loved music, all kind of music. Ever since he was a baby, he made up songs that were surprisingly good. Daily, he amused everyone in the house with his mumbling along the carols that spontaneously came him to mind.

Being born out of a Jewish mother who professionally sang opera and a non-Jewish father who worked as a jazz musician, playing saxophone, the young boy grew up in a household that was not only full of music, but filled with musical instruments as well. A large variety was available for him to play with. From a very early age on, he had not only learned to master the piano, but also the drums, the violin and the trumpet. He sang beautifully too. Clearly, he had not only inherited his mother's Jewish appearance, but her talent for singing as well. It wasn't a surprise to any of his family members when he started composing at the age of five.

The young boy succeeded with each and every piece he produced. His music was unheard before, but people loved it. The fact that he was of such young age, certainly also contributed to his ever-growing reputation. Once he had started, age seven, to use a computer in making music, he truly amazed the world with opera, pop, jazz, rock, R&B and house music of top-notch class. He became famous in just about every current in the music industry. At age ten, he was a worldwide star.

He grew up in a small town in the South of Brittany, France, a town well know for tourism because of the Carnac rock formations nearby. Even though his parents had rather lived abroad, they had stayed in the area because his grandparents had lived there all their lives too. They were the ones to raise the young Mozart since both his mother and father stayed overnight in hotels all over the world often.

When he was seven years old, the au pair first came into his life. His grandparents took a step back in raising him because of their old ages.

At this young age, Mozart already knew his path in life. He had to do what he did best. He had to make music. He thanked the angels for his blessings daily, meanwhile spreading his music and therefore his love, around the world.

His au pair had only been eighteen years of age, but he had learned a lot from her. She had taught him how to lock himself from the outside world in order to get a better focus on his work, and showed him how to stop working regularly, especially after he got stuck, to do something completely else. Most of times, even during a game of soccer with neighbouring children, the solution to any problem automatically popped up in his head. Soon after her arrival in their household, he had come to love her as his own mother. His grandparents loved her like a daughter too.

She had taken him along on many field trips in the wide surroundings, showing him everything there was to show, or told him ancient stories about the rocks nearby. For hours he had lain next to her in the dry grass, studying an ant farm, meanwhile listening to her sweet voice. There had so many exciting things happened in the area, he could never get enough of the ancient stories she told.

For example, nobody had ever understood how people in prehistoric times had succeeded in creating the Carnac rock formations. More than ten thousand standing rocks, known as menhirs, were placed in precise mathematical figures that seemed impossible for people to know in their time, mainly because the Greek Pythagoras would only discover these figures two thousand years later.

Local tradition claimed that the formations were bred by the great French magician Merlin who had turned a Roman legion into stone, but Mozart's nanny knew for a fact that the angels were responsible for them since they could be seen from heaven. They functioned as a beacon for aliens, as well as an amplifier for the Earth's energy field because it pushed the special energy of Carnac high up in its magnetic atmosphere. Strange enough, she had told him about this special task of the rock formations on many occasions, over and over again. Every time she told, she assured him that it was very important that he made his music in this area specifically. Of course, he had asked her why each time, but she had always found a way to dodge his answer. Most of times, after telling him the story, she simply stood up and walked away. Sometimes, she had briefly mumbled something about his life purpose while walking away. He had never gotten more out of her and so he had let it, knowing that he was going to find out himself one day, sooner or later.

Stories like these had been for Mozart a huge source of inspiration because, after each one she told, a musical theme came him to mind immediately. It became his way of remembering songs. He only had to rethink a chapter of one of her stories to be able to reproduce its sounds. Since he never forgot them, it had proven to be a safe way of storing and so he was able to enjoy life besides music as well. His nanny encouraged him to keep working, but also insisted that he took the time off to play. This way, his work became neatly scheduled. He grew up a happy boy, under no pressure and with enough time left to play or do his homework for school.

She had left him when he was only ten years old, just before he became a worldwide celebrity, without saying goodbye to him in person. She only left him two things upon his bedside table. He found them when he woke up one morning; a leather bracelet with a white stone tied in and a small note saying '*I will always be with you*'. It was signed by '*Nanny*', as he had always called her.

He had missed her tremendously, even though he had always felt her being around from his first lonely day on. Not only did he feel her presence, he saw her regularly too. Whenever he listened to music, he held his eyes closed and pictured her precisely: She had the darkest hair that curled around her face and neck in sophisticated twists. Thick, silky soft locks crawled over her brown shoulders, where her skin was smooth and shiny, her hands as soft as butter cream and her eyes as green as grass, with little twist of white light within.

She became his muse because every time he worked with music, he could feel her warm presence next to him, as if she hadn't left him at all. It had filled him with love and inspiration so much, he dropped out of school. Since he already could support his whole family with his musical earnings, even though his parents made enough money too, his family had let him in order to make the music full-time. They were his biggest fans.

Unfortunately, a day after his eleventh birthday, he suffered from a range of ear infections so bad, the doctors had to operate his left inner ear, removing two of his ossicles. Mozart was left with only fifty percent of his left hearing and a constant tone in his right, named tinnitus. It never stopped him from going on, even though it took him a while to recover.

Initially, his tinnitus had been so overwhelming, it had interfered with the music in his head tremendously. He had tried to ignore it and finally succeeded in switching it off when the music came, even though it was hard to ignore when he was not working. Eventually, he managed to deal with that too by accepting his tinnitus rather than rejecting it. His right hearing improved, as his brains were compensating his left loss by adjusting his mind to the current situation.

Slowly, but still within a year, his hearing for music improved, even more superb than it ever had been. He now could listen with greater focus, bigger precision and far more attention. It made him the greatest composer of all times at the age of twelve. He became known as 'Rock Boy' since he always had his snowy white rock neatly tight around his wrists, wherever he went.

***

Miles woke up pleasantly by his latest installed mobile phone alarm. The sound of croaking frogs told him that it was time to rise and shine. He listened to it, meanwhile slowly awaking in his room. Suddenly, he marveled, grabbed his phone from the bedside table and switched it off. He paused for a while, meanwhile thinking over what place he had just woken up into, but smiled next. He remembered. He lay in his own new bed, in a chamber of the house wherein he lived with several others, all students at the Technical University of Delft. Today was going to be the first day of his life as a student here. He was now in Holland, on his own, but never alone in this house. He had made his new friends quickly.

He lived downtown Delft, in a nice street that had similar houses on both sides. Between flooded a canal. Cars drove in the one-way, narrow roads aside, as cyclists cycled the streets and sidewalks in all directions. All houses were former godowns, multistory, and mostly occupied by students who in general jointly rented. It was a nice street, however it differed from the streets in his hometown enormously.

He had moved the day before, leaving everyone he knew behind. To him it had truly been a big relieve, for in the small village he grew up, everybody continuously had avoided him as ever, even though he had tried so hard to change his reputation. Fortunately, that was now all in the past. After graduating school with great marks, he had decided to move to another country, where people didn't know him, in order to start with a clean sleeve and show the world his qualities.

He had told his parents at breakfast, the morning after the graduation party, that he wanted to do a technical study. They had reacted with immense enthusiasm over the whole idea. Their problem child had finally made the wise decision to go to college! It had been no problem for them to accept that he wanted to follow his classes abroad. They simply had understood his desire for change of environment very well. Besides that, the Delft University in The Netherlands had a very good reputation throughout the world.

Still, his parents had a hard time letting their only son leave, for they knew that they were going to miss their chubby blond boy in their house tremendously. His mother had cried her eyes out and even his father hadn't been able to hide his emotions. Miles had hugged them profoundly, reassuring them they could always come over for a visit and that he would come home for holidays too. To hide his own farewell tears, he firmly had turned around and gone into the bus to the train station next. While waving his parents goodbye, he finally had felt relieved. He was able to start all over and make something out of his life.

Thinking back of his hometown, he now reached for his bedside table and picked up the stone. For a moment he looked at it, as he had done all mornings since it first came in his possession. Every time, he had bewondered its beauty: Colourful strings were orbiting around a bright core, while the outside shell changed its blur continuously. Right now it was bright pink, which was probably a good sign.

The stone had been his talisman from the day on he had found it, the day he was forced to change. For a moment, cold shivers went throughout his body when he thought back at that particular Saturday night until he remembered it was time to rise, for his first class was about to start in two hours. Quickly, he shook the shivers off and jumped out of bed. From the seat next to it, he grabbed the fresh clothes that he had laid there the night before and went on his way to the bathroom, only two doors away from his room. He was excited to start his first day in college, the first day of his brand new life.

When he stepped into the hallway, he almost bumped into a girl he hadn't met yet. Both Miles and the girl were startled by his sudden approach, both jumped backwards. The girl even shrieked, while Miles bumped into his door. Next, they laughed. The girl dramatically laid her hand at her heart. She said something in Dutch Miles couldn't understand. She laughed again and let go of her heart. 'I'm sorry,' she now spoke in English. 'I must still be a little sleepy. It hadn't occurred to me that you don't speak Dutch. You had me quite spooked by bumping into me so unexpectedly. You must be Miles, our new English housemate!' and she reached out her hand to introduce herself. Although Miles now did understand her words, he still couldn't bring out one word himself. He was too overwhelmed by her appearance. She was the most beautiful girl he had ever seen in his life, more stunning than any of the woman he had dreamed of in England: She had the darkest hair that curled around her face and neck in sophisticated twists. Thick, silky soft locks crawled over her brown shoulders, where her skin was smooth and shiny, her hands as soft as butter cream and her eyes as green as grass with little twist of white light within. He drowned in her appearance and kept staring for a while.

'Earth to Miles, Earth to Miles!' he heard her saying from somewhere far away. 'Time to rise and shine, my friend!' and she reached out her hand a little further. 'Let me introduce myself. I'm Sarah.'

Since Miles still hadn't moved, she grabbed his hand herself and shook it firmly. It brought him back, and, while his cheeks turned red of shame, he said hello to her as well. 'Still a little shy, aren't you?' she asked without awaiting his answers. 'No worries, mate, you'll get over that inhere within no time.' She then laughed and turned towards the bathroom door. 'Since I was in the hallway first, I think I'm entitled to go in the shower first,' she said. 'That's one of the Rules of House you should be learning. Don't worry, I'll be out as quickly as I can. No more that fifteen minutes of showering, that's the second rule, for we all must be in class the same time. Wait here in the hallway, or someone else is about to take your place. That's no rule, simply wisdom,' she advised him smiling and after a 'See ya in fifteen!' she closed the bathroom door, leaving Miles in utter excitement on his own in the hallway. He was glowing. How life could turn from just great into amazing!

He did as he was told and waited in front of the bathroom door. At its other side, he could hear Sarah taking off her clothes and turning on the shower. In his mind he couldn't help but picturing Sarah naked. Soon after, in his pyjamas, something grew. As he looked down and discovered the big lump his excitement had caused, he felt ashamed. Immediately, he took the risk of losing his place in line for the shower and returned to his chamber, afraid someone else might see him in this aroused state.

Only after he heard Sarah leaving the bathroom, he dared to come out. First, he carefully peeked around the corner to the hallway. Fortunately, nobody had taken his place yet. He quickly traversed, went into the bathroom and closed the door behind him. Still with a large erection, he took off his clothes and jumped under the shower. Its warm waters soon rinsed away his shame. He became his old self again. Now all confident over what he was about to achieve, he next turned off the shower. He dried himself, while whistling the latest Rock Boy, put on his new outfit for the day and stepped out of the bathroom, into his new life.

*\*\*\**

Agnus, father and the twins had impatiently waited for Vincent to finish his sandwich. All men simultaneously stood up from the table after he had swallowed his last bite. When he grabbed his glass of milk next, even Hector stood up, leaving Utopy, still snoring, behind. All left the kitchen and went to the insect barn, as promised.

Vincent hit his milk in one gulp back and put the empty glass on the table. He was about to stand up too, in order to join the men outside, when the kitchen door opened and his aunt appeared. At the doorstep she held still. Instantly, Vincent jumped up from his chair and ran to the door. He was equally glad and surprised to see her. She normally never came to their house, not even on birthdays or other special occasions, but today clearly was an extra special day.

Angela smiled, when he ran towards her so joyfully, dropped at one knee and caught him in her arms. He never withdrew his speed, so she lost her balance and fell back. Vincent landed on top of her chest. Everybody laughed, his aunt first. Remaining his position on top, he looked her into the eyes and gave her a big kiss. 'I'm so happy you are here too,' he whispered. She smiled and pressed him a big, loving kiss on his forehead, whereupon she lifted him off and got up on her feet. Vincent crawled up as well as she hugged his mother and greeted the teacher with similar enthusiasm. After that, she briefly walked outside to return quickly with a big square present in her hands. 'Surprise,

surprise,' she said. 'What I have here is the only appropriate gift for an eleven year old wonder boy.'

She handed it to Vincent and took place at his father's seat. Next to her, his mother and the teacher put themselves at the kitchen chairs as well. Vincent went back to the breakfast table too. First, he put his plate and the glass aside, whereafter he placed the wrapped up box in front of him. He looked at it for a while. It fell him hard to unwrap, for it looked so wonderful already. It had a shiny purple blazed wrapper, as if made of oil, and an alike shiny green ribbon tied around. 'Wow…' was all he could say.

'Now, come on, open it!' his aunt commanded him. 'We all are curious about your reaction!'

He was just about to untie the ribbon, when Vincent saw the fly again. It landed on top of the box and looked at him, its head slightly tilted. He looked back at it and found out it was similarly coloured as his gift. It had the same purple blaze upon its wings and the same green colour all over its body. He kept watching it for a while. Finally, he chased it away and untied the ribbon. With a cranky buzz, the fly took off and landed upon the pendant lamp above the kitchen table. There, it watched Vincent's every move.

The ribbon fell off and Vincent unwrapped the paper, making sure he didn't tear it. Instead, he carefully removed all the tapes that had held it in place. It took him a while. The three women at his side could hardly restrain their impatience, but finally, it came off and immediately revealed its content, for the box was made out of see-through plastic.

Inside, in styrofoam, lay a crystal sphere. It had a tiny hole in the top that led to its hollow interior. Next lay a crystal socket, filled with blue velvet bedding, which a tiny door gave entrance to.

Vincent opened the box. Carefully, not to break anything, he first picked up the socket and placed it next to the box at the table. He took out the sphere and landed it upon the socket, its hole straight up in the air. He stared at it, not knowing what to make of this beautiful yet breakable present.

He had just opened his mouth to ask his aunt what it was for, when the fly came down from the pendant lamp. It landed on his sphere and went through its hole next. There, it took place at its bottom.

Vincent was annoyed by the little creature and wanted to scare it off again. He never noticed how the three women beside him were smiling, but reached for the orb in an attempt to shake the fly out. Suddenly, his hands got stuck in the air. His eyes turned big.

The fly stood at the bottom of his globe, straight up, on two legs, like a human. It bowed first and spoke next. 'Hello, my friend!' a high voice resonated in his ears. 'Congratulations on your eleventh birthday!' It bowed again. 'Th…Th…Thank you?' Vincent mumbled amazed, whereupon his mother laughed aloud. Soon after, both Angela and the teacher joined her. After a while, his mother stopped laughing and got up from her chair to give Vincent a big hug. 'Don't be spooked, my boy,' she said. 'We would only like to introduce you to an old family friend, someone we've all known for many years by now. Say hello to Gaia first, we'll explain all about her in a minute.' Vincent nodded, ever surprised over the talking fly in his sphere. He looked back at it and was able to speak this time. 'Hello Gaia, I'm sorry for chasing you away earlier. I hope you don't mind.' 'Don't worry, boy,' it answered him. 'I know what people think of flies in general. They think they're dirty and spread diseases, so I can't blame you for not knowing any better. I'm only glad you didn't try to kill me.' Again everybody at the table laughed, knowing that no one in this gathering would ever think of killing her.

The kitchen door opened and the men came in. His father first, the neighbour next and finally the twins after them. Hector closed the procession. None of them bothered to close the door behind them, so it remained unshut. Suddenly Vincent felt the urge to go outside and come round over all surprises this morning had brought him. 'Not yet, my friend,' Gaia's tiny voice sounded in his head, as if she had read his mind. 'I just need to tell you a little story before we all can relax and have a good time. Do you have an extra ten minutes for me?' Vincent smiled about the amount of understanding he received from this unexpected tiny new family friend and nodded his yes. After all, it was such an extraordinary day already.

His father was enthusiastically talking to Agnus about the shed when both walked in, but ceased the conversation the moment his gaze went over the table. 'Hey Gaia!' he said, totally unsurprised. 'Finally found your stage, haven't you?' whereupon Gaia bowed again. 'My best friend,' now also Agnus greeted her, 'I'm going to miss you around the farm, but I'm sure you will have as much as fun around here as well.' Again Gaia bowed to him and then turned towards the twins. 'Hi guys!' 'Hi Gaia,' they simultaneously greeted back.

It hadn't surprised Vincent that his father and the neighbour had known all about Gaia. After all, they hadn't reacted upon her flying around earlier anyway, but that his brothers knew all about her took him by a huge surprise. He could never have imagined them to keep a secret from him, especially not a secret that was as unimaginable as this one.

'You knew…?' he stumbled. 'Ha…ha…ha…' Gaia's voice sounded. 'Yes, my dear Vincent, they knew. As did your teacher, as did your parents, your aunt and even your neighbour. Everybody knew…I mean…not everybody, for that would be ridiculous… only those who are closely related to you. Guess what…that's exactly all people present!'

It took him a brief moment to realize what Gaia had just said. Only close relatives knew…and they were all here?! This day brought him from one surprise into another. Again, he didn't know how to react. He just looked at the people around him, not even noticing that Hector had taken place at his right side. He had put his big head on his lap.

Vincent was too amazed to fear the dog this time. He gazed around questioningly, at the family he had previously thought to know so well, at his teacher and at the neighbour he had just met. All close relatives? How could that be? It left him wondering. For the first time, he now looked at Hector, but still didn't truly see him. He laid his hand upon its head and slowly stroke it, meanwhile looking back at all faces that surrounded him. Hector squeezed his eyes in showing that he liked the attention.

No one spoke a word. Even the twins were silent. All understood the shock Vincent just had received and wanted him to find out himself. He was petting the dog, still wondering. How could all people present be family members? Sure, he knew for a fact that his brothers, his aunt and his parents were, but what about his teacher? And what about the neighbour? He looked at his mother. All the sudden his eyes grew big. They welled up next. He let his tears run freely. Finally, he understood.

He looked at their neighbour, at his teacher and back at his mother again. Next, his eyes switched back and forward between faces. Her eyes, the neighbour's eyes, his teacher's nose, her nose, her cheekbones, the neighbour's cheekbones, her shoulders, his teacher's shoulders, and so on. How could he have not seen their resemblance earlier?! How could he have been so blind?! Gaia clearly had stated that he was surrounded with close relatives. Only now he was able to see!

Slowly, he got up. Tears were heavily dripping down his cheeks as Hector lifted his head in order to let him leave. He shoved back his chair and walked up to Agnus on his left side. Softly, as if he still couldn't believe, he held still in front of him and saw the tears in his eyes too. The old man synchronously smiled and cried. Without saying a word, he opened his arms. Vincent threw himself in the embrace immediately, pressing his body into his chest, until he let go and turned around to his teacher. She was crying too. He ran towards her and gave her the same hug he had just given the neighbour. He had finally found his grandparents.

Agnus had his arm put around his mother. Tears were dripping down her cheeks too. Clearly, now everyone was crying. Armed, father and daughter walked up to the grandmother who was striking Vincent's hair. He still held his arms tightly around her waist. He looked up to his mother and smiled at her. She smiled back. 'So, now you know,' were the only words she said. Her mother opened her arms to expand the circle into four. Laughing, now all four joined the family hug.

Then, all the sudden, it became warm in the kitchen. A tropical, humid air filled the room. His mother let go of everybody and nodded to her own mother. She looked at Agnus next and gave a signal to him too. Vincent still couldn't let go of his newly found grandparents, but felt that something else was about to happen. He questioningly looked up at the three adult faces above. Both his grandmother and grandfather bent at him. She gave him a kiss at his left cheek, while he kissed him at his right. They nodded at his mother and waved at the others in the room. His grandmother blew a kiss to Gaia next.

In panic, Vincent had let go of his grandparents. He looked up, first at her face and then at his. She smiled. 'It is time, Vincent,' she said, 'for we only can stay like this for a limited amount of time. It costs us a lot of energy to lower our vibration to your levels. Don't worry, because we'll always be with you, in so much love. You will see us soon anyway.' After that, Agnus shortly pressed a kiss upon his forehead and then both dissolved. They simply vanished into the humid kitchen air.

Vincent kept watching them while they disappeared until their silhouettes had fully vanished. The temperature in the kitchen turned back to normal next.

'Now we can go outside!' Gaia stated. She flew up, went through the hole of the crystal globe, buzzed over the kitchen table and through the ever-opened kitchen door. Hector immediately followed her.

Finally, Utopy woke up. Slowly, the young dog lifted his head off the edge of his basket and yawned in the biggest gasp someone could ever imagine. He stood up on all fours next, shook his furs from head to tail and stepped out, looking around for Vincent.

'Time to take him outside as well, my boy,' Vincent heard the heavy voice of his grandfather resonate throughout the kitchen. He went over to Utopy and picked him up. In protest of the lift, he uttered a tiny bark. It made the remaining family members in the kitchen laugh. 'Potty time for you, my friend,' mother said, 'outside you go! And, for the rest of us, let's all join Utopy because it's about time. I can see that Vincent getting tired.'

Indeed, Vincent hadn't noticed before, but he had become quite sleepy. Glad that his mother had felt his needs so well, he carried Utopy outside and let him go loose on the courtyard. Immediately, the young dog pied upon the driveway. After that, he went on the look for grass to do his number two. He succeeded rather quickly and happily wagged his little tail when he walked back to Vincent, as if he was very proud of himself.

'Well done, Utopy!' Vincent praised his dog, petting his head to reward until he needed his hand in front of his mouth. He yawned profoundly and struggled to keep his eyes open. With half a gaze he noticed that all his family members had come outside after him. His brothers first, his parents next and last, his aunt. She held the crystal sphere in her hands. All were walking up to him silently, as in a procession. Vincent awaited their arrival, curious about what this day would bring him.

From his left hand side, out of the insect shed, his sleepy eyes noticed Hector. The dog was running towards him at such speed, he was the first to reach him. Once at his side, he set his buttocks down and waited for the family to arrive as well. Soon after, all joined the hairy giant. Angela silently handed Vincent the crystal orb. Still, nobody spoke a word.

The moment he laid hands on his present, Gaia turned up again. She just popped up out of nowhere and immediately flew into the sphere. 'I know you are tired,' she said, 'but this won't take long. Now, where's your stone?'

\*\*\*

After Miles had dressed himself, he had put his stone in his pocket as usual and made some breakfast. He had the kitchen all to himself and quietly enjoyed his first morning meal. After breakfast, he quickly brushed his teeth upstairs, whereafter he left the house on the rear, into the backyard. Once there, he lifted his face up to the sky to enjoy the morning sun for a moment until he realized he was running late. He went into the shed and took out the bicycle that he had bought the day before. It was quite a rusty piece and in much lesser state than the one he owned at home. It had to be.

Soon after his arrival in this house, his housemates had assured him he needed to buy a bicycle as soon as possible, for it was the cheapest way of transport. It also needed to be a shabby bike because, as they claimed, the lousier his bike looked, the lesser chance he had of it being stolen. So, as seen from a Dutch perspective, this bike was perfect.

Fortunately, back home, he had learned to master the skill of cycling well. Smoothly, he jumped upon the saddle, went through the gate and quickly was on his way to his first class of Aerospace Engineering. He previously had checked the route on the internet and so he reached the impressive campus easily.

He was just parking his bike, when he all the sudden felt really tired. He assumed it to be the tension of starting his new life today and got quite annoyed by his sleepy feelings. It was definitely not something he could use in class. Even though he already had studied his new books thoroughly, he still wanted to pay attention as closely as he could, so he shook his tiredness off, locked his bike on the rack and went to the entrance. There, he met several other freshmen, all trying to find their ways with maps and ground plans, meanwhile older students were crossing them in slight contempt.

Miles didn't even try to find his way. In a straight line, he walked up to the reception, where a friendly lady helped him. Soon, other students soon followed his lead and queued up for her assistance too.

Within five minutes, he had found the lecture hall. An older student was waiting at the door to welcome him in. Miles nodded at him and passed the doorstep, beholding the strange world he had just walked into, for this room differed tremendously from the classrooms he was used to at home. Not only was the ceiling way higher, it was also fit for many more students. In front of him, over two-hundred seats rose all the way up. Stairs along both walls and one in the middle gave access to seats that were folded up on a rod. In front of each row of chairs, long, narrow table leaves were attached. Each stretched throughout a row, only leaving a gap for the middle stairs.

Several students already had taken place, some in the middle, some all the way up. One girl sat in the front row, alone. Miles liked her right away. She had thick, blond hairdo that she had tight up in a sloppy knot and was looking at him friendly. She wasn't the most beautiful girl he had ever seen, but surely wasn't unattractive and seemed very nice.

Miles decided to take place in the front row too. Sidewards, he moved over to where the girl sat and asked her politely for her permission to sit at her right hand side. She nodded an okay and so he folded out his seat, leaving his satchel upon the table right in front. ' Hi, I'm Miles, I'm from England and this is my second day in Holland,' he introduced himself to his neighbour. She smiled at him and answered in plain English that she didn't know anyone inhere too since it was her first day in college as well. She seemed to be a few years younger than he was, but that was no surprise to him because he had spent more years in high school than others in order to graduate.

Spontaneously, she stuck out her hand and introduced herself likewise. 'Hello Miles, nice to meet you, I'm Britt, currently living in Delft, but born and raised in the UK too. Quite some coincidence, don't you think?' He nodded back and smiled at her, liking her more and more because she had a nice tone of voice, something he had always been sensible about.

In front of them, high up the ceiling, a huge projection screen told them that they were in the right lecture. 'People and Engineering' it said in big writing. While Miles looked at it, Britt asked him what had brought him to Holland in the first place. He shrugged. 'Change of environment,' he answered her the truth, whereupon she smiled again and asked him the next question. Britt liked to talk a lot, he soon found out. He didn't mind, for they had to wait anyway. Secretly, he was enjoying the sound of her sweet voice. He chatted with Britt about their mutual feelings of being a stranger in this new town, their new homes and their new studies. They also talked about the places they had lived in England. Yet another coincidence occurred: As it turned out, both Britt and Miles had lived in the same village for a couple of years. They only hadn't met because Britt had gone to a school in the city all her life and had kept her friends there. She had never been in town much, at least not for anything other than shopping for groceries with her mother, which was something Miles had never done.

Next, she told him why her family had moved to his hometown several years ago: Her mother had never gotten used to city life and had always wanted to live in the countryside, but the family had never been able to afford a move until the day her father had contracted several big clients. Not only could they afford a house in the hills now, they could also afford a dog, something Britt always had wanted. It was a big German Shepherd, appropriately named Utopy. Britt had, together with her father, adopted it from the local shelter. However she liked living in Holland, it fell her hard to let go of her old home. Not only did she miss the dog tremendously, she had also come to love their house in the hills a lot. Now, living in a new house, she missed the little shutters in front of the windows, as well as their nice pond with fish and frogs in its frontyard. Fortunately, she was able to return often since her parents had enough money to fly her in on a regular basis.

Miles was in shock. He stared at her. Inside his head, her voice constantly repeated teasingly: 'Quite some coincidence, don't you think?' Britt never noticed, for she continued talking about pretty much everything in her life. His thoughts wondered off. He couldn't believe that she was the daughter of the same woman he once had encountered in front of their local pet shop, the one who had given him the push. The thought of almost having their lovely house burned down, made him feel deeply ashamed of himself, no matter how much he had changed his life around by now. Plunged in thoughts, he never noticed that Britt had stopped talking. She was looking at him and shortly even waved. 'Earth to Miles, Earth to Miles,' she said to him laughing. 'Where are you?' He excused himself for staring at her, but decided to tell her nothing about the incident with her mother. Instead, he told her how beautiful she was. She smiled at him and thanked him for it. Fortunately, soon after, she found a new topic to talk about.

She pointed her finger at the entrance, where more and more first-year students were coming in. Some in groups, others alone. Obviously, some had already made new friends, for they chatted and laughed among themselves while taking their seats. The ones alone, however, hesitated quite some time at the threshold, just as Miles had done earlier. Both Britt and Miles watched them finding their places. They made fun of some of them and shared their malicious pleasure, meanwhile feeling deeply relieved that they had found each other. Miles tried to smile, but it was short-lived. The tiredness came back, more heavily than before.

After a while, after almost all the seats were filled, their professor came in. He was a tall, bold man with a friendly face and a thick brown mustache covering his upper lip. His two brown eyes severely looked around the college room. Only students on the front row could see the twinkle within, the rest immediately stopped talking the moment he had stepped in the lecture room. All noises dimmed, fading out in seconds. Clearly, everybody was impressed by the charisma the man naturally carried. He picked up a microphone and shortly cleared his throat before he started. It scattered into the room throughout huge black speakers, high upon the walls all around.

Miles hadn't discovered them earlier, but now was impressed by so much technical ingenuity in a classroom. He pointed them out to Britt, but quickly found out that she didn't care, even though she did try to share his interest.

He renewed his focus upon the professor. It fell him hard because his eyelids truly wanted to fall down now. Meanwhile fighting the unwelcome sleep, he managed to hear the professor telling all about his former profession of being an astronaut. Even though Miles was highly surprised of being taught by a former astronaut, soon his vision started to blur. Looking at the man in front, meanwhile making every effort to stay present, he discovered a blue blaze around his new teacher. He tried blinking his eyes to see whether it would disappear, but it didn't. He was just about to rub his eyes, thinking something must be in it, when he noticed that the professor was looking straight at him. It gave him a harsh, tingly feeling throughout his entire body, as if he had just put his fingers into a power point.

Next, the professor spoke to him directly. It startled Miles because, this time, the voice never sounded from the speakers, but from somewhere inside his head. 'Nice to finally see you, Miles. I've been waiting for this moment.' Miles froze and kept staring at the professor in great disbelieve. Finally, he looked around to see if others had heard it too, but no one reacted. Everybody paid close attention to the man in the front. No one looked at him.

The professor winked. 'Don't worry,' the friendly voice in his head resonated. 'No one can see what you can see, for you are a Special One. Don't fight the sleep anymore, just go! You won't miss anything from this lecture, I promise. Just give in and go!' Then he carried on his lecture, as if nothing had happened.

Britt hadn't noticed a thing, not even how his rock was heavily shaking in his pocket, even though she clearly must have felt the trembling since the whole of Miles' chair was vibrating. He took the rock out and was shocked by its overly bright shine. It almost blinded him. He wanted to put it back in his pocket immediately, afraid people around him would notice, but sleep overtook his will to do anything. The hand that held the stone slowly dropped at the table on its way to his pocket, as if he had lost all control. His head dropped next. Immediately, he drifted away into a vivid dream, a dream wherein he could float. The moment he finally closed his eyes, he started floating upwards, leaving his body beneath. He saw himself, next to Britt, his head straight up, holding a pencil in his right hand. He was making notes. Relieved that he wouldn't miss anything, he continued his journey, unaware of where he was going. He kept watching the room until the ceiling lowered over his sight.

Soon after, he had the greatest view over the city of Delft. He looked down and discovered his bike in the rack, still at its place, waiting for him to return. He kept looking at it until he could only see it as a small dot. Eventually, it totally disappeared. Then Delft became a dot too. Without any fears, he wondered how long his rising would continue since he could now see the whole of Holland's East coast. Immediately, as if he controlled the journey with his thoughts, the rising stopped as he slowly started to float forward. His new course led him into the direction of the North Sea, The Channel, and the country behind.

He had just flown over the city of London, way beneath him, when he could feel the forward movement slowing down. Instead, he started to lower himself now. Underneath his feet, a wide, rural area revealed itself. The lowering continued and soon, he could discover several farms aside a tiny road. He wondered what could be his business there and tried to higher himself again, but his movement persisted. He clearly was out of control of where he was going.

Now he could see people at a courtyard. He figured that they were probably his destination since he was going to land in between them. A little worried about their reaction upon his falling out of the sky, Miles helplessly let himself float down. He wanted to warn them about his arrival and started shouting. The group of people, two women, a man and two young boys, stood around a third young boy who held a crystal sphere in his hands. Two black dogs, a puppy and an older dog, stood in the middle of the circle. All were paying attention to the crystal globe. Miles felt a little peculiar to drop into such a mysterious gathering and raised his voice louder. 'Hey! Over here! I'm dropping down and can't help it! Watch out!' Still, under his feet, no one reacted. In the meantime, the distance between him and the people diminished rapidly. Only a couple of yards above their heads, Miles realized they couldn't hear him. It was alike he was a ghost, and so he relaxed. 'If they can't hear me, they probably can't see me either,' he assured himself. Next, he gently landed on his feet, at the right side of the boy with the crystal globe. His assumptions were right indeed. Nobody noticed him. To be certain, Miles looked around at all faces that surrounded him. None looked his direction, all stared into the crystal sphere. Curious about what they were looking at, he also looked at the sphere. The moment he first laid eyes upon, his breath got stuck in his throat. In its middle stood a tiny person, female. He looked a little closer and then recognized it. It was a mini version of Sarah.

'Welcome Miles,' her voice resonated in his head, just alike the voice of his professor had done earlier. 'I'm glad you were able to make it. It's just about time. Relax and sit back, enjoy the show!' She winked and then turned back to the young boy at his left hand side. This time, she clearly spoke aloud since he heard her voice throughout his ears. 'I know you are tired,' she said to the boy, 'but this won't take long. Now, where's your stone?'

*\*\*\**

In the meantime, in France, Mozart was working in his studio, arranging the last details for his next release. It was a romantic song with a strong beat. He knew it was going to deeply touch a lot of people, if only the sound was right. He was working against the clock because he had a deadline. It had to be sent to his publisher by noon today, for it was due to be released three days later. It already sounded perfectly, but Mozart wasn't happy yet. The sound still needed to be mastered, which took a lot of skills and therefore a lot of extra time. In the early days, mastering sounds had been the job of a dedicated professional, but since the selling and illegal downloading on the Internet had made its entrance, producers and record companies earned a lot less money and had to cut costs. Many producers therefore had to do the mastering themselves, which didn't benefit their sounds, but everyone took it for granted. Fortunately, Mozart's record company had not cut on these costs totally, but still he had to pre-master his productions before sending it, a pretty tough job. He didn't like it because he was eager to produce, as so many new songs were queuing up in his head, waiting for a form to be poured into.

Although his music had brought him lots of success at the age of eighteen, financially as well as socially, he wasn't the least interested in all the outcome. All he wished for was his music to be heard, loved and enjoyed by others. He had an extraordinary urge to write and release since it was his way of making the world a better place for everyone. He had succeeded in finding a way to truly connect people and had therefore produced the biggest variety of music he could think of. Of course, it had been quite helpful that his age had made him famous first, which had made it easy for him to stand out in between the tens of thousands of songs that were produced around the world weekly. Sometimes, he shortly wondered whether he also would have been able to make it without having his age benefit, but every time these doubts crossed his mind, he shook the feelings off, knowing they could lead him off his path if given too much attention.

Inspired by his spiritual mother, he had made sure that his accords were constructed in such a way that they included several frequency tones that monks used in their mantra's. For example, he had tuned his music in 432 Hertz for enhancing people's heart energy instead of the globally ordered 440 Hertz, which amplifies reason and ego only. Using these special techniques, meanwhile making sure that people liked his music in the first place, his sounds of all kinds went straight into the hearts of his audience, secretly reshaping them into more loving, more forgiving and less violent people.

He had witnessed the transformation first in three cranky old men in the local pub. They were well known in town for their bad moods, for the only thing they did all day, other than continuously drinking, was complaining about pretty much everything they could think of. People were fed up with them and so Mozart figured them to be the ultimate guinea pigs for his music.

He had first asked the bartender if he could play one of his latest songs. Since the bartender hadn't mind, he had immediately gone behind the bar towards the CD-player. He had just only pressed the 'open' button in order to put his CD in, when the men, who were sitting at their usual corner of the bar, already started to protest.

'Hey kid, leave it! We happen to like this song.'

'No worries, mister. I'll put it back on in a minute,' Mozart had assured him while firmly putting his CD in the player. The man had grumbled something Mozart couldn't understand, but then had let him.

He had only played a couple of minutes, softly in the background of the rumorous bar, and had seen, to his own surprise, an immediate result. After having not even paid the music some real attention, true joy had entered the men's faces. First, their eyes had twinkled. A minute later, the corners of their mouths had started to curl up and ultimately, they even had laughed, something no one in town had ever witnessed them doing.

Now, Mozart knew that his music could make a huge difference in the world. It had encouraged him to further exploit his findings and improve its effects until it had become a technique he was urged to apply in any arrangement that came to mind. So he did.

He had always felt truly blessed to be able to do what he loved most, but not today. Today was one of those days his job almost felt like a regular working job and he was struggling to get through. Fortunately, the sounds could more and more bear his approval, so he was almost finished, little over an hour before his deadline, as he read from his atomic clock.

He just wanted to press the play-button to hear the whole song for a last time, when the rock on his wrist started acting up. It only began with a small vibration. Mozart thought it was his wrist that had caused the trembling. After all, he was working for hours now. A little worried, he rubbed it to get the blood stream flowing, his eyes never leaving the screen, but the vibrations became more heavily. Again, without looking, he placed his left hand over his right to rub it, but then instantly pulled back.

The moment his fingers touched it, a tiny electrical shock struck them with a small blizzard. He looked, his eyes big. Inside his stone, tiny strings of bright colours were circling around each other. On top of that, its walls changed blaze in the same colourful varieties as the strings inside. Besides, it moved more violently, rocking up and down as if it wanted to break free from the ropes that had it tight down at Mozart's wrist.

As quickly as he could, Mozart took his bracelet off, for the first time ever, and threw it on the ground, filled with fear of such an unexplainable phenomenon. The ropes around his rock magically pulled back and let his rock go free. Immediately, it rose in front of Mozart's eyes, causing him to faint.

As a young boy, just before the nanny had come into his life, Mozart had had supernatural, nightly experience that he had, until recently, fully erased from his memory the morning after. He had only remembered because of something his mother had asked him to do, half a year ago. She had persuaded him to go to a special massage therapist who was also a newly found friend of hers. Being raised by pretty rational parents, Mozart had never understood how it could be that such a worldly-wise woman as his mother had suddenly turned into a very spiritual human being.

Out of the blue, as it seemed, she had gone to yoga classes, had started to daily meditate and had completely changed their family's diet. In the early days, whenever Mozart had been ill, she used to drag him to the doctor, claiming for immediate help, meanwhile making a scene at the assistant's desk, but nowadays she mainly used her hands in comforting him.

The first time she did this, she had frightened Mozart quite a bit, but she had reassured him quickly that she wouldn't do anything wrong, but just wanted to find out something. He then had let her, even though he had thought his mother had turned mad, for it really had been a weird situation. Later, he had gotten used to it. However, it had never felt completely normal. Whenever he hadn't been his good old self, as she then stated, she had laid him on the couch, closed her eyes and stretched her hands to feel his aura. Something, or someone, Mozart still hadn't figured it out, then usually told her what was wrong in his body, a sign for her to take immediate action upon his treatment.

Sometimes, she had straight away gone to the organic shop in order to buy some nature based herbs and spices, other times she had only used her hands in relieving him from pains. In any case, his mother's approach had worked for Mozart and so he had let her. He had never understood why and how she had brought this new perspective into her life, but both Mozart and his father saw that it worked well for her, for she had become a truly devoted and happy household family member. Never, not even once, she had tried to force her new believes upon them, other than the organic foods and drinks they from now on had to consume, something both Mozart and his father liked just as much as their former way of eating.

However, this time, asking him to go to this friend of hers, was the first time ever that she had asked him to go along in some of her new ideas.

'All that hard work in such an electro-magnetic environment, and at such a young age, is not a normal development for a boy,' she had stated after breakfast. 'You must pay attention to your energy levels and take good care of yourself, as well as you have to protect your energetic body against any form of radiation. I know a lady who lives nearby and who is able to not only balance you out, but also clear you from any bad energy. Let me make an appointment, so she can check on you.' First, he had denied it was necessary to have himself checked since nothing bothered him, but because his mother insisted, he soon let himself be persuaded that it certainly wouldn't do him any harm. He went the same afternoon.

A little worried about what he was about to get himself into, he was able to find the house quite easily. His mother had given him the perfect route descriptions. She even had described the house to him plenary; a small, free standing house that was fully covered in pink climbing roses. Only a red front door was to be seen in between. A big bell hung at the door. It held a rope underneath.

Mozart gave it a swing and was surprised by its high, penetrant ring. He waited for a short moment in front of the door, but took a step back when he heard footsteps on its other side. Soon after, a friendly lady, in a bright pink and yellow blouse stood in the doorway. A big black dog with bristly fur appeared at her side. She looked much younger than he had anticipated, for he had expected her to be around his mother's age. She wasn't. He estimated her to be around forty years old and liked her right away because she had a friendly expression upon her face and two bright blue eyes, which were looking at him waitingly. She wore little make-up, only a bit of mascara, but quite some jewelry. A large silver amulet rested in between her breasts, hanging on a thin silver chord, as two big silver earrings accompanied the black curly hair in her neck. Most impressed Mozart was by the blouse that she wore. It looked like she was wearing big pink and yellow wings and it made him filled with joy. It clearly was a funny outfit that fitted a colourful person. He now looked at her smiling.

The woman, in the meantime, had given him the time to get an impression. She knew she didn't look like the average person and that people usually needed some time in getting used to her.

Indeed, been given this time, her attitude had put Mozart back into his comfort zone. It was like she knew that he had only come to do his mother a favour, as if she understood his situation, and so his former shield and doubts dropped instantly. He truly felt at ease with this lady.

After she had noticed his energy change, the woman stuck out her hand and introduced herself kindly. She named herself Simone and welcomed him in. Mozart stepped over the threshold, followed her into the hall and into her living room next. He was a little surprised to discover a large massage table in the middle. Three cats had curled themselves upon the blanket that laid on top, as the friendly black dog with bristly fur came to sniff his pants. He petted it upon its big head.

The whole chamber smelled nice, an odor he knew from home, for his mother had burned the incense a lot as well. 'That is Hypna,' Simone meanwhile introduced the dog to him. 'Don't let yourself be spooked off by her appearance, for she is a friendly giant and a special dog.' Mozart nodded at her as he knelt down to further cuddle it. Meanwhile Simone continued. 'She descends from a respected family that has been known to accompany the Great Souls on Earth for ages. Just by living next to such a soul, the dogs protect it from any bad energy such as demons or earthbound spirits with bad intentions. They have a habit of becoming very old, for they grow into, for dogs, matchless ages. Her very few relatives live all over the world, the nearest in the UK. Hypna has recently given birth to a puppy, just one. They are only born whenever a new Great Soul is in need of its protection.'

Being used to ignore his mother's spiritual statements about souls and spirits, Mozart neglected her remark completely. Instead, he scanned around to see whether he could find Hypna's puppy because he had always been very fond of dogs. Simone noticed him looking for it and smiled. 'It's not here anymore,' she said. 'After living with us for two months, it was time for him to move. He went to England only two days ago. I still miss the little creature. Once every now and then, I take a peek to see how he is doing, but I know I have to let go. He is going to grow up in a very warm and loving environment, close to his biological father. Hector is his name, maybe you have ever heard of him?' Mozart shook his head in letting her know he had never heard of Hector before and continued petting Hyna. She wagged her tail in utter joy. 'Well, that's a pity,' Simone stated, 'but don't worry, there will be plenty of time. Whenever you do meet up, make sure to send both dogs my love.' She turned away to the massage table and lifted all the cats off, ignoring the questioningly look upon Mozart's face.

'I'm going to give you an energetic massage,' she explained. 'Have you ever had one before?' Again Mozart shook his head. 'Okay, then let me explain further. In a couple of minutes, I'm going to ask you to take off all your clothes, except for your underwear, and to take place upon the table. I will then take special oils, made from the spices and herbs I grow in my own backyard, and gently rub you in. Through these oils, I will be able to establish a better contact with your energetic body, as well as your soul. I will remove old energy that probably got stuck within and possibly contact some of your guides and angels. Whenever you pay true attention to your gut feeling, you can feel their messages. However, it is hard to truly interpret, for humans have so many thoughts to distract. I am here to help you with that through my massage, but first I'm going to make you a cup of tea. All right?' Mozart nodded. He hadn't understood a thing of what she had just said, even though he had heard every word, but he decided it wasn't necessary for him to know it all. If only Simone knew what she was doing, it was fine by him. On top of that, she certainly wouldn't do him any harm, he instinctively knew, and so he never asked for more information. He had come to trust her completely, even though he had no idea where he had gotten himself into.

Simone brought him a warm cup of tea and told him to make himself at home at the couch. Then, she started to light all sorts of candles, meanwhile humming an evocation. Mozart looked at her while nipping from his damping hot tea. 'Raphael, Michael, Gabriel and Uriel, Great Archangels, I call upon you now.' Whether it came from the dozens of candles that Simone was kindling or from her repeated mantra, Mozart didn't know, but while she was at it, his cheeks started pleasantly glowing a tingling sensation. It went throughout his body next. He was just about to ask Simone whether this was normal, but before he could open his mouth, she told him to get undressed and take place at the massage table. Immediately, the tingling feeling disappeared. He got himself undressed and took place upon the massage table, just as he was told. Simone started rubbing his whole body with nice smelling oils next. Her soft hands touched him gently when she started the massage at his feet. It felt so pleasant, Mozart relaxed instantly. Soon after, he dozed off, dreaming a vivid dream.

He sat upon a branch of the big oak that stood aside a small road. A linked pathless beneath gave entrance to a big courtyard ahead. Mozart looked at its farm and saw how a big black dog with bristly fur alike Hypna was just entering it. He turned around and discovered more farms. All were situated at the same roadside. On the opposite side, only fields were to be seen. Several goats, horses and cows were grazing in the meadows there. It was an idyllic picture, very different from the coastal area he grew up in France, so he took the time to look around. Admiring the new surroundings, he hadn't looked down yet. Only after a couple of minutes, he discovered the young boy on the ground beneath. He seemed to be asleep since Mozart could clearly see him breathing. A big fly was buzzing around his head until it took place upon his nose. It woke the boy up.

First, he waved his hand at it. Then, he gazed around, amazed, as if he didn't know where he was. He rubbed his eyes shortly and looked above, straight at Mozart. He stared at him in such a deep way, Mozart wanted to say something, ask him why he had fallen asleep in this weird place, but he was too shy to start speaking to a total stranger just like that, so he said nothing. Instead, he kept watching his every move.

The boy, in the meantime, had grabbed his rucksack from the ground and looked at the sun. Clearly, he was running late for school because he wondered aloud, swung his rucksack over his shoulder and turned around immediately. He was just about to leave, when Mozart first dared to speak. He opened his mouth and yelled, but, as he found out, only was capable of producing a harsh crow. He tried again and heard another. All the sudden, he had lost his ability to speak. However, his crowing seemed to work, for the boy stood still for a while and kept watching him for the second time until he turned around in order to leave again. Very worried about his lost speech, Mozart screamed at the boy for help aloud, although the only sound that still came out of his mouth was the harsh crowing. Words clearly were no option.

At least, he had succeeded in getting the boys attention, even though he had nothing understandable to say to him. With his left arm, he wanted to reach for the stone bracelet at his right, something he always did in similar uncomfortable situations, only to discover that it was gone.

In panic, he looked at his arm. In absolute despair, he found out that he had no bracelet. In fact, he didn't even have an arm. Instead, a shiny black feathered wing hung aside his body. He looked at his other side and discovered another. First, he panicked for being changed into a bird, but then he somehow remembered that he was dreaming. The only thing that now worried him was that, until now, in all his dreams, he had always been accompanied by his stone. He looked around for it. To his huge relieve, he found it in his own right paw. At least, it looked like his stone. It certainly wasn't the same. This one had quite a different shape and was much bigger. He wondered for a while until he remembered that he was dreaming for the second time. Still a little unsure, he now looked back at the boy, who was captured in his gaze somehow. Next, something in his gut feeling told him that he needed to bring the stone to the boy, so he jumped off the branch elegantly. To his own surprise, he already mastered the skill of flying. Gently, he landed in front of the boy's feet, where he dropped the stone to the ground. He crowed at him for three more times and then took off, meanwhile enjoying his newly found ability to fly. He went for the clouds, rising higher and higher and was just about to reach the first, when he woke up. He opened his eyes and looked straight into the friendly, smiling face of Simone.

'Hi there!' she said. 'You've been away for quite some time, haven't you? I hope you've enjoyed the massage in the meantime. Your muscles felt so tight that, from now on, I think you really should take more daily time off. Please, do as your mother does, meditate, for you're working too hard, my boy.' Indeed, Mozart felt his body was well treated. He came up, straight upon the massage table, and stroke his right hand over his left arm. It was amazing. Nothing ached him anymore, all his muscles were relaxed and his skin felt as soft and smooth as butter cream. He wanted to tell Simone about his dream next, but when he opened his mouth to speak, he found out it was erased from his memory. He searched his mind for a while, but couldn't remember. Simone, in the meantime, started to explain how she had treated him and what she had found out. He let it and listened to her, paying attention closely.

'I took blockages away, restored your central energy point and shielded you from further attacks by disrupting electro-magnetic fields. From now on, you should come to me more often, sweetheart. You're working in such an unhealthy environment, your mother did the right thing by sending you here. If you want to stay as healthy as you are now, you need to keep your energy levels clean.' Mozart nodded to her that he had understood. 'Thank you Simone, I truly feel great and I will return soon.' He then jumped off the table and walked over to his clothes in order to dress himself, but Simone stopped him. 'Hold on a second, I'm not finished with you yet.' He had already picked his trousers from the pile of clothes upon the couch, but now dropped them, went back the massage table and climbed back upon while Simone continued.

'Your guide was here,' she spoke. Meanwhile, her voice sounded more serious than before. It even dropped a few tones, intruding Mozart's attention intensively. 'She is not a anthropomorphic spirit, but comes from nature, from a higher source than we, humans, can possibly understand with the knowledge of life we have today. This amazing spirit willingly chose your soul to be her protégé. You have a unique and very special task upon this Earth, my boy. Therefore, she told me, she wants to closely guide you, much closer and personal than most people usually are. However, this seems to be impossible, for she already has shown herself to you once, when you were only a little boy. You reacted so scared that she is not sure she will ever be able to appear to you like this once more. Only when you are capable of overcoming your fear of the supernatural, she is able to show herself again. Do not fear the divine, my boy. Otherwise, she can only communicate with you through your gut feeling, which obviously is not a clear channel, as I've told you before. Now, she gave me the following important message: You need to do much more with your music than what you are doing currently. To find out what it is exactly, you have to listen very carefully to what you feel, pay attention to your dreams, what you hear and what you see, for everything can hold a message. Clear your mind from anything that distracts you, focus and take good care of your physical body. For this, it is very important that you swim in the ocean daily. Its salty waters will rinse away any dust and give you clearance, both physical and spiritual. Only then you will be able to grow from here.'

She finished, leaving Mozart upon the massage table in great confusion. She walked up to him next and gave him a reassuring hug silently, never explaining what just was said, for it was important he found out himself.

Mozart was a little startled by all the news he had just received. Silently, he put on his clothes, meanwhile deeply plunged in thoughts. Had this guide truly showed herself to him? When would that be? He had no such recollection. Wouldn't he remember anything that clearly had made such an impact? He didn't know. Ever silent, but now fully dressed, he turned to Simone and wanted to shake her hand in thanking her. She pulled him towards her instead and gave him a hug for the second time. Whispering in his ear, her arms still around him, she first broke the silence. 'I know you have a lot of questions left, but do not worry, the answers will come soon. Whenever you have a question of any kind, call upon your guide and ask. Maybe the answer will not come straight away, but it will come in the days after, I promise. Pay attention, my boy, look for the signs. I know you can do it!' Then she kissed him upon both cheeks and accompanied him to the door, followed by Hypna. It was time for him to leave.

The whole walk home, he had been wondering about everything he had just heard. He had tried to recollect, but hadn't succeeded. Only when he walked into his bedroom to pick his swimming trunks and a towel from the closet, his memory came back.

He looked at his bed and all the sudden remembered. He was still young, the nanny wasn't in their household yet, and he was deeply asleep, lying upon his belly, his ever-favorite way of sleeping. It must have been around eleven o'clock at night since his parents still sat in the living room downstairs, he somehow knew.

Holding the towel in his hands, Mozart now went back to that particular moment in his life, to the moment he woke up by a whispering voice and a hand upon the foot that stuck out from under the duvet. He could still feel it, a pleasantly warm and loving touch. 'Mozart,' sounded in a woman's tone of voice. 'Mozart!' now more loudly. He remembered how he had raised his head and, still sleepy, had turned around to see where this voice had come from. It had sounded familiar somehow, as if it was the voice of his mother. Then, he saw the silhouette, a dark figure in which he couldn't discover a face. It was dressed in clothes alike Maria, alike the statues he had seen alongside the roads in town, at least, her contours looked alike since the whole figure was hidden in darkness. Suddenly, he realized it was a stranger who stood at the foot end of his bed. He opened his mouth to yell as she started to speak again. 'No, no, don't scream!' she tried to stop him. 'I will do you no harm!' He did it anyway, going against the gut feeling that he wasn't meant to be screaming now. Loudly, he yelled for his mother who immediately flew up the stairs and rushed into his room. 'What's the matter, Mozart? What's wrong?' 'There was someone in my room!' he stated. 'A woman stood aside my bed!' His mother laughed. 'You silly young boy! You must have been dreaming. There's no one here!' and she switched on the lights. 'Look!' she said as she dropped to her knees. 'There's no one under the bed…' She got up, walked up to the closet and opened its doors, '…no one in the closet and no one anywhere else. Go back to sleep, sweetheart, and don't worry, because your father and I are right downstairs. It is safe for you to go to sleep.' She bent over and kissed him on the forehead. She switched off the light next and left the room, leaving Mozart behind in believe that he indeed had been dreaming. Reassured by his mother's former presence, the young Mozart went back to sleep. He would wake up the next morning a normal boy, fully forgotten about his nightly experience, ever suppressing the memory. Until now.

The older Mozart, thinking back of his experience with the guide, felt a little ashamed upon the reaction he had given her. He was curious about what it could be she had to say to him, but realized it was now, so many years later, too late to find out. Still, he felt unsure he was able to react differently if she would pay him a nightly visit now. He knew he hadn't overcome his fear of the supernatural yet and silently asked his guide not to show herself to him like that anymore, at least, for now. He decided to take action upon her message and from now on pay close attention. Next, he turned around and packed his stuff to go to the beach for his daily swim in the ocean, something he hadn't done in many years.

His guide had indeed never shown herself to him anymore. Likewise, he had never experienced any other supernatural phenomenons. The floating stone in front of his eyes had been his first ever after. He still couldn't handle it and so he had fainted.

Lying passed out upon the floor of his studio, ignoring his deadline, he dreamed another vivid dream, of which he later would have no recollection either. As soon as his head touched the soft carpet, he floated out of his body, next to the ever-floating stone in the air, and raised, through the ceiling, high up in the sky, leaving the stone behind. Once really high, he moved forwards, now flying over land, over water and over land again. When he landed, his feet touched the ground in the between a group of people. Two women, a man and two young boys gathered around another young boy who was holding a crystal sphere upon a likewise socket in his hands. Two black furry dogs, a puppy and an older dog, were standing in the middle of the circle. The people didn't seem to notice him, so he looked at the dogs. He smiled. 'Hello, little one,' he said to the puppy. Immediately, the dog looked up and saw him straight in the eyes. The bigger dog looked at him next. Mozart somehow knew that this dog must be the Hector that had impregnated Simone's Hypna. 'So, only you dogs can see me, huh?' he mumbled. Both dogs nodded their heads. He laughed. 'Simone sends you all her love, my boys. Do you understand that?' Both dogs wagged their tales. He admired them for a while. His view switched between the brown gaze of Hector and the puppy's bright blue eyes, meanwhile feeling pure love for these dogs. He could clearly understand their specialties and why they were the ones suitable for the task of protecting Great Souls, as Simone had once told him. Both dogs simultaneously turned their heads back towards the boy at his right side. Now all were again paying full attention to the crystal sphere. When Mozart looked to the right, he discovered a vague silhouette behind the boy next to him. He couldn't find out whether it was a boy or a girl since it was so unclear, but it obviously was paying attention to something in the globe as well. He became curious too and looked at it. He startled. Inside the orb, a tiny version of his nanny was waving at him. 'Hi Mozart,' her high voice resonated in his head. 'Nice of you to join us too!' He wove back a limp hand. Out of astonishment, he was not capable of anything else but staring. His nanny laughed and told him not to worry. 'It will all become clear to you one day,' she assured him, whereafter she turned around to the young boy at his right. She spoke. This time, her voice sounded via his ears, so he understood that she was meant to be heard by everyone present. 'I know you are tired, but this won't take long,' she said. 'Now, where's your stone?'

\*\*\*

Vincent had been surprised that the fly had just asked him for his stone. He had never told anyone, but since this had been a day of miracles, he realized it wasn't so weird that Gaia knew. Ashamed about having kept it a secret for his family, he first brought the crystal sphere to his left hand only. With his right, he took the stone out of his pocket. He looked at his mother to see how she would take it. As if she had read his mind, she reassured him. 'It doesn't matter, Vincent. It is alright to keep secrets, as everybody does. We knew all along, but wanted you to deal with it your own way. It has helped you a lot already, but now is the time to give it its true purpose. Put it in your globe's socket and you will see what it is truly for.'

Meanwhile, his stone had started to glow its variety of colours. The familiar strings of light meandered inside. It vibrated softly as Vincent held it in front of the socket. Automatically, its small door opened to give entrance to the blue velvet cushion inside. It had three ditches in the middle; one bigger than the other two. 'Yours goes in the biggest,' Gaia stated, 'for the ditch is perfectly fit to its shape.' Vincent held the stone in between his thumb and forefinger and shoved it into the narrow door opening. He struggled a bit, but finally he was able to get both his fingers and the stone in. He was just about to drop it in the middle when his breath got stuck in his throat. The moment his stone had entered the socket, the fly in the sphere above changed. Vaguely, Gaia's silhouette flashed in between the fly and a tiny girl. He stared at it in disbelieve for a while until she brought him back.

'Come on, drop it!' she urged him. 'This hurts!' Immediately, he dropped his stone in the biggest ditch of the velvet cushion. It was glowing in the brightest flair he had ever seen. Meanwhile, the contours of the girl became more clearly until nothing of the fly was to be seen anymore. Instead, in the middle of the sphere, now a tiny person was waving at him. He recognized her immediately, for he had been dreaming about her all his life. She had exactly the same dark hair as he imagined her to have. It curled around her tiny face and neck in sophisticated twists. Thick, silky soft locks crawled over her brown shoulders. Her skin was just as smooth and shiny, her tiny hands just as soft as butter cream and her eyes just as green as grass with the same little twist of white light within. 'I know you,' he mumbled. 'I've seen you in my dreams. Ever since I was a little boy I've known you. I've always known you!' whereupon Gaia laughed. Next, everybody laughed, for it was truly funny, the way Vincent stood there, blushing. 'Okay, that's enough,' aunt Angela ended the fun. 'Come on, everybody, we've got work to do, for Vincent's almost falling asleep on the spot now.' Indeed, Vincent all the sudden felt so tired, he was even unable to stand up straight. His head felt really heavy as he had trouble keeping his eyes open. 'Hold on for a second, Vincent,' Gaia supported him, 'and look into the sphere. What do you see more?'

Barely able to keep his sight clear, Vincent did as he was told. First, he only noticed the reflection of his face, but when he looked better, he discovered two more faces on each side. Both were looking into the orb. His tiredness diminished. Startled by this sudden new discovery, his eyes fully opened. Confused, he first looked at his left, and then at his right side. In real-time, there was no one to be seen, but as he held the sphere a bit away from his body, he saw the boys' reflections in there again, both at his sides. He looked at their faces with greater precision and was little by little able to place them. He recognized the boy on his left immediately, even though he seemed older than upon the pictures he had seen of him before. He was the famous Rock Boy, the artist all the kids in school were loving, especially the girls. Some had his picture printed upon their agendas, others carried his music around to be played in the schoolyard during breaks. On some of those occasions, Vincent had heard the music, and even had quite liked it, but since he had never come out of the classroom during breaks and had always been preoccupied with his books and animals, he had never bothered to pay any further interest in the music. Still, he was honored that such a global celebrity was paying him a visit, even though it was only by his reflection. He waved at the boy in the crystal sphere as a sign that he had recognized him. Rock Boy waved back friendly.

Next, his attention turned to the boy at his right hand side. He also recognized him, but he had little trouble finding out wherefrom. 'Don't think too hard, Vincent,' Gaia helped him. 'Just close your eyes and see, for you have never met this boy in person.' Only then, the early memory of a dream, long time ago, came back.

*** 

When the boy with the crystal sphere looked at him, Miles startled. A cold shiver moved along his body while the two bright blue eyes stared straight through. Goosebumps covered his skin.

Earlier, when the boy first had spoken, he had already had a feeling of slight recognition. It had given him the creeps, but he hadn't been able to discover why. Seeing the eyes now, somehow, he immediately remembered. Instantly, his memory took him back to the frightening experience with his two friends, a hedgehog and Quagmire, reliving the moment that flames had caught his pants. When he started to shiver, Sarah comforted him. 'Don't be afraid anymore, Miles,' she spoke inside his head, 'for this boy only meant to teach you a lesson. Instead of fearing, you should be thanking him. After all, he was the only one who succeeded in turning your life around. Look at where you are right now. Do you think you were able to come this far otherwise?'

Indeed, Miles had to admit, after the promise he had made to those eyes, he had truly bettered his life. Once he had come home after that peculiar Saturday night, he had first dropped himself upon his bed and cried his eyes out. Peeling himself out of his severely damaged clothes next, he had overseen all fifteen former years of his life and had concluded that he had been a prick from an early age on. He had truly hated himself by the time he stepped into the shower, but while its warm waters were cleansing his skin from all the mud, tears and sweat, he had somehow received a strong premonition of him being highly of value for the world. Resolute to compensate for the rotten fifteen years behind, he had decided to from now on work hard in school, be nice to every living creature that crossed his path and make an effort in being a good boy. After he had switched off the shower crane that night, he had changed, determined to make a difference in the world. He had grown into the boy he nowadays still was.

He felt better, thinking back of the things that had happened to him since. He was so plunged in thoughts, Sarah needed quite some perseverance to bring him back. 'Earth to Miles, Earth to Miles!' he heard her in his head. It brought him back. She laughed, for she knew that this was the third time someone brought him back like that today. He blinked his eyes a couple of times and then looked into the sphere again. There, he saw the eyes of the boy on his left side looking at him friendly. He waved at him to let him know that he had recognized him. The boy waved back until Sarah flew up, to the top of the crystal sphere. Two tiny wings were violently flapping upon her back. Once she was out completely, she grew into her full size. Still, she hung in the air above the globe, her wings now calmly waving. They were huge.

She spoke, this time aloud. 'That's it, boys! The show is over. It is time for you to go back now. Back to the future and back to your lives, for you have a deadline…' She first turned to a gap in the circle Miles hadn't noticed before and then back to Miles. '…and your lecture is about to finish. Allright, off you go, through space and time, without remembering what you've just witnessed.'

She clapped her hands three times. Magical dust came out of her palms with a hissing sound. It twinkled in various colours and blinded Miles from seeing any more. The last thing he saw was a silhouette on the spot where the former gap had been earlier. It was the only one he saw since all others were gone up in smoke, even Sarah's. Everything blurred next. When it finally cleared around him, he could see again. He was back in college, still sitting next to Britt, leaving him with no other recollection than the class he had just attended to and five fully written papers of notes.

\*\*\*

The moment Gaia had clapped her hands, Vincent's sight was blinded by a twinkling dust. Various colours twinkled around him alike the strings in his stone.

He blinked his eyes firmly in an attempt to fight the sleep that had made its comeback ten times heavier than earlier. He couldn't fight it anymore. Cautious not to break his present, he dropped himself upon his knees and placed the crystal sphere on the ground in front of him, his eyes already closed. He collapsed to his side next, still trying to fight the tiredness. The last thing he felt was the tiny wet nose of Utopy, the only one to notice him since the dust hadn't cleared yet. He smiled and pulled the dog towards his chest. It curled up there and fell asleep as well. Vincent didn't notice anymore. He was already gone.

When the dust cleared, all his relatives immediately noticed that sleep had overcome his will to stay present. His mother smiled, knowing that her son had already put up quite a fight to stay awake earlier. They left him to sleep on the floor for a while, as all beheld the picture of their birthday boy lying deeply asleep in between the two dogs. Utopy had curled itself up at his chest and Hector had taken place against his back, a paw around his waist.

Gaia had taken the dust as an opportunity to leave as well. She was nowhere to be seen, not even as a fly. Nobody found it strange since everybody was used to her appearing and disappearing. She had been in their family for ages. Even the twins knew her from the day they were born. They all had kept her a secret for Vincent because the legend had clearly stated that it was very important for him to grow up the first eleven years a normal child, if ever possible.

Finally, his father bent over to pick him up, after mother had picked up the ever-sleeping Utopy first. The puppy had only opened one eye slightly, shortly mumbled a growl and then curled up in mother's arms to further sleep there. Everybody laughed, for it was the cutest thing ever seen.

The crystal sphere still stood upon the courtyard at their feet. Angela bent over to pick it up, but let go immediately after touching it. When her fingers had just stroked the sphere, first the stone in the socket started glowing a bright, golden blaze. The whole sphere took over next, spreading the light throughout their entire courtyard.

'Mom, look!' one of the twins screamed. All heads turned in the direction he was pointing. Behind them, just in front of the former rabbits' shed, a small Hans-and-Grettle-like house had appeared. It was purple and pink coloured and very tiny, but big enough to hold a person. As they walked towards it, the front door opened. Still holding the sleeping Vincent in his arms, father looked at his wife questioningly. Silently, she nodded at him. He walked in, leaving his wife, two sons, his sister and the dogs behind. He had to bend his head to enter the door, careful not to drop his son, but when he came in, the house was big enough for him to stand up straight.

It only had one chamber, a small bedroom chamber. Alongside the right wall stood a comfortable bed. It was made of hay, but had nice sheets and covers as well. He took Vincent upon his left arm and pulled the duvet back. Next, he carefully laid him in the bed, covered him and tenderly pressed a kiss upon his forehead. Then he turned around and walked out the door, again careful not to bump his head. His sister went in after him. She was holding the ever-glowing crystal sphere. Inside, she placed it upon the only table in the room, a small bedside table. She kissed Vincent as well and turned around to leave too.

Last, after carefully laying Utopy into father's hands, his mother came in. She sat with him on the bed for a while and looked at her son, as if she wanted to firmly imprint his image. After gently swiping some hairs off his forehead, she finally pressed a long kiss upon it and turned around to leave. Meanwhile, a tear rolled down her cheek. She stepped outside and closed the door behind her, knowing she wouldn't see her son for the next seven years.

Outside, all family members stood still upon the courtyard, in front of the tiny house wherein Vincent was sleeping. All were sad. The twins silently cried while Johannes briefly snored his nose. Even Hector had his ears down and his head low. Only Utopy didn't notice a thing. He lay, happily asleep, curled-up on Johannes' arm and only made tiny noises twice; first, when Johannes moved a bit to put his handkerchief back in his pocket and later, when he gave his wife a comforting hug. She broke down the moment her husband laid his free arm around her.

All comforted each other, meanwhile touched by the ever-shining golden light that came from the house. It warmed them and quickly diminished their grief in such a way that sadness soon made place for joy. After all, they knew this was Vincent's destiny. He was about to start his journey, his life lessons and his world changing task. Instead of feeling the loss of his company, all now were proud.

Simultaneously, they looked up at each other's wet faces and smiled. The moment they did, the house started vanishing. It slowly dissolved into the humid air above the courtyard, taking

Vincent along. Last, the lights disappeared and the whole surroundings turned back to normal. The family turned around and walked back arm-in-arm, into the farm for a last cup of coffee. Hector followed them, for he was supposed to stay in this family, as the boss had strictly instructed him. It didn't matter because he truly liked it here. Happily wagging his tail, he went into the farm behind the people, ignoring the sad feeling of having no physical touch from his boss for the next seven years.

***

When Mozart came round, he found himself miraculously seated in his studio, behind his working computer. Aware of the time he must have been away, he felt a huge amount of hurry pressing him to finish the song. After sending his work, he would have plenty of time to rethink his recent experience, he thought.

He pressed the play-button and re-listened his newest song. To his surprise, it was perfectly mastered and totally finished. Not even a single thing needed adjustment, no more work had to be done. When he looked at the atom clock, he found out it was half past eleven, half an hour before deadline. He relaxed and fell back in his chair, at ease now. He needed the moment to rethink what just had happened, but discovered that he had no other memory than working in his studio. A little worried because he knew that something had taken place, he searched his brains for it, meanwhile rubbing the stone that was neatly tied around his wrist as ever, but couldn't find anything other than working in his studio. With a shrug, he finally let go. It was about time to send the piece to his record company and mastering engineer. He clicked the computer mouse to upload his music into an online file. It was such a big amount of data, it was going to take him quite a while to upload. He made himself a cup of tea in the meantime. A loud ping later told him it was done. He sipped his tea, clicked the send-button next and fell back in his chair, glad that he again had succeeded in finishing another project just-in-time.

Immediately after, he heard the voice, his own voice, inside his head, saying 'Lift up all consciousness. Make higher vibrations. Lift up the world.' He wondered a while how he could have said that to himself until the music came.

It was alike something he never heard before, had heavenly accords and was of such an imminent beauty, he immediately rushed over to his keyboard in order to reproduce. He never noticed that the stone upon his wrist had started to glow a firing green blaze, for he was too caught up in the world-changing song he was about to produce.

\*\*\*

When Miles came home, Sarah was waiting for him in his room. As he first laid eyes on her, his ears and cheeks started to glow.

'How was your first lecture?' she asked while ignoring his blush. 'Fun,' he answered, 'and very inspiring too.' 'That's great news, good to hear. Make sure you do something with everything you've just learned, will you. Whenever you need help, I will be right next to you. Don't hesitate to ask. Can you promise that?' A little startled by her pushover and bossy acting, he promised her to ask her for help if needed. 'Fine, that's a deal then,' she concluded. 'Now, relax a bit, watch some TV and get started!' She laughed, while turning on his television and left, leaving Miles behind in confusion.

He kept staring at the door after Sarah had shut it behind her. What a strange girl. If she wasn't so very beautiful, he would probably have thrown her out of his room for telling him what to do like that. He became curious next. What had she put on and why was it so important he watched TV right now? He looked at it. The Discovery Channel was playing a documentary about sea pollution. It probably had just started since it was little over one in the afternoon. He had seen the show before, but then had quickly zapped away in shame. After being a polluter for many years himself, he hadn't had the guts to watch it earlier.

This time, he couldn't zap away, for his attention was pulled by a massive sea bass. It had big holes all over its body. Poison had eaten most of its skin. Barely alive, the fish continuously gasped its mouth, as if it was gasping for air. It died next.

Miles' eyes welled up as he watched it pass away. He felt deeply sorry for the poor animal. He sat upon his bed, astonished, and let his emotions run freely.

Still crying, he heard a voice, coming from the inside of his head. It sounded alike his own, but he was pretty sure it wasn't him having the thoughts. Something else was causing them. 'You can do something about this,' it sounded. 'You can make it disappear. Build, for you are a strong builder and an environmentalist too.' A determined look appeared upon his face. He never questioned where the voice had come from, but focused on the program with greater interest, looking for clues. He wanted to do something, if only he knew how.

Meanwhile, the television displayed more animals with marks; sharks, dolphins, whales and seals, all deeply wounded, until the view switched from under water into an image high above the sea. It showed a huge floating continent, right in front of the Canadian coast, only formed by plastic waste and about the same size as Europe.

Disgusted by what he saw, Miles firmed his attention to the program. He even grabbed his notebook and started to scratch while watching. He learned that one of the substances of plastic, named ureum, was not only causing the wounds upon the many marine animals, but also endangered the whole planet's oxygen supply, for the organisms that normally produced the oxygen, so-called phytoplankton, were now producing poison under the influence of ureum instead.

The camera zoomed out and showed a view as seen by a satellite in space. Huge clouds of red poison formed mass poisonous areas, killing everything in the high depths of the ocean, threatening to destroy all life on Earth. The program ended next, leaving an open end to all its viewers.

Miles fell back upon his bed. His notebook slid aside him. He was deeply shocked, frightened and had his head full of questions. How come people on Earth had let it come this far? Why had nobody done anything about it? He never found the answers. Instead, he got up from his bed, dried his tears and grabbed his notebook in order to write the questions down. Only then he saw what he had just drawn; the blueprint of a floating construction, a delta plane with big wings that could capture plastic. He stared at it for a while, meanwhile feeling growingly happy, until he jumped up from the bed. He grabbed his rucksack and looked for his phone. He knew he was supposed to ask Sarah for assistance, but he felt like calling someone else. He looked for the number and pressed the dial-button. Then he waited for the answer. It came soon. 'Hi Miles!' Britt's voice freshly sounded on the other side.

***

'Vincent, Vincent...' softly sounded through the room. Vincent squeezed his eyes, tried to wake up for a moment, but then pulled the duvet over his head and rolled to his side, facing the wall, away from whoever was trying to awaken him. Whoever first pulled his blanket away from his head and later, when he still refused to wake up, from the bed totally. He moaned and rolled over to his other side, now understanding that Whoever meant business. He yawned for a couple of times and rubbed his ever-closed eyelids in an ultimate attempt to get them to open. They gave him a hard time, but finally he was able to pinch through half an opened eye. Both opened next because it peeked around a very unfamiliar place.

First, he touched around to feel the soft bedding. Since he had never slept in a proper bed, it felt unusual to sleep upon sheets. Underneath, he felt the comfort of the sticky hay, but still, this was something new to him. It was very weird to not wake up in his familiar haystack.

He looked up. His grandmother, formally known as teacher, sat on the side of his bed, waiting the moment he would be fully present. She looked at him in a parental, loving gaze, but didn't say a word. Behind her, his grandfather, formally known as the neighbour who lived three farms away, awaited his awakening as well.

He scanned around. Nothing familiar stood in the room, so he had no idea where he just had woken up into. It was a tiny room with a very low roof, as if the room was especially designed to house a child, even though the adults were able to stand up straight. Its walls were made of strange materials and varied in colour, in a flaming blaze. Besides his bed, only a small table stood in the room. It held his crystal sphere, his stone in the socket, and his ancient book of Heracles. For the rest, there was nothing else to be seen, other than his grandparents. He looked at them and felt fully awakened. Even though he woke up in such a strange place, the fact that both his grandparents were there reassured him deeply, glad that he was able to spend more time with them.

'Hi,' he greeted them, before crawling upon his knees and hugging his grandmother. She pulled him up on her lap and cuddled him, rocking him softly, just as he had imagined her to do ever since he was little.

'Welcome to our world, my boy,' she greeted him back. Next, also his grandfather bent over and pressed a kiss upon his forehead. Vincent let go of his grandmother and gave him a big hug too, as if he never wanted to let go. Grandmother then wrapped her arms around them and together they stayed in the seemingly never ending embrace. Finally, his grandfather let go. Soon after, also his grandmother pulled back her arms. She signaled him to sit next to her, so Vincent shoved over to her right side. His grandfather took place upon the bed as well. As Vincent sat in between, his grandmother said: 'There's a lot we need to explain to you, for you probably have no idea of where you are right now. Do not worry, for we will be with you all the time. We are destined to guide you into your new self. If anything wrong, you must immediately tell us, for we can always do something about it. Do you understand me?' 'Yes, grandma, I understand and can't wait to find out more. I'm so happy that I finally have the opportunity to spend this time with you.' 'That's great, my boy. We are very happy to be with you too,' his grandfather responded. 'Let us show you why it had to come this far and why we couldn't be in your life earlier.' He leaned to the right and grabbed the book from the bedside table. He opened it on the first page and showed it to Vincent.

Even though he had read the book over and over again, he had never seen the text that now appeared upon its first page ever before. That page simply had been empty. Until now.

Before reading its lines, he looked at his grandfather. 'That text has never been there. I've read this book like a thousand times and almost know it by heart, how come I haven't seen it before?' His grandfather laughed while his grandmother started explaining. 'You see, my dear, it is not true that this text hasn't been there all along. It has, only you couldn't see it yet. You know, this text contains an important message, a certain prediction, and is of great importance for the whole of mankind, but only to be seen by very few people. To only those who belong to the Great Souls of this world, the text will reveal itself, but not any sooner than the moment those souls are ready to know. Before, you were simply too young, my child. Now that you're eleven years old, your time has come. Read, for the legend is yours, my son. Read it and know what you're about to step into.'

After a last empowering glance at his grandfather, unable to truly get what was happening to him right now, Vincent dared to read the text. He spoke aloud:

*After many years of plundering*
*Reaping and polluting too*
*Peace will be restored again*
*A messiah will come back to you*

*Nature reconstructs itself*
*Energy will heal the Earth*
*Mankind reunites within*
*And see what truly life is worth*

*With eyes deep blue and very bright*
*He will start the age of seven*
*And have Gaia on his side*
*By the time he turns eleven*

*Natural he must live first*
*Make his way through third dimension*
*Kept away from further truth*
*Meanwhile growing his intention*

*As the conqueror of unforeseen*
*His name shall be Vincent*
*Teach until he is eighteen*
*Then he reveals the Great Event*

*He'll awaken all mankind*
*In the Earth its latest hour*
*People will discover that*
*Everybody has the power*

*The boy needs to accumulate*
*To let his love shine bright*
*In others it will open too*
*For everyone shall live in light*

*Seeds must be collected first*
*Compassion then will rise above*
*And responsibility, but*
*Most of all the seed of love*

*Next he'll need two of a kind*
*In good luck they'll roll the dice*
*Attuned to in each separate mind*
*This energy is needed twice*

*Buried they must be at last*
*Reset the time with utmost joy*
*Will bring back another past*
*And return a normal boy*

Unsure what to make of the text, Vincent looked at his grandfather for help, though neither of his grandparents spoke. They stood still and watched him tenderly, as if they awaited something to happen.

Gaia entered the room. Slowly, she appeared in its middle. First vaguely, then more clear. She had no wings and was dressed in a bluish, green coloured veil, leaving her face unexposed. Vincent barely could see her contours. His grandfather stood up and went over to her side. Then she first broke the silence: 'None of us is allowed to explain what exactly this text means, Vincent, for we are only meant to guide you upon your quest. It is important that you figure it all out yourself, as it is your life mission. As ever, guides are not allowed to tell people their life missions. All need to find out themselves, usually by paying attention to their intuition. I suggest you do the same. It will all become very clear in the end. Don't worry. We understand your insecurity, for you are only eleven years old and have yet a lot to learn about life, as the legend states. We will teach you together, each in their own field of expertise, for the next seven years. Then you will be ready to reveal the Great Event, which will…' She was interrupted by Vincent. 'Seven years?!' he cried out. 'Do I have to stay in this room for the next seven years?' He felt true panic rushing his veins, as if he was kept a prisoner by his own family. His grandmother laughed as she saw how this prospect had spooked him off. 'First lesson,' she said, 'is that, seen from the perspective of the universe, time is no issue. Only upon Earth and in the third dimension you experience time as linear. In this dimension, time is irrelevant. There is no time, so there is plenty of time. Don't worry, for you shall feel like it has only been lasting a day.' This calmed him down immediately. Instinctively, he knew that all people around him only wanted the best for him. He took it by heart that he would trust them fully. Gaia instantly read his mind. 'Good job already!' she stated. 'That's what I meant earlier, when I spoke about following your intuition. Now you know what it feels like.' He laughed and felt better each minute in this strange gathering. 'Okay, folks, we have work to do, or else it will feel like seven years indeed,' his grandmother said. 'Gaia, you're up first!'

Vincent looked at Gaia and startled. She looked ill. She obviously had trouble breathing and looked like she was going to faint any minute now. His grandfather also noticed. He was just in time to catch her when she stumbled to his side. Supporting her by her arm, he guided her to the bed. Vincent stood up. His grandmother too, making way for her to lay upon. Sitting on the bed, Gaia took off her veil for Vincent to see her face. It was pale, but had a deep red blush upon the cheeks, as if she was developing a fever. He wanted to lay his hand upon her forehead in an attempt to comfort her, but she pushed it away.

'Not yet, Vincent,' she spoke in a whispering tone of voice. Then she started to undress herself.

Out of respect Vincent turned away, but his grandmother stopped him. She laid her hand upon his head and turned it back. 'No, Vincent, not this time,' she said. 'It is important that you'll see this.' And so he watched Gaia take off all her clothes, all layers of skirts and dresses that she wore, until she lay in his bed fully naked. Vincent's ears and cheeks immediately glowed. He even became red in his neck, so ashamed he was, but he never took his eyes off the ever-naked Gaia. In full admiration, he kept staring at her body, for it was truly something he had never seen before. Only when she coughed, he looked back at her face. Her cheeks had now turned a deeper red, so Vincent laid his hand upon her forehead in a second attempt to comfort her. He sank down on his knees, next to the bed, to be able to keep it there. This time, she let him.

Her head felt warm. A tingling feeling spread throughout the palms of his hands. It made Vincent worry about whether he was doing the right thing. Questioningly, he looked at his grandmother. 'Keep it there, my boy,' she said. 'No matter what happens, keep it there. Don't pull back!' Vincent nodded that he had understood, meanwhile ignoring the now more intense prickling.

He noticed a change in her skin, still keeping his hand upon her forehead as he was told, even though it frightened him. From where he had placed his hand earlier, her skin turned blue. It spread all over her face, went into her neck, to her breasts and belly until it reached her legs and finally her feet. She further changed next. Random green spots appeared, as a big red mark upon her abdomen started showing, covering her belly button. Vincent didn't understand, but kept staring at the marks as they were changing. Once it stopped, he could discover tiny dots within the green. Smaller white marks moved along her body, as did the huge red ones in the bigger blue. He came up from his knees, careful not to move his hand until his grandfather told him it was okay to let go. Only then he came up straight, now able to see the whole of Gaia's changed body from a further distance. This time he recognized the dots and colours. He had seen it before in a different shape. He looked at Gaia and noticed that she had become a life version of his globe at school. She even had the light within, only much weaker. He recognized Europe upon her right side and saw bits of Africa upon her legs, discovering that the white marks were clouds and therefore moved. Only the red marks made her differ. He didn't know what to make out of them yet.

Gaia tried to say anything, but she was too weak to speak, so his grandfather took over: 'She is the spirit of our world,' he explained in a harsh voice, 'also known as Mother Earth or Mother Nature.' 'Why is she sick?' Vincent asked. 'Because of what mankind has done to her, the last five decades especially. It has accelerated after the Industrial Revolution, a time in which machinery were invented. Before that, people also brought disbalance to her circle of life, for example by overhunting animals like wolves, bisons, tigers, elephants, gorillas, whales and rhinos, but after the Industrial Revolution they were able to destroy on a much bigger scale. With the use of new machinery equipment, they all the sudden chopped forests in higher numbers, fished with bigger nets on immense ships and mined for raw materials in a wider area. Also, people were able to produce new materials. Plastic, for instance. Globally, production levels of any thinkable product raised rapidly, not taking into account environmental issues such as waste disposal and particulate matter, which has resulted in Gaia's illnesses today.'

Vincent looked at her. She had fallen asleep by now. At her side, in the South American area, he could see deep brown marks appearing. Once, they used to be green. Meanwhile his grandfather went on: 'By now, Gaia is exhausted. She has trouble breathing because of all the pollution in her lungs and a short of oxygen in her air. Do you see the red spots?' Vincent nodded. 'That's caused by the plastic continent. It grew of all plastic waste people worldwide disposed in the oceans. It has drifted along its currents and was collected here,' He paused for a while and pointed at Gaia's neck, just in front of the Canadian coast. 'where the ocean hardly has a current. By now, it is even bigger than the whole of Europe.'

Vincent's eyes grew big. He could hardly believe that such a wide area was covered in plastic. 'Hard to imagine, huh?' his grandfather asked. Vincent shook his head in utmost disbelieve. 'But why are the marks on Gaia's belly red and not various in colour, as plastic is?' 'That's because the plastic disintegrates into particles. To the naked eye it looks like it disappears, but really it doesn't. It stays, forever.

One of its ground fabrics is a material called 'ureum'. Under the influence of this matter, tiny single-celled organisms, a sort of tiny trees in the sea called phytoplankton, produce a red poison that forms large sea clouds in which hardly anything survives. Only some big mammals as whales, seals and dolphins are able to quickly trespass these unhealthy surroundings. However, when they do, the poison has often afflicted their skins with large wounds.' 'That's sad,' Vincent answered. 'Only because of such a tiny organism.' 'No,' his grandfather stated, 'not because of the phytoplankton, you've misunderstood. Without the influence of ureum, or better put, without the influence of plastic waste, the phytoplankton produces oxygen at a bigger scale than all the trees in the world do. Do you see now why Gaia has such a trouble breathing?' Vincent understood very well. It made him sad. Mankind had succeeded in attacking both Gaia's oxygen suppliers, the forests and these tiny trees in her seas, meanwhile forming a real threat to its own existence. He couldn't understand why nothing was done about it by now.

'Whenever you don't understand why nobody does anything, it is upon yourself to do something,' his grandmother read his mind. Overwhelmed by all the bad news he had just received, her remark shocked Vincent. 'Me?' he asked. 'All by myself? How can I do something about this? I am just a young boy!' She shook her head and said: 'You are much more powerful than you realize, my boy. The legend has clearly stated that you are the one. Have faith, don't doubt yourself, for you can only enhance your powers with positive thoughts. It will all become clear to you soon. Don't worry, for you certainly are not alone!'

'First, we'll show you what's wrong with this planet,' his grandfather stepped in. 'Next, we'll fill you in on the true meaning of life. In the meantime, two other boys, roughly your age now, are working on restoring Gaia's health. They are due to succeed, so Gaia will wake up from her sleep very soon. She has to, for she is the key to the rest of your quest. See, you truly aren't alone. Lots of help is being offered. Now, I've got only one more thing to show you before we can proceed to the next chapter. Can you take a little more bad news?' Vincent nodded, whereupon his grandfather walked up to the bed.

He bent over and rolled the ever-sleeping Gaia upon her belly. 'Look,' he pointed her back out to Vincent. 'You see what's going on inhere?' At her back, Vincent saw a large area that glowed and tingled. Already the sight of it hurt his eyes. 'I see,' he said to his grandfather, meanwhile squeezing. Eventually, he even had to turn his head away. He looked at his grandfather instead. 'What is it?' 'It is the area around the nuclear plant of Fukushima in

Japan. After it got hit by a tsunami, it was severely damaged. People struggled to close the plant down, a process in which many gave their lives. However, they didn't succeed. As we speak, its nuclear reactor leaks water into the ground underneath, leaving radio-active water to pour directly into the sea for years now, causing high radio-activity levels in its wide area.'

In shock, Vincent looked at his grandmother. She immediately noticed it was a lot to handle. She laid her arm around his shoulders and pressed him firmly against her side. Vincent looked at Gaia again. She seemed very weak now, as she breathed hiccupping and shaking. When he laid his hand back upon her forehead, he could feel she had a harsh fever, for she truly glowed. It made him pull his hand right back.

'That's what is called 'Global Warming',' his grandmother said. 'All pollution in the air form an extra layer in her ozone, which blocks the warmth of the sun from bouncing back into space, meanwhile heating the Earth up to unnecessary high levels, causing the polar ice to melt. Everything that once was balanced so perfectly, will be destroyed by this effect.'

Vincent's eyes welled up. He had understood what was happening to his beloved planet by now, but still had a lot of questions in his head left. How could mankind have been so imprudent with their own planet and what had caused people to behave this irresponsibly?

His grandmother answered immediately, even though he hadn't expressed his questions: 'Ego,' was all she said with a sad expression upon her face.

Gaia moaned and cramped up. It startled all three. She rolled over to her side and crouched, covering the red spot upon her belly with both hands. She didn't wake up though. Probably she couldn't yet.

Grandfather, grandmother and grandson looked at her in shock. They deeply felt for the poor creature. 'Her organs are about to fail,' grandfather after a while whispered. 'The poison starts to move inside. I sure hope Miles is getting a head start upon his project.'

\*\*\*

Miles had agreed to meet Britt at the campus. After his telephone call, she had called their professor who also considered it a great plan. He had offered his help and expertise in building the construction right away. 'Drop everything you're doing and come to the workshop immediately,' he had told Britt. 'Make sure to bring Miles!' And so it was done.

When Miles just cycled on campus property, Britt already was waiting for him at the entrance. She waved at him when he looked. A warm feeling went throughout his body as his cheeks turned red. How nice that he could work on a project like this with the girl he fancied so much! Ashamed about his blushing cheeks, Miles turned his head away from her when he parked his bike. He even took longer time than necessary in locking it. Finally, the feeling diminished, so he got up straight. Only the butterflies in his abdomen remained. That was okay since Britt wasn't able to detect them. He walked up to her and wanted to greet her distantly by shaking her hand in order to hide his feelings for her, but Britt already flew around his neck. 'I'm so excited!' she screamed so loud in his ears it hurt. 'So cool that already after a day, we're able to work on a project like this, let's go to the professor, for he's super exited too!' She never awaited his answer, but grabbed his hand and dragged him through the entrance door. She turned right, almost running, while still holding his hand. Miles hardly could keep up with her, for he held his rucksack with his notes and drawing in his other hand. It bumped into his leg by every step he took, causing him to stumble a couple of times. Finally, Britt

noticed and let go. 'I'm sorry,' she said, 'but I'm so looking forward
to this. I'll slow down a bit. Look, we turn left here and then there
must be the workshop.'

She pointed out a sign that hung at the ceiling. Miles had to
look all the way up to notice it. 'Workshop' it said indeed. In the
meantime, Britt had already reached the door and knocked upon
it politely. Immediately, it swung open and the professor stepped
out. He opened his arms in welcoming them both. 'Come in,
come in,' he urged them next. 'Quickly, children, for I have got
a feeling there's no time to waste.'

Britt had already gone into the workshop, but Miles still had
a couple of steps to go before entering the door. The professor
showed that he meant business by bending over and grabbing his
arm. Smoothly, he pulled Miles, shoved him through the door
opening and stepped over the threshold himself. He closed the
door behind them.

When Miles first sat foot in the workshop, he couldn't believe
his eyes. For a moment he held still and gazed around. Britt
and the professor enthusiastically discussed his idea in front of
a blackboard that hung upon the wall at his right. It was a huge
room, for it held enough space to build an aircraft. Against all the
walls, machinery and tools were placed, above hung workmates,
much bigger than the ones he knew from his father's garage at
home. In the middle, open space was left for whatever big thing
someone might build inhere. Above, at the ceiling, he saw steel
constructions with large cables underneath to lift heavy parts or
to hang something off the ground. This place was just perfect to
build his construction.

'You like it, Miles?' the professor asked him. 'Yes, very much
indeed,' he said. 'Can we build it here?' 'Of course!' the professor

answered. 'No question of you building it anywhere else.' 'But is it free for us to use?' Britt asked.

'Sure. Normally, workshops like this one are used for giving practical lectures, but as you see,' he opened the door to the hallway and pointed out all the other doors in there, 'there are many more workshops like this one, not all of them as big in size, but all of them very much suited for classes. So, don't worry, it will be ours until the construction is finished. Now, show me your drawings, Miles, for I am very curious about what you've come up with. I've wanted to do something like this myself for years now, but I never knew how to. Let me see what you've designed.'

He walked over to a desk that stood under the blackboard and tapped upon its surface. Miles went up to it and dropped his rucksack upon. He took out his notebook and opened it up at the page of his drawing. He laid it down and made way for Britt and the professor to look at it. They stared at it for a while until their mouths fell open and they were finally able to speak.

'This...th...this is it!' the professor stuttered. Britt said nothing. Both stared at Miles in great disbelieve until Britt flew around his neck for the second time that day. It shied Miles and the blushes at his cheeks returned. This time, he let them.

'You're saving the world, Miles,' Britt whispered in his ear. The professor nodded approvingly. 'We can build this, Miles,' he said. 'There's enough know-how at this university to overcome any thinkable problem and enough equipments to make anything you want. On top of that, this university has many rich and powerful friends. Together, we will be able to raise a fund in order to pay for materials. We might even be able to produce more than one of these constructions, for there is a lot of plastic in the oceans to clean. Let's get to work. I truly believe that this is it!' 'Actually,' Miles interrupted him, 'this is not all of it.' Both the professor and Britt looked at him, amazed again. 'There's more?' Britt asked. 'Yes. Removing all the plastic waste from the oceans without processing it into something useful, will not solve the problem of plastic waste, will it?' he asked them. 'No,' Britt answered while deeply considering his question, 'that will probably only solve the problem of having plastic waste in the ocean. Still, we will then have a lot of plastic waste to deal with.'

The professor, impatiently awaiting the moment they could further specify the design of Miles' construction, didn't understand where Miles was going. 'What does it matter?!' he cried out. 'Let's first get the plastic out of the ocean and then see what we will do with it.'

'No!' Miles firmly stated, meanwhile his stone heavily vibrated upon his leg, straight through the fabric of his pants. 'We've got to think of it now, for I have a plan: We'll process it while collecting. It will save us a lot of time, for the constructions will not need to travel back and forward in order to empty their bulky loads. We want to transport in smaller and useful amounts.'

Afresh he looked at two amazed faces. In showing them the idea that had come him to mind while cycling to campus, he walked up to the blackboard and picked up a crayon from the shelf underneath. 'Look,' he said as he started to draw. 'If we are capable of building more than one construction, we are going to build this machinery on top of each one too.' He held silent for a while, meanwhile drawing the construction that he now knew by heart. Only when he finished drawing, he further continued.

'Whenever plastic is collected by the nets of each floating drone,' he said, 'a robotic arm will pick it up and put on this conveyor-belt to bring it to the top. There, it will drop it into this distillation system, where we break the polymer chains of plastic up. It will then return to its original form, which is oil.

This way, we're not only able to transport the plastic waste in a more compact way, but we'll also be able to make money on the project by selling the oil. It's a win-win situation!'

He reached over to the desk and grabbed his rucksack to take an article out. 'Look what I've found on the Internet,' he said while showing them the paper. 'Some guys in Japan have found a way to break the plastic polymers up. I have printed it out.'

The professor snatched the piece of paper out of his hands and started reading. When he finished, he immediately reached for his mobile phone in his pocket and called a colleague who was considered a worldwide expert on chemistry. He hung up and looked at Britt and Miles with a huge smile upon his face. 'He's in,' was all he said as he stared into nothing, as if his mind was miles away. Also Miles was plunged in thoughts.

'Now, let's get to work then!' Britt suddenly woke them up. Both came round immediately and together they started designing the technical details of a construction that would later be called the 'Delta Floater' because of its triangled shape.

When the chemist came in to assist them upon the technical details for their oil processor, they were almost done in specifying the construction. All looked up from their work. Only the professor wasn't surprised about his appearances, but Britt and Miles stared at him instantly, for he was a dwarf; a tiny man with a big belly and a long, white beard. First, their professor happily greeted him because, as it turned out, they were old friends who hadn't seen each other for years. Next, the chemist walked up to Miles and Britt and greeted them in a such a high pitched voice, it almost made them laugh. Fortunately, both beheld their manners just in time to further offend him. They soon regained themselves. Enthusiastically, all three filled the tiny man in upon the project, whereafter he congratulated Miles to his astonishing invention. Next, he put on his reading glasses and together they dove into their work. When the four of them were finally finished, it was already four o'clock in the morning. All had forgotten the time.

Once they were done, Miles felt how fatigued he really was. He yawned, whereupon Britt yawned too. 'Stop it,' she said, 'for now I know how tired I am. I haven't felt it earlier, but the more you yawn, the less I can keep my eyes open!'

'It's about time that we call it a day,' the professor said. He yawned too. 'I suggest we'll take a day off tomorrow, for we already have accomplished so much today. Let's rest the technical specifications and see whether there's anything we might want to change. The day after tomorrow, I will have a construction team ready and we'll be able to start the build. Let me see if I can gather some investors around that time too. In no time, Delta Floaters will cover the oceans in order to keep marine life clean, that's a promise!'

All nodded silently, for all were too tired to say anything. Then the professor majestically walked up to both Britt and Miles and gave them a hand. 'Thank you, children, for making my world a better place.' He turned around to the chemist and gave him an emotional hug, which brought tears in Britt's and Miles' eyes. In this short-run, they had become a real team, both realized.

Outside, after wishing the chemist and the professor a good night, Britt accompanied Miles to his bike. She had come to campus by car and had offered to give him a lift home, but Miles had rather cycled. After all today's work, he desperately needed the nightly air before going to bed, even though the idea of being alone in a car with Britt was very tempting.

The rack was only lighted by one lamppost that stood far away from his bike. He had trouble finding the keyhole in his lock, so he struggled for a while. When he bent over to see if he could find it on sight, he felt that Britt laid her hand upon his back. It tingled throughout his body and blushed his cheeks again, only this time more heavily. Miles secretly was grateful for the dark night and dared to come up. His bike remained locked.

In the little light of the street lamp, Britt's face lit up at one side. Her eyes were big and sparkled in full excitement. Miles had already fallen in love with her, but now his feelings rushed his body in greater speed. He knew it was the perfect opportunity and the perfect night after a perfect day. It made him nervous, but he didn't back off. He was going to persist.

He brought his face close to hers. Britt said nothing, only stared into his eyes. With a lump in his throat and butterflies in his stomach, Miles slowly tilted his head to the right. His nose slightly touched hers. He held his head still, meanwhile stretching his hands to her sides, where they slid to her back easily and crossed each other, leaving their palms firmly pressed upon her shirt. Now he was fully holding her in his arms, their noses ever touching.

Moving his head up and down slowly, his nose rubbed hers tenderly in showing utmost affection. It felt so good. The tingling throughout his body became more heavily. Meanwhile, his hands turned sweaty as he felt the blood rushing through his veins and his heart palpations accelerating by each strike.

Britt closed her eyes. His lips immediately found hers. Finally, they kissed, first slowly, then more passionate while deeper firming the embrace. His tongue examined her lips and teeth carefully. It went inside next. There, they played, teased and wrestled each other until Miles gently pulled his head back. He knew it was time to let go, even though it fell him hard.

'I'm getting tired, love,' he whispered in harsh voice. 'Don't let go yet,' she said as she laid her head upon his shoulder. He put his arms around her and laid his head against hers too. Slowly rocking her from left to right, they stayed in the embrace for a while until Britt looked him into the eyes and kissed him for the last time, passionate.

'Sleep well, my love,' she said. Next, she turned around and walked towards her car. He watched her walking. When she reached the driver's door, she opened it, turned around and blew him a kiss. Then she got in and drove away.

Miles watched her drive off the campus until the rear lights of her car totally disappeared into the dark. He stayed there for a while, staring at the road, as if he couldn't believe what had just happened to him. Finally, sleep overcame his happiness. He bent over and succeeded in unlocking his bike instantly. He jumped upon the saddle and cycled in the same direction as where Britt had vanished earlier. It felt like he was floating.

\*\*\*

'Grandpa, who is Miles?' Vincent asked. His grandfather smiled. 'Once, he was a pesky lad, but nowadays he is a true hero, a bright young man, who is about to save Gaia from her red marks,' he answered. 'You've already met him twice. Do you remember the boy at your right hand side when you had just put your stone in the crystal sphere?' Vincent nodded. He knew who the boy was, but had never heard his name before. 'Yes, I remember.' he said. 'Wasn't that boy from the future?' 'At that time, he certainly was,' grandmother now said, 'but, as we told you before, in the perspective of the Universe is time not linear, not the same as in your dimension. There, many years have passed by now, even though you probably have the feeling you've just woken up here, am I correct?' Vincent nodded again, not comprehending her at all.

'Let me show you,' she went on, pointing towards the wall in front of him. It dissolved and showed him their courtyard. 'Are we still here?' he asked, almost yelling. 'Indeed, my boy,' his grandfather said, 'we've never left. Only our vibrations have risen to such a level that people in the third dimension can't see us anymore. This room has never left its place.' 'But how come, I've been able to meet you both in that world then?' He pointed through the wall, towards the farm.

'Well,' his grandmother explained, laughing, 'guides like us are capable of lowering their vibration in order to come in touch with third dimensional creatures. However, we can only do that for very short periods of time. Gaia, on the other hand, is the only spirit who can stay in third dimension longer, especially if she disguises into something small...' '...like a fly!' Vincent adjusted. 'Exactly, like a fly. She therefore is capable of showing herself in third dimension long hours of consecutive time, as your grandfather and I cannot.'

'But you've been my teacher for many years!' he now cried out. 'Yes, I have, but don't get me wrong, I have only been yours. The rest of the class has had a different teacher. Look!' She pointed towards the wall again and swiped the image of their farm away. A new image appeared. Vincent recognized his classroom. All his classmates were neatly seated behind their tables. He discovered himself, reading a book. In front of class, behind the teacher's desk, a man was seated, a man he had never seen before.

'That's your third dimensional teacher,' his grandmother pointed out. 'You've never met him because, each time you walked into the school doors, I secretly raised your vibrational levels up to mine. This way, your body was present in your third dimensional classroom, among third dimensional classmates and in front of your third dimensional teacher, while your spirit was taught by your fifteenth dimensional grandmother. I'm sorry to have confused you like this, but it was the only way for me to stay in touch with you. Besides, without me present there, you wouldn't have been taught so many Geography, Biology and Chemistry, for those lessons were way ahead of your classmates. It has been part of preparing you for the quest. I had no choice,' she concluded in whisper.

Obviously, it had fallen her hard to have been misleading him like that, so Vincent walked up to her and pressed his head against her waist. Meanwhile, the image of his classroom dissolved, making way for a view upon their farm and courtyard again. 'It doesn't matter, grandma,' he said to her. 'I know you only did what was best for me.' He hugged her firmer and then let go because a big dog just came out of their farm. 'Hey, is that Hector?' he asked his grandfather. 'No, son, that's Utopy. He's now fully grown.' 'So I've missed out on his entire puppyhood?! Why? What's the point of owning a dog when I haven't even had the chance of raising it?' Vincent cried out, disappointed. Dazzled, he gazed around to see what his grandparents would have to say upon that, when a voice behind him made him turn his head back.

'You didn't think you were the only one living in that farm, did you?' It was Gaia. She sat up straight in the bed and still looked weak, but her eyes had regained a sparkle within. She smiled. Next to her, on the bedside table, his crystal sphere glowed its ever-golden blaze, this time very bright.

Not awaiting her answer, grandmother poured Gaia a glass of water and looked at grandfather. 'Miles is doing his job well,' she spoke softly, 'for she's obviously recovering now. Let us continue ours, for she soon will be well enough for Vincent to continue. We'd better hurry. You show Vincent his true powers, I'll stay with Gaia in the meantime. Show him as much as you can, I will call for you whenever she's ready. Now go, before we miss out the chance.'

His grandfather silently nodded. Vincent said nothing while Agnus slowly approached him. Ever silent, he grabbed his hand. He took one big step and dragged him along in a short, harsh pull. It surprised him, but he regained himself quickly. He walked behind his grandfather. They went towards the wall. Agnus stepped through. Vincent hesitated, but a second harsh pull on his hand made him clear that he had no choice. His head went first. It tingled upon his neck and the rest of his body as it followed. However, only for a brief moment. Next, he stood outside. It was dark, deep dark. He couldn't see a thing and was taken aback by this sudden darkness. It frightened him. He grabbed his grandfather's hand more firmly.

'I know it's dark here,' Agnus said. 'It frightens me too every time.' 'Where are we?' Vincent asked. 'This is the Great Nothing, son. A crossing in space and time. From here I can choose whatever time or place I'd wish to go. This is the beginning of your journey, into understanding who you truly are.'

The surroundings changed. Lights in various colours enclosed them. It circled around alike the strings in his stone until they conjuncted and formed an image. They stood in a park, still holding hands. It was night.

At his left side, Vincent saw the beginning of what he assumed to be a field, at his right the ridges of some sort of a morass. They were standing upon a path. Where it lead, he couldn't see because a dense fog blinded his view, but as they walked on, he discovered three silhouettes in front of him. He walked a couple of steps further and noticed three boys standing aside a bench, pushing each other around while smoking cigarettes and drinking from a bottle of whisky. They had just set fire to a bin. It still smoldered a little.

Vincent looked at Agnus, his eyes big. 'I know this place!' he cried out. 'I think I saw this in a dream, exactly the same situation. Why are we in my dream?' 'We're not,' Agnus answered. 'We are in the local park of a small town, not far from yours. The park is real, the boys are real and everything you're about to witness is real, even though you think you dreamed it.' 'But... how,' Vincent startled. His grandfather interrupted him. 'Do not wonder any further, just watch and learn. I'll explain everything that needs explaining afterwards.' Vincent said nothing because the three boys were now coming their direction.

'Can't they see us?' he asked Agnus. 'No, they can't. We are in a higher vibration, remember, like ghosts. However, it is still possible to materialize into their dimension. It is up to us to decide whether we want to be fully seen, heard or felt, or not. I'll show you in a minute.'

The three boys were walking very near. Vincent recognized the eldest, for it was the same face that had earlier stared at him in the reflection of his sphere. Despite that the face looked many years younger now, he knew it to be Miles'.

The boys were about to pass at Vincent's left hand side, so he stepped aside to let them. His grandfather pushed him back. 'Stay where you are!' he ordered. Vincent didn't know why, but stayed anyway. When the youngest of the three was about to bump into him, he braced himself for the inevitable collision. It never came. The boy went straight through. It tingled. Somehow, the young boy had felt the passing too because he held still and gazed around.

'Hey, slug!' Miles yelled at him. 'Hurry up, man. We haven't got all night.' It encouraged him to continue. He took a short sprint and caught up with his friends in no time. Meanwhile, the thick fog seemed to dissolve. It moved away from the field and gathered above the morass in a thick cloud. Vincent wanted to ask why, but his grandfather didn't give him the time. 'Now, watch what I'm doing,' he said as he walked over to the three boys who had just discovered a hedgehog. It had curled its head against its belly in protection and lay upon the wet grass.

Agnus held still behind the youngest and awaited what was about to happen. 'Look, it's disguised as a football!' the boy pointed out to his friends. 'Bad choice, little hedgehog, bad choice!' He was just about to give it a kick when Agnus' left leg briefly flashed a bright green light. It kicked the boy in the back and pushed him over. He fell into Miles, who was about to light the spray of an aerosol can. They almost fell together. Miles grabbed his friend at the collar of his jacket, just in time to prevent a landing on the hedgehog. He yelled at him next. While they went back to focusing upon their instrument of torture, Agnus walked back to Vincent.

'Did you see that?' he asked. Vincent nodded. 'Was that your leg materializing?' 'Yes, but only for a short moment. The boy never noticed a thing but the kick. Now, it's your turn. See how you can protect that poor creature, for they are not done harming it yet.' He pointed at the hedgehog. 'Me?' Vincent asked. 'How can I protect it? I have had no practice like you before!' 'Oh yes, you had,' his grandfather answered smiling. 'Just follow your intuition. You are so much more powerful than you think, even more than I am. Just do it, son, for they are about to continue.'

Vincent, still not knowing what to do, walked up to the hedgehog and held still between the boys. He looked at their faces, saw their drunk stupidity and became very angry, even insanely mad. He stretched his hands out towards the boys and screamed a primal roar. Nothing happened. 'True powers never come from anger, Vincent,' he heard his grandfather say from behind, 'they only come from love. Try focusing on your love for the hedgehog instead.' Vincent focused, scanning his body in search for any hidden powers. Finally, something took over. He never knew where it came from, but all the sudden he knew what to do. Automatically, as if he had done it many times before, he stretched out his hands towards the ever-shaking creature in the grass. It hardly took him the effort. The palms of his hands spontaneously produced a steam that immediately stuck upon the hedgehog. Strings of bright bluish, almost white light orbited between its spines like planets to a star.

'That will do,' he heard Agnus say. 'Don't give it too much, for it's only a little creature. I knew you were capable of doing this and secretly, you knew too. Do you see what you can accomplish by following your instincts?' Agnus tapped him on the shoulder in reassuring Vincent. 'Now, keep watching, for you and I have accomplished a lot more here, as you might remember from your dream.' Vincent shook his head. He remembered nothing, only recognized the surroundings.

In the meantime, Miles and the youngest boy had taken off their jackets and were building a goal in the grass, planning to play a game of so-called 'Hot Soccer'. Vincent shivered, feeling deeply disgusted by the cruelty he was about to witness. Miles lit the gas and solemnly pointed the growling beam of fire down. 'Let the games begin!' he even dared to say. Vincent wanted to scream and stop him from further action, but his grandfather pulled him back and laid his hand over his mouth. 'Don't!' he said. 'You are already here, remember? This poor little creature is not going to be harmed, I promise. You've already done your job protecting it. Now just watch and behold your strength, for you are here to learn about yourself.'

It calmed Vincent down, but he couldn't help feeling a severe anger for the three boys. He let it and watched what was about to happen.

The cloud of mist and lights around the hedgehog grew when the fire came closer. Once it was about a foot above, it pushed the beam away and directed it into Miles' trousers. They immediately caught fire. Miles screamed as the flames ate their way upon his sweatpants. 'Ouch…help…aaaai…aaai… aii…I 'm…on fire…On fire…Help me!' His friends laughed. Miles jumped from one foot to another next and wildly hit the flames, meanwhile cracking his friends up. Finally, one of them pointed into the direction of the swamp. 'Quagmire…' he said hiccupping, whereupon he gave himself over to the laughing fit.

Vincent looked at the swamp and startled. In the scrubs, he discovered the contours of a man. When he looked closer, he saw the curly white hair that waved a little in the wind. Two bright blue eyes were watching Miles as he was running towards him. Vincent turned his head to his side. Since his grandfather had disappeared, he sat himself down in the grass and watched.

Agnus had waited until Miles had approached the swamp by half the distance. He stretched his hands, forcing the morass to remove itself away from the ever-running boy, and kept the distance between both sustained. Vincent observed, amused, until he noticed that the swamp had changed.

A small mist rose above its waters, lifting a single cigarette filter out. It had two tiny wings, alike the wings of a humming bird and was heading towards Miles' friends upon the field. Once it reached its targets, it started pounding their heads. Meanwhile, the mist above the swamp grew bigger. Vincent saw it was filled with cigarette filters. All were heading the boys' direction. His breath got stuck in his throat when two bright blue eyes opened up in the cloud. Soon, he knew they them to be his.

Sitting on the grass, he enjoyed the show, for these boys were finally served right. While cigarette filters continued pounding their heads, he looked at his right side and saw that Agnus had stopped moving the swamp. It was now back at its original location. The ever-burning Miles dropped himself into its mud, quenching the flames instantly. He looked back for Agnus, only to find out that he was gone again. Searching the scrubs for a while, he finally detected him. Agnus had bent over to pick something up. He now held it in his hands. Vincent had to squeeze his eyes to see what it was. It was the hedgehog. His grandfather was cuddling it.

In the meantime, the cloud had changed. A large mouth, his own mouth, he realized, had manifested itself in its bottom regions. Vincent laughed as the cloud started to giggle, finding it truly funny how it had just booed the boys. Its eyes regained seriousness next. 'All three of you have made a promise,' he heard it say. 'Hailstones and flames will return the moment you break it. Remember, for my eyes are always everywhere.' It giggled again as it took off, leaving the air filled with its laughter, as if it echoed in the park.

Immediately after, Vincent's vision blurred until only darkness surrounded him. He saw nothing. Someone grabbed his hand. The roughness of Agnes' palms assured him immediately. He understood they were back in the Great Nothing.

'Did you see what you've just done to change these three lives around?' he heard Agnus ask. 'Yes, I saw and I recognized Miles instantly. I'm amazed that he is the one, once such a brat, we now rely on in restoring Gaia's damage.' 'That truly is a miracle,' his grandfather stated. 'Do you see now why you never can judge anyone upon his past actions? You never know why some things have to happen in order to bring someone upon his true path in life. You never know what powers are accompanying an action. You never know why, only,' he briefly paused to show he meant business. He went on, whispering this time, 'for sure,' as he took the moment again, lifting his index finger in the air, just in front of Vincent's nose. Vincent never noticed because he still couldn't see anything. He startled when it suddenly hit his nose. Agnus must had moved his head very close to his, he felt, since a warm breath suddenly moistened his left cheek. His grandfather continued, whispering his ear this time, '…that there is always a reason. Have you seen your powers? Do you understand?'

'Has this to do with my mission?' Vincent asked instead of answering all his questions. 'Yes, it has.' Agnus answered, still whispering. While he persecuted, his voice gradually became louder, as if he was preaching. 'You are a Protector, a Messiah, who is about to save the world from the ever-drifting spirit of mankind. You have powers which only a few souls in human history ever possessed. No one can teach you exactly how to use them, for no one present knows what you are capable of!'

Still, Vincent couldn't see anything in the Great Nothing. He closed his eyes and pictured Agnus. Through his mind's eye, he watched him bending over. He felt the kiss on his forehead next. Agnus grabbed him by his arms, knelt down in front of him and looked him straight into his ever-closed eyes. He continued. 'Only Gaia knows. You need her upon your quest, but she needs to recover first. I have shown you only a tiny bit of what you've accomplished in your so-called dreams, but I think you have a pretty good idea already. Am I correct?' Vincent remembered how he had protected the hedgehog without even knowing what he was doing and nodded. 'It's my intuition that will tell me what to do, I understand so far. I won't ever panic anymore, but from now on listen to my gut feeling. I know that whatever action I take from there will be the right one.' 'Glad you understood the most important lesson,' Agnus said while tapping him on the shoulder again.

'We are in a hurry now, for I have to show you human life next. I understand Miles has already fulfilled his task in cleaning the oceans, whilst Mozart will finish his latest symphony soon. The moment we hear his tones, Gaia will be ready, just as you must be then.'

He let go of Vincent, stood up and waved his arms in the air. Vincent opened his eyes. Darkness made way for a new sight, something that he had never seen before, nor ever dreamed off.

A huge sphere of light appeared in front of them. However vibrant and bright, it didn't hurt his eyes. Contrary to looking into the sun, he was able to just look into it. It was of such an indescribable beauty, his eyes welled up.

Both held silent for a while, beholding the spectacular rays of light, swirling around inside the sphere before their eyes. Finally, Agnus explained, in a whispering tone of voice: 'This is where it all began, The Creator of Life. All is connected through this light, for in every molecule throughout the universe, this energy is found. It is the base, it is love, it is the highest source and the highest spirit. It is God.'

He held silent again, giving Vincent the time to consume his words, to get an impression of the power in front. His grandson looked as if he hadn't understood, but clearly was busy in trying to get it. He had a large wrinkle upon his forehead and a serious look in his eyes. Finally, he asked his question, however his voice still sounded insecure. 'Grandpa, does it have a soul?' Agnus smiled, for he knew it was not for him to answer. The Voice quickly sounded after. 'I am your soul, your body and everything around you. I am your mother and your father, your brothers and your dog. I am the chair you sit on, the bed you sleep in and the house you live in. I am everything and everyone, and so are You.' Vincent was taken aback by its sudden appearance because The Voice not only came from out of his head, it also came from out of the lights and simultaneously vibrated throughout all space around him. It sounded like his own voice, but also like his father's, his mother's, his brothers' and a lot of voices he didn't know. He felt it, heard it and even smelled it as it spoke, like a freshly picked bouquet of flowers, only stronger. He didn't fear it, but was having a huge respect for it instead since he felt the intense power of this soul. Instinctively, he bowed his head until Agnus grabbed his hand again. 'Come on, let's go in.'

Vincent startled and looked at his grandfather with big eyes. 'Go in? Can we go inside God?' he asked. 'Of course, son. What better place to learn about life than inside life itself?' He then stepped into the light, dragging Vincent along.

The same tingling feeling as when they went through the wall covered Vincent's body the moment he stepped inside behind his grandfather. This time the feeling didn't disappear. Instead, it filled him with energy. He felt light, as if gravity had no place inside. When he looked down, he saw that he was floating indeed. Meanwhile, the sphere of light grew into enormous proportions, filling every space as far as he could see. His grandfather floated next to him. Vincent noticed his eyes were glowing in a vibrant blue. He assumed his eyes to do the same since he felt filled with an utmost joy and great love for everything. Next, his grandfather started radiating allover his body in various colours. He looked at his own hands. They radiated as well.

'Great feeling huh?' Agnus asked. Vincent nodded happily, but stopped when he saw other forms of radiation, floating around. He couldn't distinguish anything other than their size. Agnus noticed him looking and immediately explained. His voice sounded funny, like a vinyl record, played at low speed. 'Those forms are other souls. Some are spirits that once lived on Earth, some are from other galaxies or other universes. Others are spirits from people who are meditating. You see, you can always come back here in order to gain, purify and cleanse your energy. For that, you only have to visualize being here.'

'Is this heaven then?' Vincent asked. He laughed because he heard how slowly his own voice sounded. He giggled again as his grandfather continued. 'You could call it like that, for passed spirits who stay here are spirits who served well. If not, if they did horrible things in their lives, they stay for undefined period of time in the Great Nothing. Until they have learned their lessons. Next, they can either go to the light or choose to return to life in order to straighten things out.'

'But why are such horrible souls allowed to return?'

'That, my son, is because they have to balance and compensate for every big mistake in previous lives. The universe is always thriving for balance. It's called Karma.'

'But, if God is everything and everyone, why can't He keep those souls from disturbing the balance and doing such horrible things?'

'Because of Free Will and Ego, both creations of God. All life forms have the free will to make their own decisions, therefore their own errors and thus create their own lessons. The ego is originally designed to keep one healthy in times of scarcity, to keep the fittest of species surviving in order to maintain a strong variety of species at Planet Earth. It is a part of nature, the circle of life. However, we, humans, have outgrown this fine balance of survival. We possess knowledge about preserving food, keeping ourselves healthy and producing foods for the entire planet. Really, there shouldn't be any scarcity existing among the human race anymore. It only does because of overmuch intensified ego energies and overly decreased heart energies. Because of this enormous focus upon developing intellect and ratio, people forgot how to live by instinct and intuition, as taught by heart, which makes their society a harsh place of conflict, pollution and poverty. Until they start to live differently and follow their instincts, the Earth will remain that place for as long as Gaia can keep it up. Now is the time people start to realize that change is inevitable, that something needs to be done, by the people itself. They need to reunite within, for Gaia is about to collaps. However, it must be their collective free will to do so, for God doesn't control life. Life has to control itself. God is only The Creator and fills life with love through people's souls and hearts. If people decide not to listen, it's their own free will to do so. They can do with their lives whatever they want, but will be held responsible for whatever actions they took.'

'I don't get it.'

'I'll give you an example: Remember what Miles wanted to do to the hedgehog?' Vincent nodded. 'Well, however that was a cruel idea, to him it has become his biggest lesson ever. If he hadn't planned to burn a hedgehog, if he hadn't, together with his friends, polluted the small swamp, you weren't able to teach him the harsh lesson you've just taught him.' Vincent nodded again, unsure this time because he had no idea where his grandfather was going. Fortunately, he went on.

'If Miles hadn't been the pesky young lad he used to be, he might have missed out on his life mission: Saving Gaia from her red spots. You see how everything that happens has a reason?'

'Yes, I see. In this particular case it turned out well.'

'Well, if you see that in this particular case, you already understand a lot. Just know that every action has a consequence, good or bad, because, as I told you earlier, the universe always wants to be in balance. In Miles' case, all turned out well. Do you now see why God can't interfere? Why bad and sometimes horrible things can serve a good purpose?'

'Not really, still,' Vincent answered. He was very confused because everything he previously thought to know about life was now rocked upside down. So many questions filled his head, he couldn't think straight. Without noticing he did, his head automatically rocked left and right in trying to process whatever he had just heard. 'I know, I know,' his grandfather said reassuring while grabbing his shoulder in order to calm him down. 'Let it rest for a while, I have much more to show you. It'll all become clear to you in the end, that's a promise.'

He swayed his hand again and the sphere of light around them disappeared, making way for a new vision. The Earth popped up. They floated in space and watched the Earth from a distance. 'I never get tired looking at this planet,' Agnus said. 'It is such an incredible phenomenon. Once you're uphere, you truly understand how extraordinary this planet is. Every astronaut who's been in space experiences the same feeling, so I've heard. You gotta love this planet, for it's the most beautiful, utmost fragile system in the universe. Do you see the thin layer that's covering it?' Indeed, Vincent saw at the North Pole a yellowish layer of dust. Green lights meandered it. Immediately, he knew what it was. 'It's the ozone,' he whispered. In school, at Geography and Environmental classes, he had learned all about its importance. He had always thought it to be a thick layer of protection against outer space radiation. Only now he saw how thin the ozone truly was, how vulnerable life on Earth.

He held his breath and kept staring at it in great disbelieve. 'Do you see now how living on this planet comes with certain responsibilities?' his grandfather asked after a while. As the Earth was turning before them, Vincent looked at the massive amount of blue waters. He noticed the red spots and some green spots around the equator. They were still massive, however accompanied by large brown areas. He knew those areas were the result of deforestation, the results of mankind chopping woods on a huge scale. He nodded in silence to his grandfather, impressed by the stupidity of mankind. 'If only everyone was able to look at our planet from this distance,' he whispered to Agnus at last. 'Well, that's the key issue here,' he answered. 'Humans have to cope with these responsibilities and to take care of themselves in the meantime. They have to feed, dress, keep themselves warm and take care of all other desires, while taking care of each other as well as their planet. In the early days of life on Earth, that never was a problem, but now human population grew into problematic proportions, causing scarcity of products. Not because there's not enough, just because people grew into an unhealthy system of wanting too much. There's hunger on one side and greed on the other. It is difficult to do the right thing because one first has to transcend the ego that's continuously commanding to grab more of what seems scarce under the influence of Marketing and Commerce campaigns, no matter what consequences. The more people get used to luxury, the harder it gets to set aside their egos. Fortunately, there's a great movement going on. It's truly growing as we speak. More and more humans realize this is not the way to continue. In meditation and in training their thoughts to be positive, large amounts of people are now training themselves in setting aside their egos globally. They start to listen, to their intuition, to their soul and to their true nature. However Earth is a planet of contradictions and polarities, this movement will deeply penetrate into the human awareness. It will succeed, for more and more people are waking up as we speak. You, my boy, will play an important role in making it happen, as you've already started to do in one of your so-called dreams.'

Vincent wanted to ask how, but Agnus swiped his arms again. The vision before them zoomed in. They went through the ozone and through the atmosphere until they encountered a thick layer of clouds. They went through them as well and stopped a mile above the surface. This time, Vincent saw himself floating through the sky. However he had no recollection of doing this, seeing himself flying made him experience a strange tingling feeling in the palms of his hands. He never had to ask why because, in front of him, he noticed how he stretched his hands. Rays of light came out, the same lights as he had seen in the sphere of God earlier. They rayed downwards, to the people underneath. Each time a ray hit someone, the person lit up for a brief period of time. 'What am I doing here?' he asked.

'You're preparing mankind,' Agnus explained. 'Look,' he said as he swiped his hands again. 'Let's go in deeper.'

He showed the image of a man. 'This is a man before you hit him with your rays. Nothing to be seen, huh?' Vincent shrugged. 'Let's go in a dimension or two deeper.' Agnus swiped his hands again. 'Now, what do you see? Describe it to me, while you look at him, please.' 'I see the same man, but now vaguely,' Vincent started his description. 'I can see through him and notice his energy. It is light, moving around in lanes from in- and outside his body. It is God!' he yelled surprised.

Next to him, Agnus laughed. 'You understand now why He said that He is everyone? He is the energy that forms us all, everyone and everything. Now, tell me, what do you see next?' Vincent looked back at the blurry vision of the man in front of him. I see how the energy creates a field around the man and…' He stopped for a while because he had to squeeze his eyes to see what was happening inside this field. Finally, he was able to further describe. 'I see a second man standing behind him. Is there another man present?' 'No, son, that's all part of the one man we're looking at. Think hard, for I know you must have the answer already.' 'I know…I know…' Vincent's brains were working overtime, but finally he found the answer. It was so clear and simple, he felt stupid not to think of it straight away. He even hit himself upon his forehead, meanwhile shouting his discovery to his grandfather. 'It's his soul!' Now Agnus laughed aloud. It took him a while to regain himself, but finally he managed to speak. 'You see how the soul is connected to the man?' Vincent was still smiling because of his grandfather's laughing fit. He looked at the man's soul. A tube stuck out. It ended in the man's energy field, at his back, in front of his lower vertebras. Lights meandered through it, travelling in and out. 'Do you mean that tube?' he asked. Agnus nodded. 'It's called the Kundalini. It brings energy from the soul, or messages, as you can call them, directly into the man's energy

field. It's his decision then to either listen to his Higher Self
or to neglect the messages. He'll probably feel them as a gut
feeling or a tiny voice within. It's an indirect connection, as
you can see, for the Kundalini ends in his energy field, not in
his body itself. Only people who are truly enlightened have a
direct Kundalini connection, but those are very few cases. For
people like this man, who is living his life in duality, a direct
Kundalini connection would definitely kill him. All he needs
to do is listen to his intuition, pay attention to his dreams and
feel his gut feeling in order to live his life as it was meant to be
lived. This way, the soul reminds people upon their quests in
life, for everyone has unique tasks and holds unique lessons.
Remember I told you how the Universe is always thriving for
balance?' Vincent nodded.

'Good, then let's go in a dimension deeper, for the soul that
you see is only a tiny part of a bigger whole.' He swayed his
hands another time. As the image zoomed out, he asked 'Do you
still see the man?'

'Yes, I see, only now he's smaller. What's that cloud above
his head?' 'It's his complete soul. That's the part that wants to
be whole. However, it's too big to communicate with one man
alone. It would crush a person, for it holds too much energy. To
prevent the man from exploding, it divides its energy into pieces,
whereafter it sends each piece into life, each with its own specific
task. They are spread throughout space and time. Look into the
soul, you'll see the different lives that it's living right now.'

Vincent stepped forward and saw many different faces, men
and woman, boys and girls, busy in their daily activities. Some
of them looked alien to him, others normal. He saw people in
strange outfits, but recognized the gaze of the man in all their eyes.
Agnus meanwhile continued: 'They live their lives throughout
the universe, facing the specific challenges their specific

environments offer them. All are connected through this single soul, as you see. If one of those pieces of a living soul dies, it'll come back to the light, where it will gather up with its personal angels, guides and teachers to see how it succeeded in learning its lessons. If not completely mastered, it will be sent back in order to recapture. Sometimes, a piece of a soul needs several lifetimes to learn a certain lesson, but that's alright. Since the universe doesn't know time as you do, are, as seen from the perspective of a single complete soul, all pieces lived simultaneously, having a constant effect upon each other through Karma.'

Because his grandfather had backed his explanation up with such clear images, Vincent understood this story. Only, out of his new understanding, more questions about the true meaning of life rose. Agnus must have felt that. 'Only humans, whether here on Earth or somewhere else, have a divided soul. It is unique to the human race because other life forms like animals and plants only have one soul to share. They are part of a collective, however it is little divided in breeds, but I won't go too much into that chapter now.'

He swiped his hand and showed the blurry image of a dog. A tube, alike the Kundalini tube, but much longer, stuck out of its energetic body. At its other end was a large soul connected. Vincent looked into it and discovered many other dogs, all different in sizes and shapes. 'So that's why dogs have much more instincts than humans,' he concluded. 'Indeed, that's why,' Agnus answered. 'Animals, other than humans, have a collective purpose. They hold their place in the circle of life, to balance the system. Dolphins, for example, are here to connect to humans, reminding them of how life began in the seas. Other animals, such as elephants and whales, are here to boost the energy of this planet. They are its keepers. However, humans treat them poorly, causing their vibrations to diminish. If you see, how on all levels, humans are forming a plague for Gaia, you'll be able to understand more about your quest.'

'But I don't. How come animals have a collective soul, whilst humans are actually mammals too? Why don't they have a soul like the animals then?' 'Great question, son!' his grandfather exclaimed. 'I almost forgot. Indeed, humans have a collective soul as well, I'll show you.' He swiped his arms and the image of the man came back. Vincent saw his body, his energetic body, his piece of soul, his complete soul and another, large cloud above. The man's complete soul was connected through a very small Kundalini tube into this big human soul.

'Now, watch what happens as your rays of light strike the man,' Agnus said while pointing his finger. Vincent had almost forgotten, but now remembered seeing himself floating over the surface of the Earth, meanwhile hitting the people underneath with his beams of light. The moment he remembered, his hands started tingling again.

A ray of light appeared out of nowhere. It hit the man. First, his body lit up, causing a direct burst of energy inside, whereafter its effect reduced. However, the body remained slightly charged. The full effect floated into his energetic body, causing that to light up severely until it went through the tube, into his soul, into his complete soul and last, twirling around in the collective soul, leaving all previous stations slightly charged. Its power seemed negligible compared to the enormous magnitude of the collective soul, but once he kept his focus upon it, he noticed more and more of the tiny strings of his lights were meandering in it. 'You see, how you've been recharging mankind for what's now to come?' Agnus asked. Vincent nodded. He began to understand more and more about what was expected of him. In his mind, he repeated some of the phrases he had remembered from reading the legend. Pieces of the puzzle were falling into place. Not all of them yet, but he gained the confidence of being able to solve it.

As a mantra, two couplets of the poem repeatedly beat in his head:

*He'll awaken all mankind*
*In the Earth its latest hour*
*People will discover that*
*Everybody has the power*

*The boy needs to accumulate*
*To let his love shine bright*
*In others it will open too*
*For everyone shall live in light*

He repeated them aloud, feeling glad that he finally understood what they meant. The lessons his grandfather had taught, clearly had paid off. Agnus smiled and said: 'I'm glad it has brought you this far, for it is exactly the point I wanted to make clear. Now, there's only one thing we must complete before we can send you back to your dimension, to the day you'll turn eighteen. Remember the tingling spots upon Gaia, the nuclear plant of Fukushima? Let's go there, for I have a feeling you'll know what to do about it, now that you've seen what you are capable off. Follow your instincts,' he said as he swayed his arms for the last time.

The image of the Earth reappeared. Both Vincent and his grandfather now floated in space, just above the atmosphere. Beneath them, Vincent discovered large industrial terrains, situated at the seaside. Lots of buildings were destroyed. He couldn't see any radioactivity, but felt the shivers all over his body. He knew something was very wrong here.

'Gaia has done this to herself,' his grandfather said. 'She had brought up a hurricane, an earthquake and a large tsunami to destroy this plant. It was poorly maintained for several years. The Japanese people were treating it laxly, as all over the world people are forgetting the great dangers of such plants. Gaia needed to set an example in order to remind the world that nuclear plants are no solution in providing the world with energy. She had to take her loss by making it happen, but had not foreseen that large amounts of radioactive fluids would pour into the sea. She figured people would find a solution for restraining the radioactivity, but clearly underestimated this disaster. It is one of the main reasons she became so very ill. Could you think of anything to prevent the radioactive water from pouring into the sea?' Vincent nodded. He gained a determined look upon his face, for he knew what to do. He thought back of how he had protected the little hedgehog and looked at his grandfather, in need of his assistance. 'Do as I do,' he said. 'Stretch out your hands and pull as much of the bluish, white energy out of the universe as you can. Fill your body totally, then wait for my signal. If we're both fully loaded, we'll build a dome around it, just like I did to the hedgehog earlier. It will form a counter radiation, which will first lock the contaminated molecules inside until it will eventually turn all radiation back to normal Earth levels. Focus upon that, for it needs your intention to become reality. Now, go!'

Both closed their eyes and focused upon the energy that was in tremendous amounts available around them. As they did, they lit up. Vincent felt the tingling feeling all over his body, only much stronger than he had ever felt before. When it started to hurt, he kept it on for little longer. Next to him, he could hear his grandfather softly moan, so he stretched out his hands.

'Now!' he yelled and with a primal scream they directed their rays of lightning mist into the plant underneath them. It sizzled as the beams touched the ozone and roared when it touched the ground. To his relieve, Vincent witnessed how it formed a huge dome around the plant, meanwhile ever spurring the rays. He closed his eyes and imagined how the dome would continue in the soil, through the crust of the Earth and meet up way below its surface, forming a perfect circle of light around the plant, above as well as below.

He pulled his arms back. Next to him, Agnus did the same. The beams immediately stopped raying. Both held silent for a while and beheld their perfectly shaped dome. Vincent was the first to speak; 'It will lower the split molecule's vibration and cause them to cluster again. In less than a year, nothing dangerous will remain but clean air and water, so I hope that humans from now on will build…'

Vincent was interrupted by the music. It was of such indescribable beauty, he couldn't help but listening. There were chords and melodies he had never heard before. It went straight through him, moved him. Agnus was also moved, for in both faces, eyes welled up.

'What's that?' Vincent asked him with a tearful face. 'That's our sign. Mozart has finished writing his symphony. Let's go back, for I have a hunch Gaia is about to fully recover. This part of his symphony will raise her vibrational levels up to standards she only knew once, millions of years ago. You'll see.' He grabbed Vincent's hand, wiped his face and gave another harsh pull on his arm next. Again, it shocked him. He would never get used to someone pulling his arm like that. When he overcame his shock, the first thing he saw was his crystal sphere upon its socket. It still stood upon the bedside table and radiated its ever-golden blaze. They were back in the room, only to find out that it was empty.

*\*\*\**

Mozart was very proud of himself. He had been able to produce chords, melodies and strings that truly were new. Sure, all the used tones were well known, but not in these particular settings. It was something considered to be impossible in the world. Even scientist had stated that all possible combinations of tones yet existed, so people figured that there was no new sound to be found. Mozart had just proved them wrong.

He had used the low frequency-tones of the biggest African Elephants, the high-pitched voices of random Californian Dolphins and the raying squeaks of qualified Antarctican Whales, simply because he had felt like using them. For the first time in his life, he had created something purely based on intuition. It was a new technique Simone had taught him. Whenever an idea came to mind, he first examined what effect that particular idea had upon his stomach, throat and jaws. If his jaws cramped up, it meant a no-go. If his stomach ached or if his throat felt alike someone was choking him, he let it as well. But, if all three areas of his body felt warm and relaxed, or sometimes even glowed, the new idea was definitely something worth investigating. This way, he had learned not only to waste time in ideas that weren't going to bring him much, but also to follow up on ideas that he normally might have rejected for being too farfetched. It had enhanced his creativity enormously and had made things possible for him that had, until now, been proven impossible to the rest of the world. He had a reason to feel proud.

He had only played about a third of his master piece, when something deep inside warned him not to play it all...yet. He didn't know how he was told, but, over the years, he had learned not to ignore such hunches. He quickly jumped up and switched it off.

He looked at his atomic clock, a clock that would never be wrong or out of time for its solar cell power charge and exact satellite time, to see if it was time for dinner already. He was taken aback immediately. It showed him six o'clock in the morning.

He shook his head, very sure he had gone into the studio at eleven, so, even though he knew it was flawless, he started doubting its accuracy. Fortunately, it was only the time that was given incorrectly, for the date was still the same, he saw.

He climbed upon his table, stretched out to the clock and tapped upon the glass. Nothing. He pressed the 'reset' button next. Shortly, the digital 06:00 blinked and then returned. He sighed and gave up. If nothing wrong with the clock, it really must have been morning again. Discouraged, he climbed down the table. He was just about to make himself up for going again through this day, when his mother walked into the room to warn him it was time for breakfast. He nodded at her and with a last shrug he went after her, knowing exactly what he was about to have for breakfast. His second that day, apparently.

\*\*\*

The stone in the socket of his crystal sphere softly glowed a variety of colours when Vincent and Agnus entered the room, as if it welcomed them back.

'Do you think you've learned enough, Vincent?' Agnus asked. 'Yes, grandfather, I've understood. Not only have I seen what I'm truly capable off, I know a lot more about life now. Seeing myself touching those people with pure energy, gives me a pretty good idea of what's expected from me next. I'm ready.' 'Alright then. Let's go outside and gather up with the rest. We're celebrating your eighteenth birthday today, remember? Congratulations again, my boy. Never knew you were going to grow up so fast, huh?' He laughed hearty about his joke as his whole body trembled. Vincent laughed along, although not as loud as Agnus did. He knew that time was no issue in other dimensions, but still it struck him that on Earth, in the lives of his family members, already seven years had passed since he was gone. To him, it had only felt like a day. Once he knew, he was curious to see what time had done to his beloved family. He wanted to see what his brothers looked like, couldn't wait to hug his parents, looked forward to meeting Utopy and was curious about his own appearances. All the sudden, he was in a hurry. 'Can we go out then? Now?' he urged Agnus. 'Only if you bring your crystal sphere, Vincent. Pack it well, for it's about to go upon a short trip.' Vincent nodded happily, turned around to the small bedside table and picked it up. It sparkled pleasantly upon the palms of his hands. For a moment, he cuddled it. Then he pressed it tight against his chest and let his grandfather know he was ready to go. Immediately, a small door inside the wall opened. Agnus turned around and went through first. Vincent stepped after him.

The moment his left foot stepped over its threshold and upon the courtyard of his home, he could feel the now familiar tingling feeling going throughout his body. He smiled when he remembered how surprised he was the first time he had experienced it. How little had he known that day. Still, he couldn't have foreseen that this time it would bring him a surprise too. Once his right foot touched the courtyard as well, the prickling feeling enhanced. When Vincent looked down, he saw the soil moving away. Taken aback at first, he soon after smiled. He realized that he was growing into the size of an eighteen year old boy.

***

Maria woke up slowly, automatically awakened by her inner clock that had told her it was six in the morning and thus time to rise and shine. Immediately after, their rooster confirmed. She stretched herself. It had been a good night sleep, but she still felt tired. Waking up felt as if she had worked all night. At her right side, Johannes was still asleep peacefully. She yawned and stretched herself again. Then she turned on her bedside light.

When her left leg touched the floor, it struck her. Today was the day! Her heart accelerated as she was filled with joy in a split second. She smiled, jumped out of bed and put on her dressing gown. As she went down the stairs and into the kitchen, she sang aloud. It was a song she hadn't sang for a long, long time. She didn't even know why it was this song that came her to mind, but before she even realized, she was already singing it. Climb Every Mountain from The Sound of Music sounded throughout the house. It woke up her family pleasantly.

Normally, when she walked into the kitchen in the mornings, their two dogs would only open half an eye in order to greet her. This morning, they were both fully awake, up on four paws and greeting her happily, meanwhile enthusiastically wagging their tales. They obviously had noticed today was a special day too. She petted Hector upon his big head, cuddled Utopy and then started feeding them. When she turned to the coffee machine, she realized that she had to prepare breakfast for more people than usual. It made her heart pound with utter joy, for it was such an exciting feeling to finally be reunited with her eldest.

She could hardly await. Happily, she sang again while setting the breakfast table for eight.

Johannes woke up by the sweet voice of his wife singing. He smiled. It had been a while since he had heard her singing that song. He got out of bed and walked towards the window. However it was still dark outside, he opened the curtains and the window to open the outside shutters.

First, he noticed the golden glow outdoors. Immediately after, he realized today was the day. He stuck his head out of the window to view their entire courtyard. At exactly the same spot as it had disappeared seven years ago, the tiny house had appeared. It glowed a variety of colours. He didn't await the moment someone stepped out, but pulled his head back, turned around and ran for the stairs.

'Yahoo!' he shouted aloud, while he rushed down in his pyjamas. 'They're back! They're back!' It caused the twins, Michael and Raphael, to come out of their beds and step into the hallway, surprised and only dressed in their boxer shorts. They looked very sleepy and were a little grumpy over this harsh morning excitement. It took them quite some time to process what was going on. When it also struck them that today was the day, their faces lit up immediately. Next, they ran back to their rooms and dressed quicker than they had ever done in their lives. Simultaneously, as good twins do, they came out of their rooms and ran down the stairs, as their father had done only minutes before them.

When Johannes came down, he first ran into the kitchen. On the doorstep he held still, using his arms as breaks by grabbing the sides of the door opening. His body flexed inwards first, but then bounced back to the level of his arms. He glowed in full excitement when he next, calmer, walked up to Maria who was preparing for breakfast. She turned around when he stepped inside. He laughed when he saw the huge smile upon her face, for he knew she felt the same. Without the use of any words, he kissed her profoundly, whereafter he grabbed her hands and span her around, in front of the sink, dancing. 'They're back, they're back, they're finally back,' he sang again.

When they bumped into the breakfast table, it suddenly shoved to the side an inch. All empty glasses upon it fell over. They held still for a moment, laughed and, with a shrug, started dancing again. After all, none of the glasses broke.

Their dogs were startled by the noise for a short moment, but then joined in on the excitement. Both span circles upon the kitchen floor and chased their tales while happily barking. Soon after, the twins ran into the kitchen and completed the chaos. They jumped up and down in utter joy, danced, while continuously repeating 'They're back, They're back,' along with their dad. Now everybody laughed, danced and cuddled each other, dogs and parents in turns. It was a happy sight, that morning rumble in the kitchen.

In all the excitement, nobody noticed that the front door had opened. A woman walked in. She had a fly circling rounds over her head. At the kitchen threshold, she held still. The fly flew in. It landed on the top of the pendant lamp above the breakfast table. There, it started washing itself. The woman's eyes twinkled when she watched what was going on in the normally so tidy kitchen. She smiled.

It lasted for minutes, but finally Raphael noticed her first. 'Grandma!' he shouted happily. Immediately after, he let go of the hands of his brother and rushed towards her. His brother continued the spin alone and bumped into the stove. Fortunately, he was caught by his father just in time to prevent a fall.

Raphael, in the meantime, had reached his grandmother. A little harsh, he threw his arms around her and pressed her tight into his chest. He had grown since the last time they met and was now way taller than she was. Seconds after him, his brother did the same.

Their parents had stopped their dancing and watched the three of them. Johannes had put his arm around Maria's waist. Together they leaned against the kitchen sink as they awaited their turn to great her as well. 'Okay, okay, boys, that's enough,' grandmother finally said. The boys let go. She rubbed both upon the top of their heads, kissed them on the cheeks and walked towards her daughter and son-in-law. Johannes' arm let go of his wife as she opened her arms. 'Hi, mom,' she said and she wrapped her mother in the warmest embrace one could ever imagine. A big tear dripped down her face. For seven years she had profoundly looked forward to this day. Now, it finally had come.

\*\*\*

First, Vincent walked the courtyard behind his grandfather slowly, but when he heard the laughing and singing coming out of the farm, he started running. Carefully, not to break the crystal sphere in his arms, he entered the front door. He was just about to rush into the kitchen, when he heard his grandfather call after him. 'Put down the sphere first, boy!' Understanding it would be hard to hug his relatives without the chance of dropping it, Vincent slowed down. He turned around in front of the kitchen door and put the sphere's upon its socket on the small hallway table underneath the coat hangers. Then he rushed in.

'Tadaa!' he yelled to surprise them. 'Vincent!' Raphael and Michael simultaneously cried out. Again, the twins were the first to welcome a long lost relative. They bumped into Vincent in such a speed, all three boys fell on the ground. It didn't matter since nobody got hurt and even if one of them had, nobody would have noticed. Their joy was simply too overwhelming. They rolled around, laughed and cuddled each other while being on the floor.

Agnus came in. As if nothing was going on, he stepped over the boys in the door opening. His eyes laughed. 'What's all the fuss about?' he asked, now laughing aloud. He walked up to his daughter and enclosed her in the same embrace she had just given his wife minutes earlier.

Hector barked. It was a high-pitched, surprised bark that caused everyone present to laugh again. Immediately, Agnus dropped upon his knees. 'My boy,' he spoke emotionally, 'how much have I missed you.' The dog didn't know what to do with his feelings. He jumped around Agnus, wagged every limb in his body while squeaking and licking Agnus' face. Finally, he buried his big head into boss' lap and lay down, his eyes spreading both joy and loyalty. He clearly was happy.

All three boys had stopped their riot and now sat on the floor to watch boss and dog being reunited after seven years. The sight moved them. It brought the highly exited energy in the room into a calmer, loving state. Vincent looked around to see if he could discover Utopy. He found him, under the table. The dog was quite overwhelmed by his way of entrance and had found a safe spot to stay and watch. Once everybody had calmed down, he dared to come out. When Vincent called him, even though he had known his dog only for a day, Utopy immediately recognized him. Calmly, he walked up to Vincent, who was still sitting on the kitchen floor, wagged his tale and then licked his face all over. When he laid his big head upon his shoulders and into his neck, Vincent was deeply moved for the second time that morning.

'Now you see, it is truly your dog,' grandmother finally spoke. 'It's unbelievable how such a bond could be made in such short time. Well, aren't you going to greet the rest of us, or are you going to stay on that floor forever?' Vincent stood up and hugged his parents. For the first time, he experienced how much he had grown since he was way taller. His mother took his head in her hands and looked up to him to see him in the eyes. 'Look how big you've become. I've always known you were going to be a big boy, but this is ridiculous, unbelievable!' She had to stand upon her toes to kiss him on the lips next. Vincent bent his head forward to meet her in between. Then they hugged. He closed his eyes in order to feel his mother's energies profoundly. He was home again and truly felt happy.

When all the hugging and greeting was done, the whole family took place at the breakfast table. Vincent looked around. All seats were taken, except two. One, of course, was his mother's, who was pouring everyone coffee and milk, but the other one... Vincent was shocked and quite ashamed to not have missed her earlier. 'Grandma, where's Gaia?' he asked. She never had to answer.

'Over here!' a high-pitched voice sounded from above the breakfast table. All looked up. Vincent saw her first. On the top of the pendant lamp, the big fly was waving at him. The moment his eyes crossed hers, she flew down and landed upon his milk glass. 'Where's your sphere, Vincent?' she asked him. 'I need it in order to join you guys in this breakfastivity.'

'You clearly feel better now,' Vincent answered as he stood up, 'since this is the first joke I've ever heard from you. I didn't know Mother Earth had a sense of humor.' He winked at his brothers and left the table to get his sphere out of the hallway. Behind him, the kitchen burst into hilarity. He returned to the frolicsome space quickly and placed his globe upon the table, in the spot that was laid for Gaia, while his family members still were laughing. Immediately, she flew off his glass and landed upon its side, just over the edge of the table. She first turned into her tiny self and then started growing. Next, her hands slipped off the side. She fell.

As she went for the ground, Vincent's mother shrieked a short yell. His father, who sat in the chair next to Gaia's, tried to catch her. In a quick reflex, his arm just reached under the table when a large 'Pooff' sounded. Suddenly, the whole kitchen was covered in mist. Once it cleared, Gaia, in her full size now, sat on the chair smiling. She was lubricating a roll.

'Man, I'm hungry,' she said. 'It's been ages since I've had a proper grasshopper sandwich.'

De kitchen almost exploded in the laughing fit that followed. However, not the whole kitchen since Gaia was the only one who wasn't laughing. She stopped lubricating and gazed around the table, hugely surprised, at the shrieking faces around her. It only increased the blare.

The funniest sight was that her knife hung in the air still, a curl of butter stuck upon its blade. Slowly, it slipped down until it fell off, right into her freshly poured glass of milk. Immediately, it sank to the bottom, leaving a fatty trail upon the milk's surface. Of course, her startled gaze caused a renewed outburst of laughter. Finally, she saw the humor in it as well and laughed along.

After a while, everybody calmed down. They wiped their happy tears hiccupping and were gasping for air in their seats. 'Wow,' Agnus said. He was the first to recapture his ability to speak. 'That truly was something! Nothing better than to start the day with a good laugh. Makes me hungry!' 'True words, dad,' Johannes adjusted, 'let's all eat.' It wasn't needed to be said twice, for everyone was pretty hungry by now. Happily conversing, all dug in on the bug delicacies that were waiting for them upon the table. For the first time in seven years, the family was finally able to enjoy a meal together.

\*\*\*

After there was no food at the table left and everyone was fully satisfied, all helped clearing. Meanwhile, Johannes prepared the sink for the dishwashing. Michael and Agnus took a towel and dried the freshly washed plates, cups and glasses. Maria and Raphael were busy putting the dried crockery in the cabinets, so only Vincent, Gaia and Grandmother were left at the table. 'It's time, Vincent,' grandmother said and out of nowhere his book of Heracles appeared upon the table, right in front of her. Gaia shoved his crystal sphere aside, so the three of them were able to focus on the book.

'Do you remember the prophecy still?' she asked Vincent next. 'Not entirely,' he answered. 'Well, let's see again then, shall we?' Without awaiting any answer, she turned the book her way and opened it at its first page. Vincent and his grandmother shoved their chairs to her side. All family members at the sink stopped their activities, turned their heads and listened as Vincent started reading aloud.

*After many years of plundering*
*Reaping and polluting too*
*Peace will be restored again*
*The Messiah will come back to you*

*Nature reconstructs itself*
*Energy will heal the Earth*
*Mankind reunites within*
*And see what truly life is worth*

*With eyes deep blue and very bright*
*He will start the age of seven*
*And have Gaia on his side*
*By the time he turns eleven*

*Natural he must live first*
*Make his way through third dimension*
*Kept away from further truth*
*Meanwhile growing his intention*

*As the conqueror of unforeseen*
*His name shall be Vincent*
*Teach until he is eighteen*
*Then he reveals the Great Event*

*He'll awaken all mankind*
*In the Earth its latest hour*
*People will discover that*
*Everybody has the power*

*The boy needs to accumulate*
*To let his love shine bright*
*In others it will open too*
*For everyone shall live in light*

*Seeds must be collected first*
*Compassion then will rise above*
*And responsibility, but*
*Most of all the seed of love*

*Next he'll need two of a kind*
*In good luck they'll roll the dice*
*Attuned to in each separate mind*
*This energy is needed twice*

*Buried they must be at last*
*Reset the time with utmost joy*
*Will bring back another past*
*And return a normal boy*

When he finished, Agnus came over and held still behind him. He laid both hands upon his shoulders and rubbed them for a second. He took his right hand off and bent over, towards the book next. 'Let's go through it, so we know where you're currently standing.' With his index finger, he slid over the first five stanzas. 'Look, you've gone through everything that's mentioned in these first five couplets, right?' 'No, grandfather,' Vincent protested, 'not everything. I haven't completely restored peace on Earth, as the first stanza states, haven't I?' Now it was Gaia's turn to respond. 'You're right, Vincent, but only if you take that phrase to the letter. It has never meant that everybody on Earth would live in peace. That's impossible for one alone to accomplish, sorry to say, but Earth is a place of duality. It can only go without conflict if a majority of people decided in free will to stop feeding their egos, remember?'

Vincent nodded, but the rest held silent for a while, trying to process the statement. Their faces looked serious, especially those of the twins, who were totally new in this matter. Finally, Raphael joined in on the issue. Everybody looked at him as he started speaking.

'Does that mean that the Earth is created to be a planet of constant wars, hunger and suffering? That's hard to believe since I've always thought God was equal to love. How could He create a place where continuously people are suffering?' Now their heads turned back to Gaia, for they were curious about her answer. Vincent smiled.

'That depends on how you see God and what you mean by Him,' Gaia said as she turned to Vincent. 'Grab your sphere, my boy, and show your family where you have been.' Vincent understood immediately. He took his orb from the table and placed it in his lap while his family surrounded him. He closed his eyes and thought back of his visit to God. When he opened them, he looked straight into the sphere. It showed some blurry lights first, but then an image appeared. Vincent saw himself stepping into a huge globe of golden light next to Agnus. They held hands.

'You see,' he pointed out to his brother, 'God is not a man with a beard, living high up in the sky, He is an energy, a soul, a thought form that connects everything that is, for everything holds this energy within. You are part of God, I am, Gaia is, as well as this table is. All is, and so we are all the same.' 'Okay, I can relate to that,' Raphael answered, 'but why then, if we are all the same, do we make others suffer? How could that ever be part of a bigger plan?'

Maria hadn't spoken for a long time. She had been watching her boys trying to figure this one out and she was quite proud of Raphael showing so much sense for others. Now she gave him the answer: 'It is difficult to understand, son, but God is not the captain upon this ship. You must understand that he is just a part of life, the creator. He teaches people what is good and what is bad, but it is up to ourselves to listen. We're no prisoners who are told what to do, are we? You have a mind of your own and a free will to choose. That is what makes life worth living. However, every choice will have its consequences, good or bad, in this lifetime or in another. It is up to you to decide what choices to make. God can only help you make the right one, that is, if you decided to listen.'

Raphael nodded, but Michael, at his side, still looked confused. Gaia noticed and so she explained further. 'Listen, Michael, there is so much more life out there. You, yourself, have been living lives on other planets too, but none of them is as beautiful as the Earth. However beautiful, it is also the most difficult planet to live upon, for inhere we are incarnated to learn our lessons in a very difficult society of conflict and war. Inhere, our egos are way more powerful than anywhere else and so it is the most difficult place to make the right choices. You are distracted by wanting to possess more than your neighbour, collect more than you can handle, eat more than you should and other addictions. In these surroundings, people have to deal with earning money, having power over others and things as status in society, all things that don't matter in God's view. What is important, is that you live your life the way it was meant to be lived, as God is constantly telling you. You need to walk the path of your soul, not reach for status or power over others. What matters are the choices that you make, whether they are made in the best interest of others, thus in love. Remember, we are spirits having a human experience, not the other way around, even though we have to deal with human life every minute of it.'

Both twins showed an understanding look upon their faces. Even Johannes, who until now was always left out of spirituality, nodded comprehensively. Only Vincent gazed questioningly. He was still thinking over the quest that lay ahead.

'But what peace do I need to restore then?' he asked Gaia. She smiled at him again and rubbed the top of his head. 'Not you alone, son,' she said. 'Do you remember how bad my health was, before you went into other dimensions? Do you remember what the human race had caused their beloved planet and who were there to do something about it? ' Vincent nodded silently as he felt he was about to understand. He looked back to the prophecy and read the first stanzas again.

'After many years of plundering, Reaping and polluting too, Peace will be restored again…Aha!' he suddenly yelled out. 'It's not referring to the peace among mankind; it speaks about living in peace with the Earth…with you!' Gaia applauded for a while until she urged him to go on: 'Now, come on, go further. Let's see what you can figure out more.' He went back to the book and mumbled a few words as he read on. At one phrase, he got stuck. He mumbled the words a couple of times until he repeated them louder, meanwhile thinking over what they could mean. 'Mankind reunites within…Mankind reunites…' His face lit up next. 'The Human Collective Soul!' he now cried out. 'It refers to the human soul, I have to empower it, for God to be heard more clearly…How in Heaven's name am I gonna do that?' he asked next.

His grandmother smiled at him. 'Just go on,' she said, 'for you'll find the answer yourself as well.'

'I'll help you,' Agnus, still behind Vincent, said. He pointed at the seventh stanza 'The boy needs to accumulate'. 'This is what you have already done when you flew over and touched all people of the world with the light out of the palms of your hands, remember?' He waited until Vincent confirmed. Then, he went on. 'You've already prepared mankind for what's coming, so leave that behind. It'll all become clear to you soon, each step at its own time. Now, your next step is in the following stanza.' Again, Vincent bent his head over the book and started mumbling. This time, he read a little louder, so everyone present could hear as well. 'Seeds must be collected first…What seeds?' he asked Gaia. She never had to answer because, immediately after he had asked, a high-ringing bell sounded. First, Vincent gazed around to see where it came from. Gaia let him find it out himself. She smiled and looked at him with an amused look upon her face.

Michael was the first to see. 'Your sphere, Vincent, look!' All heads now turned towards the sphere, while the high bell still rang. The sound clearly came out of the orb, or better, out of its socket.

There, Vincent's stone was floating above its soft velvet bedding. It trembled violently. The moment Vincent laid his eyes upon, it stopped trembling and landed. Immediately, the ringing ceased as well.

'So my stone is a seed,' he concluded, 'but that is only one. The prophecy speaks about seeds, so more than one. Am I correct, are there more than one?' Gaia nodded. 'But where then?' Vincent asked her desperately. 'Do I have to search the planet now for more tiny stones?' His grandmother first laughed about his despair, but then reassured him. 'I understand that seems quite an impossible task, my boy,' she said smiling, 'but don't worry. There are only three stones alike in the world, since there are three ditches in your sphere's velvet cushion. One is yours, as you already know, the other two are also in possession.' 'You were not alone upon this quest, remember?' Gaia now fell in. 'Who else were helping you lately?' It took Vincent a while to understand, but finally, two names came him to mind.

'Miles and Mozart,' he whispered.

\*\*\*

Miles sat in the workshop. Together with the Chemistry Professor, he was busy improving the process of chemical breakdown. However already very efficient, he felt that more could be reached, and so he had contacted his professor in order to have another look at his ideas. Behind them, the blackboard was filled with formulas while both were covered in crayon dust. They never noticed, for they were totally caught up in working out their calculations. Their working desk was filled with fully scribbled papers. Even though it appeared a mess, they were about to solve their problem.

After the first day that he had, together with Britt, spoken about his ideas to both professors, things had happened so quickly, time had flown. Immediately after showing his designs, his professors had not only gathered a whole team of builders, but also brought in a lot of people with influence and power. As it turned out, Britt was the best in persuading the sponsors, and so she had been in charge of the fundraising immediately. She had succeeded big time since, from day one on, an enormously huge amount of money had been available for them to build their Delta Floaters. Already three were working the seas, cleaning them from any plastic material that floated in, meanwhile producing oil for the sake of their investors. Number four was about to be baptized and take off too.

The world press had picked up on what they were doing and all over the world, images of both Miles and the Delta Floaters were shown. People called him a wonderboy, for no one had understood how a fresh-year student at eighteen years old was able to come up with such a brilliant plan. Some papers had even called him The Messiah for his ability in saving the world. By now, it had become clear to everyone that 'the Plastic Continent', as people usually named it, had formed a serious threat to all life. Miles had become world famous.

His parents were utmost proud of him and even the people who had avoided him earlier for being a rotten brat, now told around that Miles originated from their town with a high hand.

In spite of all the fame and fortune that came along, Miles hadn't changed. He had pretty much stayed the same since he first came to Delft, only quite happier. He still lived in his room, in the same house, slept in the same bed, wore his stone in his pocket, and ate the same breakfasts as usual. The only difference was that he enjoyed his life with Britt now, for she had moved in with him. Miles felt truly happy, having nothing more to wish for, as long as the oceans were being cleaned.

Often, he had thought back of Sarah, who miraculously had disappeared out of his life. He had asked his housemates about her, but no one had ever known or seen her in their house, even though she once clearly had stated to him that she lived there too. Every time he had brought her up to his friends, they had declared him crazy and out of his mind, so he had let bringing the subject up, even though she remained a mystery to him. Only one time he had seen her in what later had appeared to be a dream, even though he remembered it very clearly.

It had been the night after the baptism of his first Delta Floater, the day they had celebrated its completing under a huge interest of the worldwide press. She had appeared to him when Britt had just fallen asleep at his side. She looked ill, but had a huge smile upon her face. She had thanked him profoundly and had even pressed a kiss upon his forehead. When he woke up the morning after, with a hangover from all the wines and champagnes he drank the night before, he hadn't taken her appearance very seriously. Because he had never seen her since, he had totally focused upon his study, his work on the Delta Floaters and Britt. He was hugely surprised to meet her again this morning.

The calculations were of such difficulty, they got stuck at a certain point, very near the solution, both knew. The chemistry professor shook his head and then sat back in his chair. He stretched himself. 'If only I hadn't had this feeling that we are overlooking something, I would have ceased it for today and concluded it to be impossible,' he said while yawning, 'but now, I can't stop anymore. What about a coffee, some fresh air and then having another look?' Miles nodded that was probably a good idea and then both stood up. The professor walked over to the coffee machine, while Miles let him know that he had to go to the toilet. 'Alright then,' he answered. 'You go, I'll prepare some coffee in the meantime and then we are taking it outside. It's a beautiful day today, so the sun will do our overworked brains some good. How do you take your coffee?' 'Very seriously, professor, nothing else,' Miles answered before stepping over the threshold. When the door of the workshop closed behind him, he could just hear the professor nicker hearty.

The door to the public restroom squeaked plaintively when he opened it. He stepped through. It smelled quite bad inside, an odour he probably was about to enhance.

Even though he didn't like to do a number two in public toilets, he had no choice. Once you gotta go, you gotta go. Quickly he checked the toilets to be sure no one else was in. To his relieve, he found out that he was alone. Still, he knew people could walk in any moment and so he prayed for the entrance door to stay closed. Then he went in the last toilet of the row, the furthest away from the door. He took his pants down and sank his naked behind at the seat. He relaxed. Fortunately, this time he didn't smell too bad, he concluded.

He had just wiped his bottom, pulled his pants back up and was about to flush, when he heard someone speak. It was a woman's voice. 'He's in here,' it said. Clearly, there was someone else present too. He assumed it to be Britt together with someone who probably needed him for something. He first wondered how they had managed to enter the restroom without him hearing it, but then became angry. After all the time they had spent together, did she still not know he needed moments like these alone, in order to relieve himself in private?

He flushed, opened the toilet door and was just about to tell her off, when his breath got stuck in his throat. In front of him stood Sarah. She looked amazingly beautiful and healthy. Next to her stood a young man. They held hands.

When he looked into the bright blue eyes, he shortly was in shock and kept staring at them for a while. The man gave him the creeps. He knew for sure that he had seen those eyes somewhere earlier, but couldn't remember when or where. Since the man stared back at him friendly, his fears diminished rapidly.

'Hi Miles,' Sarah finally greeted him. The man said nothing.

Miles didn't know how to react upon their appearance in a public restroom, so he said nothing. Quietly, he walked over to the sink and washed his hands while the two waited patiently for him to be done.

He closed the tap and turned aside to pick a paper towel out of the dispenser. When he ripped it, his eyes crossed the mirror in front of him. To his amazement the space behind him was empty.

He wondered if they had left and turned his head over his shoulder, where Sarah and her companion acquiescently were waiting until he was done. His eyes flashed the mirror for a second time. No one. He looked back and there they were again. 'How…,' he mumbled. He never managed to finish his sentence.

'We're not really here, Miles,' Sarah responded, 'we're only appearing in your space and time and so there is no reflection. However, we did come here for a reason, didn't we Vincent?' 'Yeah, we did,' the man next to her now spoke for the first time. 'Sorry to say, but we need your stone.'

A little hesitant, Miles picked his magical stone out of his pocket. He looked at it and wondered. For the first time in over a year, it was glowing its green coloured flare. Although Miles instinctively knew that to him it had no further purpose, it fell him hard to give up. He stroke its surface a couple of times and then reluctantly handed it over to Vincent. The moment they touched, it glowed an even brighter blaze, this time in a variety of colours.

'You did well, Miles,' Sarah now said. 'You were personally responsible for a great deal of my health and I have to thank you for that.' She bent over and pressed him a kiss upon his cheek without letting go of Vincent's hand. After an empowering glance at Miles, Vincent then nodded him goodbye. Miles nodded back. 'Keep up the great work, Miles!' Sarah's voice resonated throughout the restroom as both started to disappear. Miles kept looking at them until they were truly gone. They simply evaporated into the ever-smelly air of the public restroom. He kept staring at the empty spot for a while until he turned around for the door. He had work to do.

Quite dazzled, he opened it. Again, it squeaked complainingly. Plunged in thoughts, he then stepped through and walked straight into the tiny chemist, who was waiting for him outside with two plastic containers of coffee in his hands. He had quite some trouble not to spill any. Fortunately, he managed to keep all the hot substance inside.

'Ho ho...not so fast now, nutty professor,' he said laughing. 'You took such a long time, I almost was sure you had fallen through that toilet. Is everything alright?' Miles nodded that he was okay, excused himself mumbling, took him a coffee out of hand and walked towards the main exit. His professor immediately followed.

Once outside, they looked for a bench and sat themselves down. Quietly, both sipped their coffees while enjoying the sunlight. Then, as if a miracle occurred, simultaneously, the solution to their problem came to mind. Instantly, they looked at each other, their eyes big and joyful. Without the use of any words, both poured the remaining coffee to the ground and ran inside, back to their workshop and back to their papers.

Delta Floater five was completed a couple of weeks later. It had a renewed and far more efficient processing station on top.

***

For the first time ever, Mozart was working in his studio together with someone else because Simone sat in the chair next to him. He was showing her all about his latest discovery in tones and frequencies and what effects his music could have on people. Simone, being an expert in the field of human energies herself, first was very impressed by what he had achieved, but had given him later quite some useful tips and tricks for his latest piece 'Killer Whale Orchestra', that was due to be released in a month.

They were just finalizing the final chords together, when all the sudden the temperature in the studio drastically rose.

Mozart got up from his chair as he wanted to check on the heating sensor that was at the other side of the room, but Simone grabbed him by his arm and pulled him back into his seat. 'Let it go,' she said, 'for it's not the heating. We're being visited.' Indeed, Mozart could feel a presence too. He turned the back of his chair towards his monitors and watched the empty space in the middle of his studio. There, first vaguely, but then clearly, two silhouettes appeared. They were a man and a woman holding hands.

Immediately after his first astonishment, Mozart recognized his nanny. He literally jumped off his chair and flew around her neck. After almost squeezing her tight, she started protesting. 'Okay, okay, that's enough,' she said laughing. 'I've missed you a lot too. Do you know Vincent already?' Mozart let go of his nanny and turned to the young man at her side. He looked at him. The man looked back in a friendly way. For a while they stared at each other, Mozart in full admiration, for this man had the brightest blue eyes he had ever seen, and the man still waitingly. Vaguely, Mozart had the feeling he knew this man before, but he couldn't remember where, and so he answered his nanny with a negative. 'Let me introduce myself then, Mozart. Hi, I'm Vincent,' the man said as he stretched out his hand. Mozart took it and shook it for a while, meanwhile still thinking over where it could have been they had met. His nanny read his mind. 'No, Mozart, you have never met Vincent in person before. It has only been in your dreams, so you probably don't remember anymore. It's okay though, Vincent doesn't blame you for it.' She turned to Simone next. 'Hi Simone! Nice to meet you again too. Is everything ready for the next step?' 'Hi Gaia,' Simone answered. 'No, not yet entirely. Sure, the boy is ready, but I have to let Angela know it's about to start. Just give me a minute.' She closed her eyes and went into meditation, meanwhile locking the three people around her outside.

'Nice,' the nanny next said. 'All is arranged then. Mozart, do you know why we are here?' He wanted to shake his head in order to let her know he had no clue, but in the meantime, his magical stone had started to shake violently in its leather ropes. Clearly, it wanted to be taken off his wrist now.

He untied the strings and freed his stone. The moment his fingers touched, it ceased the trembling. When he pulled it off, it was glowing a bright green blaze. He stared at it for a while. 'Good guess, Mozart,' his nanny broke his wonder. 'We're here for your stone indeed, aren't we Vincent?' 'Yes, we are. Sorry to say, but we really need it.' Although Mozart instinctively knew that it couldn't serve him anymore, it fell him hard to give up. He stroke its surface a couple of times and then reluctantly handed it over to Vincent. The moment they touched, it glowed an even brighter blaze, this time in a variety of colours.

'You did well, Mozart,' his nanny said in a whispering tone of voice. 'You were personally responsible for a great deal of my health and I have to thank you for that.' She bent over and pressed him a kiss upon his cheek without letting go of Vincent's hand. He could feel his cheek glowing long after she had pulled her head away.

'You're leaving already?' suddenly Simone's voice sounded from out of the chair behind them. His nanny smiled. 'Yeah, Simone, there's plenty of work to do for us. Are you ready for the next episode now?' 'All and everybody is in place,' Simone answered, 'except for his previous symphony. Where is it, Mozart? Can you put it on, so we can play it later?' A little dazzled, for he hadn't told a single soul about his last creation, Mozart nodded. He turned around his chair, took place upon and grabbed his computer mouse. Seconds later, it appeared on both monitors in front of them.

'Great,' his nanny said. 'I'll give you the signal in about an hour.' Mozart wanted to ask what she had planned to do with his symphony, but she didn't give him the chance. She bent over for the second time and kissed him on the cheek profoundly. This time, she let go off Vincent's hand.

'Till we meet again, my boy,' she whispered in his ear. She turned back to Vincent, grabbed his hand again and nodded her goodbye at Simone as both disappeared. They simply evaporated into the ever-hot air that still hung in the studio.

Mozart kept watching until he couldn't see them anymore. The temperature turned back to normal next.

*\*\*\**

When Vincent and Gaia reappeared at the courtyard, his father, mother, Raphael and Michael were awaiting them outside together with his aunt. She was holding the prophecy as Michael held his sphere, Vincent noticed. Utopy and Hector leisurely lay upon the ground in front of their farm. They were wagging their tales for him, but never went through the trouble of standing up. He quickly scanned the surroundings for his grandparents, but they were nowhere to be seen, nor was the little house wherein Vincent had stayed with them for the last seven years.

Gaia saw him scanning and assured him they were gone: 'Their task is fulfilled, Vincent. It's entirely up to us now.' He mumbled to her that he had understood, meanwhile deeply feeling sad for not having had the chance to say them farewell. He missed them instantly.

His aunt felt his sadness. She took the book in one hand, walked up to him and laid her arm around his shoulder, hugging him profoundly. 'Don't be sad, Vincent,' she said. 'You must know by now that nothing lasts forever, yet everything does.' She rubbed the top of his head next and kissed him. 'Now, come on. There's more for us to do here.'

She opened the book and showed everyone the prophecy. All gathered around her. 'You've collected the seeds by now, I assume?' Vincent nodded and took them out of his pocket, showing them from out of the palms of his hands. They were pleasantly glowing their variety of colours. Inside the socket of his globe, his stone was acting the same. 'Put them in then, Vincent,' Gaia urged him while Michael already took a step forward to hand his sphere over. He took it from him and automatically, the tiny glass door in its socket opened. He laid the other two stones upon the blue velvet bedding carefully. 'Let's see what is says that we must do next,' his aunt said as she reread the prophecy:

*Next he'll need two of a kind*
*In good luck they'll roll the dice*
*Attuned to in each separate mind*
*This energy is needed twice*

*Buried they must be at last*
*Reset the time with utmost joy*
*Will bring back another past*
*And return a normal boy*

'So, now I understand why we are all here,' she finally said. She looked at his father and closed the book. 'Truly two of a kind, aren't we?' he answered her smiling, while she bent over and laid the book on the ground. 'Us too!' now Raphael first spoke. 'Indeed, nephews,' Angela responded him, 'you two as well, for this two-of-a-kind energy is needed twice.'

Gaia smiled. She had always known what was needed to be done next, but she wasn't allowed to dictate. Videlicet for the prophecy to come true, it was essential that people found out themselves. She felt proud they had uncovered it this far.

Suddenly, all looked at the sphere in Vincent's hands. It was changing. Under the influence of the three stones in its socket, it now produced a bright green cloud inside its crystal orb. 'What's that?' his mother asked amazed. 'That, mother, is the Human Collective Soul!' Vincent answered her. 'I've been wondering how to reach it, ever since I first figured out what to do. What a convenience it appeared to be inside my sphere all along. All we had to do was to collect the seeds to produce it.' 'Fair enough, but still not easy,' his father now stated. 'How are we going to get it out?' 'Together,' Angela answered. 'All four of us. "In good luck they'll roll the dice", remember?' She turned to Vincent next and took the crystal ball off its socket. 'Let us hold hands, our arms crossed,' she ordered the twins and her brother. 'The two eldest go in the middle.' 'How can you be so sure, Angela?' Maria now asked her. 'Only because of my best friend Simone, Maria. Although she lives far away, she's always with me, even right now. Do you remember her?' His mother nodded. 'She knows as she has always known. She's the one to guide us into our next step, for Gaia is not allowed to. Am I correct, Gaia?' This time it was up to Gaia to nod.

'Alright then, let's proceed. Michael and Johannes, you go in the middle, Raphael and me are covering the sides. Let's all cross arms and bend over, for you two…' she briefly looked at Johannes and Michael, '…are going to smash that ball against that wall,' and she pointed towards the brick wall of the shed. 'Just roll it over the ground in great speed. Make sure you touch it both, swing it back and let go simultaneously.' She handed the sphere to Johannes next.

While all four walked closer to the wall of the shed in an uneasy run, their arms already strangled, Gaia applauded. She had been worried over this part of the prophecy and was very relieved to see how Angela was solving it.

Vincent, who stood at her side, couldn't share her gladness. He felt sorry for his crystal ball. Sadly, he looked at the socket in his hands, where the stones were ever violently glowing. He understood it had to be done, but still wanted to save his sphere, if only he knew a way to spare it. He thought about it, but nothing came to mind and so he rested in the thought of sacrificing it.

Maria, Gaia and Angela counted down. They started at three. At each count, both Johannes and Michael swung the ball back. Johannes held it in his left hand, while Michael swayed it with his right. When they reached 'one', they had managed to give it an enormous swing. The next count sounded 'go'.

They released at the same time and launched the ball at an incredible speed. First, it bounced back from the courtyard and span in the air above. The second time it hit the ground, it bounced back slightly less high. Vincent held his breath, for he was afraid it would break too soon, but after another two bounces, it stayed in touch with the ground and neatly rolled into the shed's brick wall. With a loud bang, it burst into pieces. A large, green cloud grew out of its remains.

\*\*\*

After Vincent and his nanny had left, Mozart gazed around his studio. So many questions popped up in his head, he couldn't comprehend what just had happened. Simone noticed his struggle and suggested a cup of tea. He agreed, infatuated.

Once in the kitchen, he sat himself down at a chair and shoved it underneath kitchen table, still looking dazzled. Simone poured him a cup and took one herself. Then she sat down across him. They sipped their teas quietly for a while until Mozart was finally capable of asking her the most important of the many questions that were circling around in his head.

'Simone, who is my nanny really? I mean, I've always known her to be someone special, but something like this…' he said as he raised his arm and pointed towards his studio upstairs, '…I couldn't have foreseen in my wildest dreams.' Simone started laughing. 'I understand,' she said, 'for it is truly an amazing experience you've just had. Let me tell you a little story before we dive into answering all the questions that you have. It'll clarify a lot for you, I'm sure. Is that okay?'

Mozart nodded. He took his cup of tea in both hands and leaned forward, his elbows on the table, eager to hear what she had to say. Simone took her time. She first blew her hot tea, took a last sip, placed her cup at the table and leaned back. 'Well,' she said as she crossed her arms. 'Where shall I begin?'

She thought for a while, searching for words, whilst Mozart felt an enormous urge to rush her. However, he understood that she was looking for the best way to bring it to him and so he said nothing. Meanwhile, he couldn't help but putting pressure upon her in a non-verbal way. He leaned forward even more, his eyes big and focused as if he wanted to pull the words out of her, until she, finally, started telling. Only then he sat back and relaxed, absorbing her words.

'Once upon a time there were three little boys, about the same age, but living in different times, growing up normally. Two lived in England, one lived in France. These three little boys were destined to save the world from devastating habits of mankind, something all three were unaware of until the day they, all three, received a stone. It was a magical stone that enhanced specific abilities in the boys. One boy received it from a spirit, the other from a crow and a third from his nanny. By conceiving these stones, seeds were planted to be nurtured until the time was right for them to be grown. The stones were not just stones, you see. They actually were seeds.

One was the Seed of Love. It came in possession of Vincent, the boy you've just met upstairs. He enhanced the power of true love throughout the world.

Second was the Seed of Responsibility. It was acquired by Miles, a boy you've never met in person. He made people aware of their liability for a globally clean environment.

Third was the Seed of Compassion.' 'My stone,' Mozart interrupted her. 'Your stone indeed. It enhanced your ability of making music that touches people, meanwhile growing mercy throughout the world.

All you boys were working together, without knowing that you did, in improving Gaia's health, the spirit of the Earth.' 'My nanny!' Mozart cried out. 'You've earlier called her Gaia!' 'Don't rush me, Mozart,' Simone said smiling, 'but you are right. The woman you've always known to be your nanny, actually is Gaia.

She is the one who was guiding you into your destiny, as she did to the other boys in one way or another as well.

Now, the time for growth is due to come. However, it takes extra magical actions for that to happen, for these seeds can only grow in a specific environment, far beyond our comprehension of space and time, such as an angelic realm, a collective soul or another place of true light.

There is a prophecy. It mainly speaks about a quest that Vincent has to make…' '…in order to collect the stones and bring them to their place of growth,' Mozart finished her sentence. 'So that's why they appeared to us together. They're about to finish his quest. What role does my symphony play in that?'

Simone was about to answer when both were startled by a loud bang. It frightened Mozart, for it never came from outside. It seemed to sound inside his head instead. 'Did you hear that too?' he asked Simone. 'Yeah,' she said, 'I think that's our signal. Come on, quickly now, let's go upstairs and play your symphony entirely. You're about to find out what important part it plays in our little story.'

Mozart immediately put his tea at the table. He quickly shoved his chair back and then followed Simone who already had reached the stairs. Both ran up and into the studio, for they somehow knew they were in a hurry by now.

*\*\*\**

The loud bang had also startled the dogs. With a frightened bark, both Hector and Utopy suddenly were up on all fours. They howled as wolves intensively while they approached the remains of Vincent's sphere carefully. When the green cloud grew their direction, they withdrew and lay down again, showing it their greatest respect. Their eyes, however, followed what was growing above anxiously until the music started. It was of such an indescribable beauty, it left all humans motionless upon the courtyard. Even the dogs forgot their fears and tilted their heads to listen.

'It is time, Vincent,' Gaia after a while said. 'Be quick now, for it'll soon start to disappear.' Vincent nodded. He knew he had to place the socket inside the Human Collective Soul, but he hesitated. Somewhere in the back of his mind slumbered the thought he could do more. He turned around to Gaia and looked at her, his mind working overtime. 'Come on now, hurry!' his mother urged him from behind. 'It's already starting to shrink!' He ignored her and kept looking at Gaia. Then, finally, he handed her the socket. 'Here, hold this,' he told her. Gaia didn't understand what he was up to, but neatly did as she was told.

She took it out of his hands as Vincent bent his knees. He wrapped his arms around her waist and picked her up. To his surprise she felt as light as a feather. Then he stepped forward and lifted her into the Human Collective Soul. When he let go she stayed in, floating in its middle. She was crying.

'Thank you Vincent,' she said while the tears were rolling down her cheeks in happy little currents. 'This is more than I could have wished for. Now, I'm finally able to fully control mankind. Thank you. You've done more than you were destined to.'

She blew a kiss into his direction, whereafter the stones inside the socket exploded. A bright light blinded all upon the courtyard from seeing any further. With another loud bang, the Human Collective Soul next disappeared, taking Gaia along. All that remained was a tiny cloud of sparkling white smoke. They kept staring at it. No one said a word as it also vanished. It simply evaporated into the humid air above the courtyard. 'Guys, look!' Michael yelled out. All looked at him. He pointed at the book that still lay at the courtyard. It was dissolving. By every chord of the ever-playing music, it progressively blurred.

As they were watching it surprised, the final chords of Mozart's symphony sounded. Suddenly, all vision became obscure. Utopy uttered a surprised bark, while Hector cried a short shriek. Vincent looked at his mother for help, but he couldn't see her anymore.

Next, everything that once was faded out.

\*\*\*

Vincent woke up by his two brothers jumping up and down his bed, meanwhile singing the 'Wakey Wakey', a song their mother used to sing while waking them when they were little. He immediately was wide awake, laughed and crawled from underneath his duvet. Then he joined the twins.

Their mother, fully dressed already, walked in to see what the morning fuss was all about. She smiled when she saw her three boys having fun so early in the morning and beheld the spectacle from the threshold. Soon, her husband, also dressed, joined her. He kissed her good morning and laid his arm around her waist. Together, they watched their boys for a while. Both truly felt blessed to have their three boys getting along so well. Finally, mother decided to end it. 'Okay, boys, that's enough already. Cut it and get dressed quickly, for we have a big day ahead.' All three stopped the riot instantly. They wondered. A big day ahead? Why?

Michael was the first to remember. 'Of course!' he cried out as he flew Vincent around his neck. 'Congratulations!' Raphael did the same next. After hugging his brothers, Vincent jumped off his bed, meanwhile wondering how he could have forgotten. Today was the day of his eleventh birthday, the day he was going to finally get his puppy.

His parents also congratulated him tenderly. 'Now, come on, birthday boy,' his mother urged him. 'Grandma and grandpa are about to join us for breakfast, as Angela and Simone will be here for coffee soon too. You don't want to leave their present too long in its box, won't you?' 'No, mom, I won't,' Vincent said as he grabbed his clothes before rushing into the bathroom to get washed and dressed quickly.

His father walked over to the bedroom window. He opened the curtains and the window to open the outside shutters as well. It was getting light outside. The first morning sun beams were touching the courtyard and warmed it. Steamy air hung above its surface, forming a wonderful sight. Even though already November, it was going to be a beautiful day, Johannes knew.

He discovered the crow next. It sat upon the biggest branch of the old apple tree and was watching him curiously. Its shiny feathers reflected the morning sun so brightly, he had to squeeze his eyes in order to keep seeing it. Johannes wanted to greet the black bird happily, but suddenly his breath got stuck in his throat. It had something in its eyes. He leaned out of the window to get a closer look. A gasp of air escaped his longs when he first noticed the tiny strings of colourful lights that circled its irises, orbiting around like planets to a star. He kept staring at it until the bird took off. It crowed three times as it floated above their courtyard. Then, it went up.

He watched it fly high, straight up, as if it went straight back to heaven. His eyes kept following the bird until they couldn't distinguish it anymore. It simply disappeared in the waking morning skies.

For a while, he wondered about what he had just witnessed. Finally, he shrugged and closed the window. He turned around and went downstairs to join his wife in preparing for breakfast. After all, he had a birthday to keep busy with and a lot to prepare for their future dog. He looked forward to having a puppy in the house, especially since it was an offspring of the two dogs he loved most in this world.

Plunged in thoughts, he took the final steps of the stairs and walked into the kitchen. There, he kissed his wife for the second time that morning and wrapped her in his arms next. Throughout his experience with the crow he had felt as if a new era had just begun, a feeling he now wanted to share with the one he loved most dearly.

For minutes, they stayed in that embrace until their boys came down and joined them. Maria let them for a while, but then unwrapped herself and started to pour coffee. All others took place at the breakfast table and were about to dig in on the bug delicacies upon it, when the boy's grandparents, who lived only three farms away, came in, followed by the ever-loyal Hector. Seconds later, aunt Angela entered the kitchen too. She held a big box in her hands. It had a blue ribbon tied around and several big holes in it. Something scratched its walls inside.

Soon after, aunty Simone joined them with Hypna. Their meeting again was unusually warm. All hugged profoundly, as if they hadn't seen each other for ages. Vincent quickly unwrapped his gift and soon all three boys were preoccupied in playing with the puppy.

From his parents he received a nice big basket with beautiful blue coloured soft velvet bedding, his grandparents had brought him a food and drinking bowl which could be placed at various heights, and from his brothers he received a big chunk of topgrain cowhide.

'How are you going to name your dog, Vincent?' aunt Simone finally asked him curiously. 'I don't know why,' he responded,'and I don't even know where or how I have picked it up, but I have always liked 'Utopy' for a dog's name.' 'That sounds familiar,' his mother said. 'Then Utopy it is,' his grandfather solemnly stated. All liked the name immediately and so their new family member was added to their household smoothly.

In the days and months that followed, ordinary family life took over, having Hector, Hypna and Utopy ever at its side.

Every now and then, in the subsequent years, a big green fly would pass by their living rooms. Most of times, it would land upon on a big dog's head and nest inside its bristly fur in order to catch up on lost times.

All dogs would be happy to see it again, glad to be reunited with a long lost family member.

\*\*\*

A seven-year-old boy in Italy played in the attic of his grandparents' house. His parents were abroad for business and so he was allowed to stay overnight with his grandparents. He loved it, for their ancient Roman house was so full of stuff, there was always something new for him to play with.

Their three cats also liked having the youngster around and followed him wherever he went. All three were present in the attic and watched his every move.

He had just found an ancient coffer behind a pile of old clothes and other junk. Having some trouble to clear its top from books that lay upon, he finally managed to pull the coffer from underneath. All books slid off. He opened it. Inside were more books; novels of all kinds. He took some out, shortly inspected them and laid them next to the coffer at the floor, curious to see what more he could find.

One book drew his attention in particular, for it looked very old. He grabbed it out and blew a thick layer of dust off. It was a book of ancient Greek mythology, he now saw. He took it to the middle of the attic in order to have a better look in the light of the single pendant lamp that hung from the ceiling, sat himself down underneath and opened it. As he started reading, he was immediately seized by its tale. It told the story of Heracles, a Greek man and son of chief god Zeus, who had concurred demons and gods on behalf of mankind.

The boy rolled over to his belly and placed the book in front of him. Lying flat upon the floor of his grandparents' attic, he read until sleep overcame his will to peruse.

He never noticed how a huge green fly departed from the pendant lamp. It flew up with a big buzz, circled around his head for a while until it went downstairs and outside through an open, bedroom window.

His grandmother had never noticed that her grandson had gone up the attic. Since it was way over his bedtime by now, she searched the house, meanwhile calling his name. 'Adamo, where are you? Adamo?!' Finally, one of her cats heard her calling and answered with a querulous meow. It came from the attic.

Knowing that her cats always followed him around, she went up the stairs. When she came up, she found him peacefully asleep with his head upon an open book and their three cats curled up at his side. She knelt down and swiped a tuft of hair off his forehead. When she was about to press a kiss upon, she noticed what book he had been reading. She smiled, came up straight, picked a duvet from a shelf and covered him with it. She heaved a sigh. Finally, her boy had found it. She stood up and turned around for the stairs. At its bottom, she turned off the light, leaving her grandson peacefully asleep in the dark.

As she walked the hallway and down the second stairs, she smiled again, feeling happy that all was about to begin. She went into the kitchen and poured two cups of coffee. When she returned to the living room, she told her husband the news while handing him a cup.

In one gulp, he immediately hit his hot coffee back, put the empty cup on the table, took his long black leather coat off the hanger and went into the shed. There, he took a small box off a shelf, wiped it clean and tied it to his bike's carrier. He put his coat on, jumped upon the saddle and cycled through the shed's open door next.

He was in the greatest rush ever. Breathing heavily, he pushed himself to go faster until he went at full speed. He knew that there was little time, for this crystal sphere needed a long time to energize. They only had four years left, as the legend had stated, only just enough.

CPSIA information can be obtained at www.ICGtesting.com
Printed in the USA
BVOW07s1042200614

356935BV00001B/27/P